CRY OF ANGELS

The Wrath of War

A Novel Based on Real Events

ARIF PARWANI

iUniverse, Inc.
Bloomington

Cry of Angels
The Wrath of War

iUniverse books may be ordered through booksellers or by contacting:

iUniverse
1663 Liberty Drive
Bloomington, IN 47403
www.iuniverse.com
1-800-Authors (1-800-288-4677)

ISBN: 978-1-4697-5619-6 (sc)
ISBN: 978-1-4697-5620-2 (e)

Printed in the United States of America

iUniverse rev. date: 2/29/2012

More praise from subject matter experts
for
Arif Parwani's approach
to Literary Realism in *Cry of Angels*

"A can't-be-put-down and eye-opening novel that unfolds history, culture, politics and war with a sizzling human touch. A felicitous and pertinent encyclopedia of the past three decades of Afghanistan with both implied and explicit messages."

—Sayed Zafar Hashemi, Afghan journalist based in Washington, DC

"The most eloquent novel ever written about the horrors three decades of war have had on Afghanistan and the heavy toll paid by Afghan women."

—Dr. Nilab Mobarez, author, and Afghan women's-rights advocate

To my wife, Homa, and my daughter, Hadia

Dear Hadia,

    I always had my heart full of words for you. But I didn't want to tell you all of them. Parents do this…..they don't share with their children everything they know. When I started this book you were ten years old and still my little princess….. for your eighteenth birthday, I let you read the only happy chapter of my book, which is Laalla's love story….. I am happy my book is being published on time for your twentieth birthday. You are now my grown up lady and emotionally competent to read the entire story. The world changed faster than you grew up, and it continues to change with an even faster pace….. It's a struggle between the forces of change and the forces of resistance. With the world being dragged in chaos and divisions, may you remain strong and dedicated to responsible thinking for your fellow human beings, without regard to their geographic locations, race and religion.

INTRODUCTION

CRY OF ANGELS PORTRAYS the results of three decades of chaos and turmoil in Afghanistan under the Communists, the mujahideen, the Taliban and the post-Taliban regimes. The book is based on interviews I conducted beginning in November 2001, when I traveled from California to Pakistan to take part in the first post-Taliban conference on Afghanistan reconstruction hosted by the United Nations Development Programme (UNDP). Upon my arrival in Quetta, Pakistan, I heard the story of a young Afghan journalist, Laalla, the protagonist in *Cry of Angels*, a woman who had been forced at gunpoint to marry a member of the Taliban regime. The search for the truth behind Laalla's story and her whereabouts led me to the tragic and shocking stories of dozens and perhaps hundreds of other women who were widowed by the Communists, gang-raped by mujahideen gunmen, forced at gunpoint to marry Taliban warriors, used as bargaining chips by tribal elders, stoned to death by decree of Traditional Justice, or forced into prostitution by drug dealers and warlords. Meanwhile, young Afghan boys, rejected by society because of the stigma of their sisters and mothers, were joining the Taliban movement and becoming volunteer suicide bombers.

The past three decades of turmoil in Afghanistan—the rise of the Taliban, and the emergence of militancy in the region—and Afghanistan's geopolitical importance as a country smashed between four nuclear powers are the main factors fueling this expensive, complicated, and unprecedented war. Although analysts profess to make a distinction between the wars in Iraq and Afghanistan, one sees, reads, and hears on a daily basis that parallels continue to be drawn between the two wars. Much of this confusion can be blamed on a lack of attention to recent history and the hegemony of Afghanistan's neighbors. It also can be blamed in part on the misleading legends embodied in phrases like "the Great Game," "the Land of the Lions," "the Graveyard of Empires," and "the winners of the Cold War," which add an aura of glamour to war stories and make them interesting and entertaining to readers. The truth is that those brave lions have become the denizens of one of the world's poorest and weakest nations, whose pride and dignity are stolen, whose culture is destroyed, whose unity is shattered, whose history is being rewritten by the neighbors. Afghanistan is on the brink of fragmentation, and if it is not saved, its pieces will dissolve into neighboring countries who will have no choice but to share power with a militant Taliban state.

While Pakistan's interest in the Taliban as an anti-India regime in Afghanistan is no longer a secret, that Iran has started to support the Taliban may sound awkward to the ears of those who still remember the slaughter of nine Iranian diplomats by the Taliban during the Mazar-e-Sharif massacre in August of 1998. In the spring of 2010 at a conference in Kabul, the Iranian foreign minister delivered his speech in Persian and said, "The spoken language in this part of the world is Persian." The truth is that Iran plans to benefit from a Taliban comeback by marginalizing the northern part of Afghanistan, a gateway to yet another Persian-speaking country, Tajikistan (long coveted by the Islamic Republic of Iran).

While *Cry of Angels* is a story about the plight of women in Afghanistan, there is a great deal of cultural, political, and religious information incorporated into the story to familiarize readers with the situation in Afghanistan and Pakistan.

This work would have not been possible without the advice and support of two great friends. My first motivation to interview Afghans in refugee camps and to keep a journal of my visit came from my ninth-grade teacher, a Pashtun from Helmand. He lived in Quetta, the capital city of Baluchistan, a city famous for its terrorist training camps and now the headquarters of the Quetta Shura. I met with him in his home in November 2001. It was his request that obliged me to write the stories of Afghans' lives and to keep a journal for the past ten years. Thousands of miles away from Quetta in the DC area, my friend Brad Little and I often discussed Afghanistan, the Taliban, and the Great Game. We discussed Pakistan's three inharmonious governments—the ISI government, the militant government, and the civilian government that are collectively known to the West as Pakistan. Before the 2009 presidential election in Afghanistan, Brad and I both worked at the US embassy in Afghanistan.I requested that he read an article I had written on the upcoming election and told him about the notes and articles I had collected over the past nine years. He encouraged me to write them into the form of a novel. "People like novels. They don't read essays and articles," Brad told me.

These two great men, although from two different worlds, share a common wisdom: the knowledge of one another's culture, history, and faith. My high school teacher, Mr. Khan (I refrain from mentioning his full name for his protection), has a melancholy expression and a long white beard, wears a white turban, and lives in the deserts of southwestern Afghanistan. There, at the age of seventy, he works for one of the American Provincial Reconstruction Teams (PRTs) as a translator to feed his wife and contribute to the cause that he believes in as an educated Muslim. As a victim of Communism, a force of tyranny,

Khan is unwilling to surrender his children and grandchildren to yet another force of tyranny, the Al-Qaeda mythology. Khan knows a great deal about American history and the European renaissance. When he talks, he makes reference to historical facts, dates, and statistics. He believes no form of government is perfect, but governments and forms of governments should be studied in historical context. "Read history and compare historical events. Learn from history, because you don't live long enough to experience it all by yourself." I still remember hearing Khan saying those words when I was a ninth grader.

Brad Little, my middle-aged American friend, has a sanguine personality and a cheerful demeanor. He shows up every other week in DC for business, and usually, over a cup of coffee, we continue our unending debate on Al-Qaeda, the Taliban, and AFPAK issues. He has an in-depth knowledge of Islam, the Middle East, Al-Qaeda, and the Wahhabis. Indeed, he is the only American I know who uses the word Salafi for Wahhabi. And not only does he use the term, Brad knows a great deal of the politics and history behind it. If Khan does not consider Americans an occupying power in Afghanistan, Brad does not consider Islam a religion of terror. If Brad knows that Al-Qaeda and the Taliban are not leaders of Islam, Khan has never thought of the Chicago and New York City mafias as Catholic radicals.

After thirty-seven years, I still remember as if it was yesterday a time Communist students went on strike in our schoolyard using the political peccadilloes of the Afghan parliament as a pretext for indoctrinating young kids with Marxist ideology. Mr. Khan went down the hallways telling students to gather in room 12-A, because he needed to talk to them. Most students didn't listen to him, but a good number of boys and girls did follow him to the room, which was usually used for twelfth-graders. After we had brought more chairs from the room next door, we curiously waited to hear from Khan. He put his black leather briefcase on the desk. As usual, he asked one of the students to come and clean the chalkboard with a cloth eraser, a small white cotton pillow that we voluntarily begged our mothers to make for us and brought from home. We also carried bundles of soft chalk in our bags or pockets that we heated on a stove and brought to school for better writing and to prevent the black paint from scratching off the board. While the blackboard was being cleaned, Khan gazed through the large window out at the flowers in the schoolyard, and we gazed at the reflection of the sun on his pink, bald head. He was dressed in gray slacks and a blue shirt. He said,

"These Communists are denying your rights to free thinking and democracy. No one can talk about politics in the Soviet Union except to praise the ruling Communist Party. And look at the power of democracy in America; they are about to impeach the president. Let's talk about Watergate instead of listening to empty slogans." He did talk about current affairs in America, and we listened. Watergate was not the only topic that took our thoughts to America; Mr. Khan talked about the retirement system and the health care Americans enjoyed at retirement age. Then he sighed and looked out of the window at the petunia flowers and turned and went on, "Who's paying for Baba Azam's retirement?" Azam was an old gardener whose son was among the students who wasn't taking part in the strike. "You are your father's retirement investment," He looked at Ahmad, the son of the gardener, who sat in front row of the class. Then Khan went on. "The real investment in a child's life is education." He stopped suddenly as if he wanted to correct what he had said. Then he sighed again, and after a concentrated silence, he continued, "It doesn't always have to be a university degree, though." All of us, including Ahmad, knew that the teacher had said this because Ahmad couldn't afford to attend university. After school, he and his younger brother sold vegetables on the street. The produce was from a small school garden where the dean let Baba Azam plant vegetables to take home to feed his children. As if Khan was somehow able to predict the financial situation of today's America in 1974, he told us on that day, "Banks can go bankrupt; properties can depreciate; and stocks can crumble; but knowledge is sustainable. It grows and provides a return on your investment. It's unimaginable how damaging this demonstration by the puppets of the KGB is—they are holding students back from a week of education. Education is the best gift for a child." He paused for a moment and then went on. "That's what they say, but I say you are not children anymore. Successfully finishing school is the best gift you can give to your parents. In the absence of retirement, stock, or savings, you are your parents' future, as we are for ours and our fathers were for their fathers."

The Communist students who had taken part in the strike told Ahmad the next day that Khan was a landlord, a member of the CIA, and from an aristocratic family, that there was an irreconcilable animosity between the working masses and the upper class, and that Khan's intention was to belittle and embarrass the son of a proletarian in front of the sons of corrupt bureaucrats and bourgeois capitalists. They also told him that Steve and Doug (two Peace Corps English teachers) had paid Khan to keep the students busy during the strike and he was a traitor and would be held responsible for his actions once the *khalq,* the people, took power. This was not the only day Khan talked to us about America. He also told us the stories behind American holidays. His favorite was Thanksgiving tales. After three decades, I heard another Muslim talking about Thanksgiving and encouraging Muslim Americans to celebrate Thanksgiving with their fellow Americans. Dr. Farid Younnus, an Afghan American professor at Cal-State University, Hayward, who hosts a talk show for the Afghan community on a cable channel every Saturday, speaks out for peaceful Islam and warns Muslims against the preaching and spread of what he refers to as Wahhabism. I refer to it as *Saudism*, a sect in the service of the Al-Saud oligarchy that denies the right of Muslims to free elections and democracy. The closer the kingdom gets to the end of its oil reserves, the faster Wahhabism has spread. It has been prolifically adding to its followers since the early 1980s, from Manila to Sarajevo, from Islamabad to Mogadishu. Followers of Wahhabism call themselves Salafis. Egyptian scholar Tawfik Hamid, who also advocates a peaceful understanding of Islam, argues that followers of Salafism believe that Saudi influence is sanctioned by God. I was watching the news coverage of the recent Egyptian revolution at Al-Tahrir square and heard a young man shouting, "We are Muslim! We are Arab! But we are not Saudis." He was right: not all Muslims are Arabs, and not all Arabs are Saudis.

Four years after that strike in our schoolyard, the Communists did take the power in a Soviet-backed coup d'état on April 27, 1978, and the next day Mr. Khan's erstwhile students were in charge of the Helmand provincial government. Khan's close family members and relatives were jailed and subsequently killed. Some of them were allegedly dropped from a military airplane over a lake near Ghazni, because the Kabul Pul-e-Charkhi jail was packed with newcomers despite the fact that the prisoners were being killed in groups every night. One of Khan's students, whose brother was a member of the Communist politburo at the time, helped Kahn to escape safely to Pakistan. According to Khan, he still owes his life and the lives of his wife and children to that student.

Shortly after the 9/11 tragedy, when the Taliban were still in power, I heard on CNN that the first reconstruction conference on Afghanistan was being hosted by the UNDP in Islamabad in a matter of weeks. I picked up the phone and called the UN in New York and volunteered to attend the conference and offered my construction and engineering skills. From day one at the conference, there were Pakistani officials who were against schools, the only form of formal education in Afghanistan before the war; they were against education for girls and against educational reform. Instead, they promoted madrassas, traditional justice, and tribal shuras. I had met many people from my college time, who had worked as engineers and administrators with NGOs and IOs in Pakistan during the Afghan-Soviet war and the Mujahideen era. Some of them are now in the Afghan cabinet, in the presidential palace, or serving as ambassadors.

After the reconstruction conference in Islamabad, I flew to Quetta in search of my teacher, Mr. Khan. I had Khan's telephone number from his relatives in California. My schedule was tight; I had only three days in Quetta. Finally, on the night before my flight to Peshawar, I found Khan over the telephone. Late that night he and his son came to my hotel, and the three of us drove to his home in his son's Suzuki jeep. During an emotional four hours, he told me about his life as a refugee in Pakistan and the struggle to put his children through school. His son, his only retirement insurance, was working with an NGO. While talking, Mr. Khan constantly stared at a computer on top of a metal trunk covered with a hand-embroidered white cloth. I asked him what it was about the computer that distracted him so much; he told me with joy that he had bought this used computer for his grandson using his wife's savings. He was very proud to be able to teach basic computer skill to his two grandchildren, who were in the elementary school.

During the course of his story, he named some of the Communists who had been high-ranking officials of the short-lived Communist government but were working for the Taliban in 2001. Some of them were in the city of Quetta working for the mujahideen before Taliban took over. He also told me that the gardener and his oldest son had been killed by the Communists for not becoming members of the People's Democratic Party. It was my teacher's wish that I interview Afghan refugees when I visited them in the refugee camps and take copious notes. Upon my arrival in Peshawar and during my subsequent visits to Afghan refugee camps, NGOs, and civil society organizations, I took notes about their stories. I quickly learned from my conversations with refugees, aid workers, activists, and young journalists working underground in Afghanistan that Khan's story paled in comparison to what many had experienced.

The stories of these victims did not end in Peshawar. Starting in 2003, I worked full-time in Afghanistan on various development projects, from physical reconstruction to human capacity–building and governance projects, which put me into contact with Afghan villagers, victims of the wars, refugees returning from Pakistan and Iran, and internally displaced families and farmers and gave me the opportunity to bring the story of the suffering of Afghans to their fellow human beings in the West. Thanks to the advice of my friends, I am now able to share part of that story with you in *Cry of Angels*. While the international community is preparing to withdraw forces from Afghanistan, *Cry of Angels* is the voice of the forgotten majority, the real victims of three decades of war, crying for help.

PREFACE

THE CAPITAL OF THE Kushan Empire and an important city of the Kabul Shahan and the Mogul Empire, Kabul, the city of seven gates and defensive walls, has always been a proud storyteller. From Alexander the Great to Genghis Khan, from the Persian assault to the Mogul invasion, and from the British wars to the defeat of the Soviet Union, Kabul has marked the story of her ruins in the history books. There are stories of the bravery of her sons and daughters behind every broken minaret and lost monument. A center of Zoroastrianism and then Buddhism, praised by Persian and Turkish poets, and noted in the history of the Rigveda, Kabul has shed the light of civilization on other parts of Asia. The first European to visit Kabul in the eighteenth century, the English traveler George Foster, described it as "the best and cleanest city in Asia." Over the past three thousand years, Kabul has had many visitors. Some came as adventurers and left, some came in order to stay, some came and left and forgot they had been there. While some looked forward to coming back, others came to help but will ultimately return home, leaving the wounded body of Kabul behind. Perhaps I visited Kabul just in time to hear her story before the wrath of history shrugged her off forever. When I met her, Kabul, with a chronically ill soul and broken limbs, lying wounded and mourned, barely had the energy to tell her story to the world. In fact, she was shy and embarrassed whenever her name came up. The good old days of the 1980s, when her name made headlines in the West and her heroes inspired Charlie Wilson and his war on Communism, were in the past. When I asked Mother Kabul why she had been quiet, she murmured, "My story of honor is gone with my heroes; I can't praise cowards."

It was the autumn of 1996. The city of Kabul was nothing more than a ruined ghost town, and there was barely anyone to be seen on the streets. You no longer could hear hopeless young girls screaming for help and jumping from rooftops to escape gang rape by warlords' gunmen, former mujahideen who had once encouraged those same girls to join their brothers in the holy jihad against the Communists. The fearful sound of aimless rockets and the crying of widows and orphans in the middle of the night had finally stopped.

Taliban clerics had imposed a draconian form of Islamic law whose harshest edicts fell on women: they could go out but only in the company of a blood-related man; they were beaten if their ankles or hands showed from beneath their burqas. They were barred from working and studying outside their homes. Women and men in Kabul had only one wish: "We wish we had not been born." The only type of employment for men was in the war industry of the Taliban—fixing pickup trucks for holy warriors, preparing food in restaurants, tailoring clothes, and selling gasoline on the side of the road. Most families were headed by widows. You can imagine a household headed by a widow barred from working outside her home.

The silence of the city and the traumatized faces of Kabulis were like the quiet moment after a tornado or a hurricane has left people homeless. Maybe Mother Nature cannot compete with the devastation caused by a conglomerate of gunmen and warlords, the so-called former mujahideen factions, in the name of God. One cannot describe the physical and cultural destruction of Kabul in words. The once-elite neighborhood of Macroyan, the Soviet-built apartment complexes, and the Western-style residences of Kabul's officials had been looted and burned. Doors and windows had been taken away and used as firewood; plumbing and fixtures had been taken to Pakistan and sold as scrap metal. In the late 1970s and early 1980s, the non-Communist residents had either been killed by the Soviet regime or had fled the country. The Communist residents faced the same fate during the Mujahideen era. Many residents left their homes and escaped to safer districts of the city during the factional fighting of the mujahideen that followed the Soviet withdrawal.

Those who repeat history are dominated by their aspirations and ignore the past, and those who are aware of the past can prevent history from being repeated.

CHAPTER 1

ALL DAY AND NIGHT, the dust from the streets had blown in through General Qassim's missing windows. The summer heat of Kabul was relinquishing its grasp to the early fall breeze, a warning of a cold winter ahead. Far off in the distance, a rim of mountains was visible beyond Kabul, and you could see a thin line of snow capping the highest peaks. When the bakery across the street baked its bread, the smoke from the clay oven mixed with the red dust from the roads and drifted all around the inside of his apartment. After the long, dry season, the dust and smoke had begun to cake in his throat and lungs. It was causing his eyes to water. It gathered all day long in a fine layer upon the family's bedding and prayer mats.

When the Taliban first came to take control, before the first snow fell, General Qassim's wife Shah Jaan had already wrapped burlap around pieces of cardboard to board up the windows, but General Qassim had yet to install them. As it was November, the nights had grown quite cold, but he had been too weary to board up the windows, and the house was still filled with fine dust and the scent of freshly baked bread all night and day.

On that particular afternoon, General Qassim was lying on a pile of several neatly folded blankets, his eyes blinking against the dust, his mind lost in dreams of bygone years. He had been a military man before the Soviets invaded. He had been promoted to the grade of general in the wake of their invasion, but ever since the mujahideen had come to power, his country had found little use for his only set of skills. He was fifty but looked closer to seventy now. His once-straight back was bent over. His once-dignified appearance had deteriorated from hardship and grief. The formerly sharp, penetrating eyes of a strict general now looked more like those of a surrendered soldier. His heart was heavy. His mind was filled with many regrets. His eyes often gazed blankly off into space.

General Qassim lived with what remained of his family on the sixth floor of the third corridor in block thirty-six of Macroyan 2. It was the only apartment in Macroyan 2 still occupied. Wild dogs had taken up residence everywhere else in the building. He often heard them fighting at night. From their numbers, he could tell they were breeding.

Only two rooms of General Qassim's five-room apartment were still habitable. He and his wife, Shah Jaan, used the living room as a sleeping area. General Qassim's four surviving children used the dining room as their bedroom. A long, narrow hallway led from the dining room back to the front door. A gray blanket hung in place of the missing door. At the other end of the hallway were bedrooms with huge holes blown in the walls. There was also a small guest bathroom with no remaining fixtures or running water. The former mujahideen gunmen had looted most of the furniture, and that was why everyone in the family now slept on the concrete floors. There were enough blankets to cover those floors in a single layer and to double up as bed mats with yet another left over to fold up as a pillow. All the blankets in the apartment had UN and Red Crescent markings on them.

General Qassim's wife, Shah Jaan, was also aging quickly as she neared the end of her forties. Her hair was graying. Dark rings had grown under her eyes, and what little was left of her jet-black hair only served to accent that dark, sunken quality. As a wife, she shared her husband's grief and regrets, but as a mother raising four children, she hardly had time to indulge in his hopelessness and daydreams and empty gazes.

The oldest of their children, Laalla, had just turned twenty-six and was still a beautiful woman, but she wandered through the days now with her own lifeless expression. The general and his wife also had a twelve-year-old daughter, Sahar, an eight-year-old son, Mirwais, and a four-year-old daughter, Mina. There had been another daughter, Shabnam, but she had died about four years earlier. Shabnam would have been nineteen, had she still been alive.

General Qassim spent much of each day helping Mirwais and Sahar with their homeschooling. He went to the mosque five times a day for prayers. In the evenings, he lit a candle and sat next to the apartment corridor with his head down, holding a wooden pole flagged with many pieces of red and green fabric. Some of the fabric was four years old. Some was new.

Laalla spent every morning mixing dough for the family bread and then took the uncooked loaves to be baked at a bakery run by women across the street from their apartment building. Since it was not permissible under Taliban rule for a woman to leave the home without a blood-related male escorting her, Laalla always took her young brother, Mirwais, along for the journey.

When she went down to the street level and across the old playground to the next apartment building, Laalla no longer saw the neighborhood children at play. The playground had once been filled with playground equipment, but that had been carted away for salvage along with the plumbing fixtures. Once the playground equipment had disappeared, the children had turned to playing soccer on the dusty, makeshift field, but the Taliban had soon proclaimed that sort of entertainment to be equally un-Islamic.

With no school or schoolmates and little else to do with her young life, the twelve-year-old Sahar was slowly becoming as remote and depressed as her older sister Laalla. When Sahar wasn't busy with the school lessons her father assigned her each day, she lay on her blankets and pretended to sleep. In her mind, and in the mind of everyone in General Qassim's family, there was the ever-present fear and memory, even the expectation that all three sisters would one day face the same fate as Shabnam. That sooner or later, one of these holy warriors would come to claim each of them as a bride, and the three sisters would either have to acquiesce or do what Shabnam had done.

Laalla had been only sixteen when she had been inspired by verses of Mawlana Rumi through her home teacher and guru, Sufi Burhaan, one of the very few Sufis alive in Kabul during the Soviet invasion. As Laalla wrote in her diary, "It was Ustaad Burhaan who opened my eyes to the world and taught me love, created an attitude of hope in my heart, and lit a candle of enthusiasm for life in my mind." From the very first months of her lessons on Sufism, perplexed by her guru's story of life, passion for forgiveness, and resistance through love, Laalla came up with her own explanation for hope and overcoming misery:

Sometimes by force of nature I am lying on ashes,
Sometimes at a look from him I am in a garden of
flowers

Sufi Burhaan was a man in his late sixties with a distinguished smile. He lived with his wife in a modest home in the Khair Khana district in the northern part of Kabul. After his young son and only child had disappeared in the early days of the Soviet invasion, he had sold the house and large rose garden in the Chel Setoon district that he had inherited from his father and moved to Khair Khana.

Laalla learned from her ustaad how his only son, Nawid, had gone to America on a student-exchange program and how that had led to a scholarship studying law in the United States. Nawid's fiancée, Zainab, was a student at Kabul University at the time, and Nawid's plan was to return to Kabul and marry Zainab and help to make Afghanistan the greatest country it could possibly be.

Not long after Nawid returned home from America, the occupying forces covered the beauty of his country with the ashes of war. Zainab's father was a colonel in the Afghan army and was killed on the first day of the coup. The family tried for years to learn what the Communists had done with his body, but nothing ever came of their search.

Days after colonel's death, the Communists arrested Zainab's uncle. He was a judge, but the Communists rounded him up like a common criminal. They arrested Nawid on that same day, and no one had heard from either one of them since.

A rumor was swirling around Kabul at the time that when prisoners were flown in from places like the Helmand or Kandahar provinces and it was clear that no space remained in the Kabul prison that particular day, the pilot of the military transport was sometimes instructed to drop his prisoners into a lake north of Ghazni instead. That is the way things were done during the Soviet occupation—no respect for human life. The Communist politburo could issue a decree in Moscow in the morning, and by that afternoon people would have disappeared in Afghanistan. A two-sentence memo, and your life came to an end.

Zainab's two brothers disappeared during the winter of 1978 in a similar fashion. A blacklist of some three thousand men was posted in public one day, and soon all three thousand of them had been executed. There was never any attempt to find out who was guilty among them and who might be innocent. Subsequently Zainab committed suicide after she was forced by Communist officials to marry one of her classmates at

Kabul University who was a junior member of the Communist Party.

During the years of the Soviet occupation, Laalla herself came to be a student at Kabul University. She got a lot of attention and respect from fellow students for her famous poems. Her major was English literature. She also received violin training from Ustaad Mohammad Hussein. It was her father's dream to have her win a scholarship and study the violin further in Kiev.

It was in the summer of 1991 that the Communist regime promoted Qassim to the rank of one-star general. President Najibullah himself came to honor the general. An elegant dinner reception was arranged at the military club in Shashdrak. The military club was directly across from the American embassy, and hundreds of the general's colleagues and friends were in attendance, along with their wives and an abundance of children.

As the oldest child, Laalla was entrusted to arrange the seating and greet the guests at the door. She was also responsible for the music and chose a classical sitar and tabla band in place of Western music.

After dinner, General Qassim grabbed the microphone and asked if the musicians would allow his daughter, Laalla, to join them for a few songs with her violin. The musicians stood up. The audience applauded. General Qassim revealed the violin, and Laalla came forward in embarrassment. She quickly thanked the musicians for allowing this novice to play in the presence of masters after one song, but then turned to find the guests coming forward with their arms filled with bouquets. One of these was a young man named Farid, an engineering student whose parents were also dear friends of the general. Farid placed a beautiful ring of red roses around Laalla' neck, and the guests and musicians went on applauding until Laalla felt obliged to play another song on her violin.

Later that evening, as Laalla and her parents were saying good night to their many guests, Farid stepped forward, this time with a bouquet of tulips. *Laalla* means "tulip" in Farsi-Dari, and her father, who had been holding Laalla's hand, let go to accept the bouquet. Farid bowed, said good night, and left without another word, but Laalla found a handwritten letter attached to the bouquet. She quickly hid the letter under her dress and, upon arriving home, promptly went to her bedroom and took it out. It appeared to have been torn from a student's notebook but was very carefully folded. Laalla carefully unfolded the piece of paper and slowly read the beautifully written words. She read them again and again, and her heart filled with joy and inspiration each time she finished the letter.

The next morning, Laalla went down to catch the cable car in front of their apartment building. It was Wednesday, and she had a midmorning class at Kabul University and knew that Farid also had a midmorning class on Wednesdays. They usually crossed paths at the bus stop, but on this Wednesday, Farid was nowhere in sight.

Assuming that Farid was embarrassed by his own gesture of love, Laalla decided to wait for the next bus, and sure enough, Farid came walking down the street a few minutes after the previous bus had departed. Laalla had always thought of Farid as a nice young man. He was polite. He was always respectful. When there were no other seats left on the bus, Laalla had watched him give up his own seat many times to various women. But on this day, Laalla saw Farid in a completely different light. Now he was a handsome young man in blue jeans and a white, short-sleeved shirt. His short, curly black hair and trim, black mustache made her heart beat.

As he approached the bus station, Laalla's eyes were locked on Farid and counting his steps. He came toward her without smiling, serious now and intent.

When he was near, Laalla said, "Salaam. Thanks for the beautiful flowers and kind words you honored me with last night."

"Words are meant to bow at the feet of beauties," Farid said. "Unfortunately, the words of an engineering student don't do justice to the beauty of a musician and poet and writer like you. But please accept mine as a green leaf, the gift of Darwesh, as they say."

Before Laalla was able to think of anything to say in return, the bus arrived, and Farid politely gestured for Laalla to get on first. She stepped onto the bus and found it was full of mostly male passengers, some of whom had spilled over into the aisle. A man dressed in a white Afghan dress stood up and offered Laalla his seat. Laalla said it was okay; she would be changing buses very soon, but the man insisted and she sat down. Then the young woman sitting next to her also stood up, allowing Farid to sit down next to Laalla.

At the Froshgah station, they both got off the bus and found out the next bus for the university would not be coming along for thirty minutes. The summer morning had already grown hot, and having forgotten the umbrella she usually carried to shade herself from the sun, Laalla felt a headache coming on in the heat.

Seeing Laalla's discomfort, Farid suggested they walk along in the shade of the vendors' stands together and perhaps find something pleasant to drink. When nothing appealed to Laalla, Farid suggested they try a rooftop restaurant there in Froshgah instead.

"They have good frozen yogurt," he said. "Anyway, I have missed my first class."

"So have I," Laalla confessed to him. "My class just started five minutes ago."

In the end, they shared a glass of fresh carrot juice in the underground restaurant across from the bus stop and took a later bus over to the university. They met again the next day, and the next. Instead of arranging the time they spent together around their classes and other responsibilities, everything in their lives was now being moved here and there so they could fulfill their longing to see each other, and they did long for each other—night and day, day and night.

CHAPTER 2

THOSE TURNED OUT TO be the happiest days of Laalla's life. She found herself so deeply immersed in feelings of love that time escaped her. Day in, day out, she completely lost track of where she was in this world.

Within the week, she and Farid were planning their engagement. Various ways to arrange the ceremony were discussed with both their families, but all the while the mujahideen, like a dark storm, were gathering at the outskirts of Kabul.

Fearing the worst was to come, Farid's parents had already arranged to sell their house and were leaving for Moscow. It was hoped that from there that they would find their way to Western Europe or even America.

But Farid would hear nothing of this. He had long waited to see the mujahideen take power and imagined his dreams of Islamic justice were finally about to be realized. The oppressed masses of Afghanistan would at last have their day in power.

General Qassim too had high hopes for the new mujahideen government. If it was based on Islamic law, if the Quran and the word of God were the final judges, then no innocent person would ever have to suffer from injustice again. The general further hoped that the many Afghans now living abroad would come back home and help to rebuild their battered country with their wealth of knowledge. He imagined every Afghan child having a better education, the economy booming, and future generations living to see a happy and prosperous nation.

As an impartial soldier, General Qassim expected the mujahideen to honor his service to the Afghan flag and constitution. Yes, it had been in the service of a puppet Soviet regime for many years, but in General Qassim's eyes, he had done his patriotic duty, nothing less, nothing more.

When he listened to the radio broadcasts of young student followers of the mujahideen, General Qassim's hopes were only reinforced. The future Islamic government, inspired by the Muslim Brotherhood in Egypt, would be a glorious one, its justice laid down according to Islamic sharia law. National TV and radio stations broadcasted President Najibullah's speeches on how bloody the streets of Kabul would be if the puppets of the ISI stole the government of the people, but the followers of the mujahideen played the recorded speeches of Hekmatiar and Rabbani about the future government of brotherhood and the Islamic masses. Rabbani's message to Afghans was that he would follow the model of Malaysia, a modern Islamic state with trade and diplomatic ties with the rest of the world.

General Qassim saw no need to flee the country, even though street vendors came knocking on the door every day to ask if anyone had any furniture or household goods for sale. He persisted in this belief even when food prices skyrocketed and women took to wearing headscarves and conservative dress to work and girl students at the colleges stopped wearing makeup altogether or even walking in the streets with their fiancés. Never mind that women had quit their jobs driving the cable cars and that movie theaters had gone out of business; never mind that people were stockpiling food and fuel for the winter. General Qassim still felt certain such hysteria was unjustified.

After all, even the Afghan Jew down on the famous chicken street, who sold the souvenirs to Laalla that she gave to Farid's parents as a farewell gift, was not leaving.

When Shah Jaan asked her husband what his plans were, he replied, "I can't understand what person would leave their motherland to live overseas in a strange culture and foreign environment. My own family left to live in New York City, but I will stay and die here in the land of my ancestors. Who are these criminals and bearded puppets of Pakistan to think they can chase us away from our own homeland? Even the Prophet Mohammad, peace be upon him, instructed all Muslims to tolerate the Jews."

Still, General Qassim understood the stigma attached to the Soviet-style apartment in which they lived and decided to move his family into their house in Wazir Akbar Khan as a precaution.

A few days after they moved, the first snow fell that year, and that evening, the general was surprised to find Farid knocking at his front door. With all the fear and panic swirling around the city and Farid's parents hoping to depart for Moscow with his two sisters as soon as their house was sold, the general naturally had assumed that Farid would want to be with his family as much as possible during this trying period. Also, Laalla's final exams were approaching, and all her time was consumed with studying for them. That left only one explanation in the General's mind for why Farid was standing outside his door.

I know, he thought. *Farid is bringing us a taste of the first snow.* It was a tradition called *barfi* among the Kabulis and Afghans in the north to surprise friends with a handful of the first snow and receive a special dinner treat in return. However, upon opening the door, the general quickly saw that Farid had no snow in his hands, and he was not smiling as he usually did, so the general began to think something must be wrong.

"Welcome, Farid jaan!" He gestured him to the living room as usual. "How are your parents? Is the exam going well?"

"No, no, Uncle," Farid said. "Everything is fine. I came to see Laalla and to get her opinion on something … I have news for her. It could be good news—it depends on how you look at it—but I would like to share it with Laalla first. With your permission, of course."

Relieved, General Qassim told Farid, "Just remember, if you are having trouble at all with your exams, allow Laalla to help you. She excels at math, as demonstrated by the frugal accountant she is with our household finances. Just yesterday, for instance, we were all told to cut back on our meat and dried fruit consumption. With all the pessimistic forecasts in the air, she is sure the sky will soon be falling down on our heads." He followed this with his distinctive long laugh. "Ah, but forgive me," he said, seeing the awkward smile on Farid's face. "Of course you are here to see Laalla. Laalla!" he called out, and after a few moments she appeared from the back of the house.

"Farid jaan, salaam," she said, surprised to see him. "You told me that you would be preparing for your exam tonight. Is everything okay?"

"Please. I need to talk with you alone."

Laalla looked at the general, who waved the two young lovers out onto the balcony through a sliding glass door. The snow was falling around them as the general slid the door closed.

"What is it?" Laalla asked, as troubled as the general had been by Farid's unexpected appearance.

"It is mostly good news," Farid said. "My parents have sold their house. And even at the price my mother had been asking. But they are leaving in a week and don't want anyone to know about their trip or even to let anyone know that they have sold their house."

"Is that all, Farid?" Laalla said. "You had me worried." She slid the door open and shouted inside, "Don't worry, father! It's all good news! Everything is fine!"

While Farid discussed with Laalla how to plan a surprise farewell dinner for his parents, a knock came from inside the door. Laalla slid it open again, and the general passed out two shawls from behind the curtain.

"Thanks, Uncle," Farid said, "but it is not that cold out here tonight."

The General stuck his head out through the curtain and smiled.

"When you are a father, *bakhair*, and especially if your first child happens to be a girl, you will know how a father feels to see you take his little princess out into the wind and snow and torture her in this way. Perhaps I should bring you two a cup of hot tea."

"Thanks, but we will be inside in a minute, Father," Laalla said.

Farid also thanked the general, who disappeared back inside. General Qassim rarely called Laalla by her name; he called her his princess, his hope, and his *modarak* ("little mother").

At the general's request, Farid stayed for dinner. "We went to the dinner table," Laalla wrote in her diary. "Dad sat at the head. To his right was Mom; next to her Shabnam, and at the end of the table sat Sahar, who loved Farid so much that she couldn't stop gazing at him. To the left of my father was Farid, and I sat next to him. My mom fed little Mirwais in his baby chair. Our newborn sister, little Mina, was in her crib."

Based on the plans that Laalla and Farid made that night, a farewell dinner was arranged at General Qassim's home less than a week later on what turned out to be Shab-e-Yalda, the longest night of the year, which was celebrated with special food and pomegranate but had been declared un-Islamic by the Taliban. After a grand meal, everyone drove over to Farid's parents' house for a cup of tea. Shah Jaan wanted to throw a large party in honor of Laalla's engagement so that Farid and Laalla could officially be proclaimed engaged and Farid could move with them to Wazir Akbar Khan. Farid's parents also wanted to proclaim the engagement to all their relatives and friends, but in the end it was agreed such a celebration would simply have to wait until things had settled down a bit.

For the time being, Farid's parents suggested that Farid stay in their apartment in Macroyan. General Qassim assured Farid's parents that once they reached their final destination, the general and his family would celebrate Farid's engagement and wedding as if Farid were their own son. Farid's parents offered terse thanks for the general's gesture and went back to talking about their plans for living in the West. This left Laalla and Farid embarrassed and General Qassim quietly angry.

On their way back home that night, he told Laalla, "You are lucky, my princess, that Farid's mother will not be in your life. I love Farid as my son, but this lady is rude. While I am planning the biggest wedding in all of Afghanistan, she is going on and on about living in the West. She even talked about you playing the violin at your own engagement party. What a cultureless woman—a bride playing music in her own wedding? "

The departure of Farid's parents only added to the uncertainty and upheaval surrounding the two young lovers' lives, but despite this, they both graduated from the university a few months later, and Farid found a job as an intern with the Afghan Construction Unit and Laalla was hired to teach English at Malalai School in Shar-e-Naw.

Not long after they had taken their jobs, the mujahideen arrived in Kabul. The Afghan National Army was dissolved. President Najibullah promptly sought refuge in the UN compound. General Qassim was told to leave his post and stay home until further notice.

Farid's wishes for a new mujahideen government had at last come true, but this new government was not what he and many other young idealistic students had envisioned. Instead of order, gangs of untrained young warriors draped in bullets soon roamed the streets of Kabul. The looting and raping began in a matter of days. Everywhere you looked there were guns and heavy weapons.

Ironically, thanks to a nearby neighbor, Farid became one of the first victims of this shoddily run government. This neighbor, knowing that Farid's parents had left the country, used their absence as a pretext to claim that Farid's father had actually seized the apartment from his family many years earlier. Accordingly, the neighbor demanded his apartment back, along with the unpaid rent for the past twelve years. As he had a relative close to one of the new warlords in power, this neighbor had instant credibility. As a prominent official in Dr. Najib's fallen government, Farid's father and his entire family were automatically suspect.

In court, Farid had no documents. His mother had taken all their legal papers along with her to Europe. The neighbor brought three holy warriors with him as witnesses. They put their hands on the holy Koran, and the Court of Justice and Brotherhood ruled in the neighbor's favor. He got the apartment, along with Farid's car, furniture, and expensive silk rugs to cover the supposedly unpaid rent

Some of General Qassim's former military colleagues now worked as advisors to the new mujahideen government, and General Qassim approached them on Farid's behalf only to learn that these men were now fervent believers in the mujahideen cause. In fact, as the general was told so that everyone within earshot might hear them, these men had always been believers in the mujahideen cause and had actually been working as undercover agents within the former Communist regime.

General Qassim knew this to be a blatant lie and left the government offices that day feeling greatly disturbed but still believing things would eventually work themselves out toward a better Afghanistan. Every revolution had its ups and downs, and the General assumed it was only a matter of time before things in the government got better organized.

Farid, meanwhile, had come to regret his previous support of the mujahideen. After Farid's hardship, with General Qassim having moved his family into the house they owned in Wazir Akbar Khan, Farid was given the keys to their Soviet-style apartment in Kabul. It was now late summer, and an engagement party for Laalla and Farid was finally arranged. General Qassim had not liked seeing his daughter date a man without this usual formality. Up until that point, it had been understandable. There were the new jobs Laalla and Farid had taken, and Farid's parents' departure for Moscow, and all the upheaval associated with the new mujahideen government, and of course now the loss of Farid's home and car and most of his belongings. The timing had never been quite right, but finally a date was set, and that Thursday afternoon, General Qassim went to the Intercontinental Hotel to make sure everything had been properly prepared for the engagement party. Shah Jaan and the children stayed at home wrapping gifts and preparing candy. Farid and the general's old driver borrowed a new white Toyota and went to Karte Parwan to have it wrapped with tulips by a florist. Meanwhile, Laalla's friends and coworkers arranged to have her hair done at a local beauty salon, and Shah Jaan and Laalla's sister Shabnam were scheduled to meet them there around two o'clock.

Shortly after the noon prayers, a loud explosion shook the windows of the beauty salon. This was followed by several more explosions, and they continued every few minutes for over an hour. Inside, the explosions seemed far away and completely incongruous with getting one's hair done in a beauty salon in a nice part of town, but outside people were shouting "Allah akbar" and running desperately around in every direction.

An older man sitting in a teahouse next to the salon was busy cursing the new regime throughout the whole affair. "So this is the gift of our new prime minister to the people of Afghanistan! Mr. Gulbudden will go down as the only prime minister in history who detonates rockets in his own capital city! I am sure he has marked his name in the history books of mankind forever!"

Given the danger, the lady who ran the salon insisted that Laalla and her friends stay with her until the shelling had stopped, and two hours went by before the city grew calm again. At that point, the salon owner sent her young son off to find a taxi. When he returned, Laalla and her four friends squeezed into the tiny Volga car.

On the way back to General Qassim's house in Wazir Akbar Khan, the taxi was stopped at checkpoints by armed gunmen three times. The five women were made to step out of the car each time, and each time they were searched in a way inappropriate to the teachings of Islam. When one of Laalla's friends asked the gunman was bothering to search them when the explosions had taken place far away, he slapped her on the face and beat her on the back with his Kalashnikov rifle.

"How the hell do you know where the rockets are landing? You probably slept with him last night," he added, referring to the taxi driver.

When the five women were at last on their way again, Laalla insisted that her friends stay with her for the night. That way their parents would know where to find them and everyone would be assured of their safety.

When they finally pulled up to the general's driveway, Laalla saw her mother and sister Shabnam standing on the roof of the two-story house. Shah Jaan came down quickly and said she wanted to take the taxi to go look for the general and Farid. Smoke was coming from the area of the Intercontinental Hotel, and she felt certain they were in trouble, but Laalla would not let her go.

An hour later, one of the neighbors came and told them that on his way back from the Froshgah station, her husband had found all the roads blocked by gunmen, but otherwise things seemed to be okay. There were no injuries. The rockets had landed mostly in the mountains. She expected the general and Farid to arrive as soon as the roads had been cleared.

Laalla tried the TV and radio stations and found them broadcasting recitations from the holy Koran. This was followed by speeches from Professor Rabbani, the new president, who had been elected by a "council of persons of discretion and consensus." The council of persons of discretion and consensus was a *jirga*, which, for the purposes of the new government, simply meant that the election had taken place secretly behind closed doors.

Around eight o'clock, Uncle Ahmad, a friend of the family who had gone to the Intercontinental Hotel with the general earlier in the day, came back to the house. He looked nervous and unwilling to speak but finally confessed that the general and Farid had taken the general's driver to the hospital for a minor injury. They should expect all three of them back home very soon.

"I don't care if they kill me," Shah Jaan said. "I'm going to the hospital."

Seeing her mother's determination, Laalla said she would go along, and by the time they got to the front door, Uncle Ahmad said he was going as well.

The four-hundred-bed military hospital was just a mile away from the house, and they arrived there without meeting any more gunmen. Inside the hospital, however, they were confronted with hundreds of wounded civilians. Men, women, and children were lying all over the floors. Nurses and doctors were rushing here and there along the halls.

Laalla found the famous female general and surgeon Sohaila Siddiq standing with General Qassim.

Thank god, Laalla thought to herself. *My father is alive— but where is Farid?*

With her heart in a panic, Laalla hurried over to her father and listened in a daze while the doctor explained that her fiancé had also been injured. He was okay, but the condition of the driver was serious. They were running out of blood and needed donors fast. They were also running out of IVs.

"We were not prepared for a situation like this,' Sohaila told them.

A nurse came up to them and explained that there were hundreds of men and women on the first floor ready to donate but there were not enough staff to draw the blood. Sohaila excused herself and ran off with the nurse. Laalla went with her family to see Farid. He seemed pale but alert, weak but not suffering from any serious injury. The sun was setting, and Laalla, fearing that her family might well meet more mujahideen gunmen on the darkened roads, said that her family should leave before dark and that she would stay with Farid for the night, but Farid insisted that she go and get a good night's sleep and told her to be back early in the morning.

At six the next morning, Laalla called the hospital and learned that Farid had passed away in the night. Stunned, she handed the phone to the general as a nurse explained that Glulam, the driver, was still in a coma.

For three days, Laalla wept over Farid's dead body. She walked around in a state of mourning for another forty days, and all the while Gulbudden Hekmatiar, President Rabbani's rival prime minister, shot rockets into the city and Rabbani responded by shooting rockets into Hekmatiar's headquarters. Exchanges of artillery rounds between the two men became a daily routine.

Within months of the revolution, fractious divisions had arisen between Hazara and Uzbek, Pashtun and Tajik. The city was divided into five zones, each belonging to a different group of warriors based on ethnicity. Matters around Kabul were in such a total state of chaos that Laalla had not received her salary for more than three months. Everyone was told the government had no money and that it was about to print up new Islamic currency in order to pay its debts, so as soon as the forty-day period of mourning for Farid had passed, General

Qassim decided to move his family back into their apartment, hoping they could rent out their house in Wazir Akbar Khan for some additional income.

After several days of moving boxes from the house in Wazir Akbar Khan to the apartment in Macroyan, Laalla went to the apartment with Shabnam one more time to clean up and make room for the furniture. The general was out visiting a friend. Sahar and Mirwais and Mina were helping their mother pack the final boxes in Wazir Akbar Khan.

Around noon, Laalla left Shabnam and went home to pick up her mother and the other siblings in a taxi, but upon arriving there, she found a note tacked to the door saying they had already left for the apartment.

Laalla had the driver turn around and head back the way they had come only to find a crowd of people standing outside the apartment building when they arrived. Laalla pushed through the crowd and found her mother passed out on the ground. Sahar, who was eight years old, ran up crying to Laalla. "They killed our Shabnam! The killers dropped her from the balcony!"

The women gathered around Shah Jaan were wetting her face from a bucket of water. Shabnam's body was lying on the lawn in front of the building covered with a white sheet.

Laalla went to sit by the body but had no tears left to shed. They had all been spent over Farid. She just sat next to the body and listened without emotion as an old neighbor lady explained what had happened. Gunmen had come to raid the apartment and, seeing the beautiful young Shabnam, had tried to take her with them. Shah Jaan and Sahar had thrown themselves at the feet of these men, a copy of the holy Koran in their hands, begging them not to take their young daughter and sister away, but the commander in charge had had lust in his heart and would not be dissuaded.

It was then, in all the weeping and wailing and confusion, that Shabnam had managed to break free and jump from the sixth-floor balcony.

Later that same day, Laalla awoke in the hospital lying next to her mother. The general was standing between the beds, holding his wife's hand and stroking Laalla's hair. Laalla stared at her father, unable to remember a thing about being taken to the hospital.

It was only later that she learned from the neighbors how the general had placed Shabnam's body on his shoulder and had started down the street toward the nearest mosque, crying out to his fellow citizens to witness his grief and shouting that if the people of Kabul did not stop these barbarians, Shabnam would not be the last one to die like this. For his troubles, more gunmen came and beat the general with clubs while he carried his daughter's body.

The general was right about one thing. Shabnam's death was only the beginning. The raping of young women soon became a matter of rivalry between the various factions. The killing of innocent people was soon a commonplace thing.

Following the advice of his friends, General Qassim chose not to have a formal memorial service in the mosque for his daughter. Rocket shells were falling randomly everywhere. Just moving from one part of the city to another was taking your life into your own hands.

Not wanting to be anywhere near their Macroyan apartment and any reminder of his daughter's tragedy, and especially not wanting his wife to see that place again, the general decided that the family should go stay with one of their relatives. After the burial of General Qassim's daughter, many of his neighbors came to offer their condolences and invited his family out for a stroll and a lunch or a cup of tea, but the general did not accept any of their invitations. He had no interest in seeing any part of the war-torn city.

After cleaning the apartment one last time and packing Farid's belongings, Laalla went downstairs to find that their neighbors had marked the place of Shabnam's death with a wooden pole draped in red and green flags. It was one week to the day since Shabnam had leapt to her death, and they had come to mark that Thursday evening with candles and prayers.

In the weeks to come, Laalla saw more and more of those flags and altars with candles in memory of the many women who had been raped by gunmen and the many innocent people who had been killed by random rocket shells and gunfire.

When the General finally had the strength to return to his home in Wazir Akbar Khan, he found it completely gutted. Thieves had stolen all of his belongings. They had even taken the lightbulbs from their sockets and the foot mat from in front of the door.

As the general and his family stood around in front wondering what to do next, four gunmen pulled up in an old Russian jeep and ordered them to leave immediately. When General Qassim told them that he owned this house, he was told to shut up. The house now belonged to the mujahideen, and as a Communist, he was lucky to escape with his life. If he really wanted to claim ownership of the house, he would then be held responsible as a former Communist owner for all criminal charges lodged against it.

With nowhere left to turn, General Qassim took his family one more time back to their Soviet-style apartment, and with little left in their possession, they unpacked Farid's belongings, things they had packed away for charity only five days earlier.

Within weeks of the family's move back to the Macroyan district, a rainstorm of bullets and rockets began to fall on their apartment building, and General Qassim was forced to lead his family on one more exodus, this time to live with an old friend and Laalla's teacher, Sufi Burhaan, who owned a modest home in the Khair Khana district. General Qassim and his family were provided with one room and one bed. The general and his wife slept in the bed. Laalla and the other three children slept on the floor, but at least they were able to live in relative safety from falling rockets.

This could not be said of the once-upscale Macroyan district. The buildings there went on being shelled week after week. Most of the general's old neighbors had long ago gone to live in Russia or America, and the homeless came to occupy the ruins of these once-luxurious buildings. What the homeless did not take, the wild dogs came to possess.

General Qassim and his family lived for four years on the money he had on deposit with a money exchanger and from the car he had sold. Laalla sat around at home this whole time, depressed over Farid and Shabnam and fearful of being kidnapped by the warlords if she dared to go outside. In time, the family became so impoverished, she was forced to return to work, though it did little to allay their financial hardship. Six months went by without any pay from the government. Even without rent to pay, the family was barely getting by from week to week.

Then, as summer turned to autumn that year, the Taliban came to power. The incessant shelling stopped, and the general led his family one more time back to their apartment in Macroyan. Their particular building had been the hardest hit, so that even the poorest of the poor had not thought to live there. All that was required of the general upon returning was to chase off some wild dogs and, of course, to live with the holes left over from all the artillery and rocket bombardments.

It was that November that Shah Jaan came into the living room with burlap wrapped around her pieces of cardboard. It was well past dark, and a kerosene lamp was burning in the room.

"If you feel better tomorrow," she told the General, "please nail these to the windows. We are inhaling dust from the street all day long. The wind blows smoke from the bakery into the house, and it is getting cold now at night. Little Mina and Mirwais have been coughing all day long."

Shah Jaan sat on the prayer mat facing toward Mecca. The general lay on his back, staring at the smoke-stained ceiling.

"I am worried they may die from hunger," he said quietly enough that the children could not hear him. "With the new Taliban policies in place, women cannot have photo coupons, and the UN is not accepting any of our food coupons without a photo."

The General lay on his back with his eyes staring up at the ceiling. A folded blanket from the UN lay underneath him.

"This morning," Shah Jaan said to her husband, "UN employees brought big buckets of chlorine powder to the bakery. They asked Aunt Sakina to distribute it to all her customers. We are to wash our vegetables and fruits before eating them. They also told her the UN had reached some kind of agreement with the Taliban, that the religious police will allow women's photos on food coupons for the time being, until they come up with another solution."

"If that is true," the general said, "we should get our food rations from the past two months."

"Also," Shah Jaan said, "that journalist NGO will reopen next week in Wazir Akbar Khan. You can go ask them for the fifty dollars they owe Laalla for the article she wrote a few months ago."

"That's a good idea," the general said. "Laalla should write a letter to them in English. Something granting me the power of attorney."

"The lantern is burning the last drop of kerosene," Shah Jaan said.

The General did not respond. He lay there on the double-folded blanket, thinking about the day ahead. His children would have nothing to eat until he got his food ration from the UN food distribution center the next morning.

Let it be the will of God, he thought, *for everything that comes to us is from him.*

Laalla, lying on her bed, she was listening to her parents. She had already experienced three different political regimes, three different philosophies of change, and three different philosophies of resistance. She spent sleepless nights comparing the degrees of torment her fellow human beings had suffered because of clashes between the various factions of the former mujahideen. She wondered whether others had suffered the same degree of despair under the Communist regime or during the reigns of kings as her family had suffered during the mujahideen era and was continuing to suffer under the Taliban.

Amazing, Laalla thought, *the way the intensity of a people's torment grows with the level of commitment of the politicians to imposing fundamental changes onto a society.*

CHAPTER 3

MULLAH BAARY CAME TO Kabul as a young member of the Taliban movement. Since his birthplace was the same as that of Mullah Omar, the Taliban leader, he was fortunate to have a better job than most of his fellow holy warriors. He was made a member of a religious police force called Promotion of Virtue and Prevention of Vice. It was a prestigious position, and he was very proud of that fact.

The garrison where Mullah Baary lived had once been the Afghan military club, the very place where Laalla had preformed her first violin concert, a place that had been surrounded by a beautiful rose garden. In those days, it had canopies and an outdoor café and European-style garden lighting. Only the highest ranking officers and their spouses had been privileged to enjoy the club, but whatever it had been before, it was simply a half-collapsed concrete structure now, with no running water or electricity. Just as in the general's apartment and most of the other structures across the city, the doors and windows had all been stripped away by the gunmen long ago.

Mullah Baary lived in a small room with five other Taliban soldiers, all of whom were in charge of enforcing sharia law. Upon joining the religious police a month ago, Mullah Baary had been given a brown shalwar kameez and black turban to wear, and he had been proudly wearing the same outfit ever since. It was the first time in Afghan history that a religious police had been established, and Mullah Baary was very proud of this ground-floor status as well.

The garrison where he lived was roughly one kilometer away from the Macroyan apartments, so he had specifically been put in charge of the Macroyan area. His duties included ensuring that women did not walk the streets without the escort of a blood-related male and that their ankles and hands did not show from beneath their burqas. Also, if male shopkeepers did not go to the mosque five times a day for prayers or men did not wear their beards long enough to satisfy Taliban sharia law, it was Mullah Baary's job either to whip these men or arrest them. In fact, any man or woman more than seven years old who did not comply with the Taliban's version of sharia law could expect to be whipped by Mullah Baary.

He carried a brown leather whip for this purpose, and the whip was very special to him, since it had been a gift from his Pakistani trainer, Qazi Mufti Rayhan. It was made with a handle from the branch of a date tree and had Rayhan's personal signature on it.

Mullah Baary remembered what Mufti Rayhan had once told him: "Beating women and violators of sharia law with this whip has seven times more reward in the afterlife than a regular whip. Of course, it is even more rewarding to stone a woman to death for committing adultery, but unfortunately there has not been a single case of stoning in Afghanistan in recent history. That is because the judges and authorities in your country were not real Muslims, but I am sure with the help of God you will change all that and bring these women to justice."

Each day before dawn prayers, Mullah Baary left his barracks wearing his black turban and went to stand in front of the mosque. After the dawn prayer and prayers during the course of the day, he would stand there and shout out to the crowd of men coming out of the mosque, "Oh, Muslim brothers, may Allah give you the reward of your prayers in the afterlife! Now go home and make sure your females are praying as well. Remember, you can beat your wives for not praying, and you can ultimately divorce them after they have defied your orders for a third time."

Mullah Baary conducted his duties with a fervor that came from being an illiterate young man who honestly believed everything the Taliban had told him. In his mind, he was fighting a holy war, a crusade against unbelievers and corruption and immorality.

Everyone in the bazaar knew that Mullah Baary would turn down even a cup of tea from a shopkeeper. He always went back to his barracks for lunch, and for only one hour. He believed that eating someone else's food or eating in a restaurant, even if you paid for it, was *haraam*, since his God had appointed his meal for him through his employer, and that by not eating his lunch at the barracks, he would be defying God's invitation.

On one Wednesday morning after dawn prayers, Mullah Baary left his barracks for the city's tenth district, but not on religious duty. Instead, he was off to see an old friend at the Ministry of Interior, Mullah Abdul Satar. Mullah Baary and Mullah Abdul Satar had fought alongside each other for three months at the outskirts of Kabul, and now that the Northern Alliance had finally been defeated and the mujahideen were no longer in power, Mullah Abdul Satar had been made the district governor of Garmser in Helmand province, and Mullah Baary had learned that he was in Kabul to socialize with Mullah Abdul Qayoom, the deputy minister of the interior.

On that day, Mullah Abdul Satar had gone to share breakfast with Mullah Abdul Qayoom, who was from Helmand province and often acted in the minister's position when his superior was in Pakistan on official business.

After a forty-five minute walk from his barracks, Mullah Baary arrived at the Ministry of Interior offices and went directly into the main building. All along the darkened hallway, he passed broken chairs and desks scattered around the concrete floor. A bald old man with a bushy beard was sitting crossed-legged outside the deputy minister's office door. He wore the same brown shalwar kameez as Mullah Baary and had a kerosene lantern burning beside him.

"Is Hajji Rayeece Sahib's office moving somewhere else?" Mullah Baary asked the attendant, referring both to Mullah Abdul Qayoom, who was addressed as Hajji Rayeece Sahib when he was acting in the place of his superior, and to the several pieces of furniture scattered along the hallway.

"Hajji Reece Sahib has ordered all departments to get rid of any vestiges of the Communist and Rabbani regimes," the old man said. "And yesterday we received our delivery of floor cushions and pillows from Peshawar, so now all officials are instructed to sit on the floor, the way our grandparents and our great-grandparents once did."

Mullah Baary dismissed the old man and went through the door into the adjacent small room. Four young boys were inside making a breakfast of fried eggs and french fries on two gas burners. Mullah Baary passed through that room into a much larger one, which was the deputy's office. It was furnished with the new Pakistani floor cushions, a Pakistani red carpet and enough thick, round green pillows for each man to take one under his shoulder and lean on it.

"Assalamu Alaikum to all Mawlawis," Mullah Baary said and touched shoulders with everyone sitting in the room, first with the deputy minister and then with the several other people gathered around him. Lastly, he greeted Mullah Abdul Satar, his best friend and fellow warrior.

Among those in the room was a distinguished businessman, Hajji Wakil, a close relative of Mawlawi Jalaluddin Haqani, who had businesses in Dubai and was renowned for importing right-handed SUVs into Afghanistan and then smuggling them into Pakistan. Also among the guests was Mullah Babak, a great singer-storyteller who was renowned for his religious legends about jirgas and jihads and the Taliban and especially Mullah Omar's successes. His songs were always a blend of a warrior's true exploits and his own wishful fabrications; in leader Mullah Omar's case, the songs were usually about how he would conquer the world one day and rule every Muslim. Mullah Baary knew that Mullah Abdul Qayoom was a compulsive listener to these songs and enjoyed them so much he could hardly take his afternoon nap without hearing Mullah Babak's voice.

"I am hungry!" Mullah Abdul Qayoom shouted to the four young boys making breakfast. "My guests are waiting! Where is the food?"

"Only two minutes more, Hajji Rayeece Sahib," one of the boys shouted. "We are waiting for fresh bread. It is coming any minute."

"Hajji Rayeece Sahib, with your permission, I have to leave," said Hajji Wakil. "I was here with a very important favor to ask of you."

"Tell me what can I do for you," said Hajji Rayeece.

"Hajji Rayeece Sahib, my cousin was wrongfully put in jail for drug trafficking. His Land Cruiser, weapons, and large amounts of money have also been confiscated. He is a good Muslim, but soldiers from the Promotion of Virtue and Prevention of Vice have arrested him, thinking he was part of one of the Pashtun wings of the Northern Alliance from Kunduz."

"Why?" Hajji Rayeece asked. "Does he look like one of them? Does he speak Farsi? Is he shaving?"

"Sir, my cousin has the perfect appearance of a Talib brother, so I assume it was a misunderstanding. The boys are new to Kabul, and it takes time to distinguish a friend from the enemy."

"Where is he jailed?" Hajji Rayeece asked him.

"Sir, he is under surveillance in district ten headquarters, just next door from here."

"Have you something in writing on his behalf?" Hajji Rayeece asked.

Hajji Wakil handed him a letter, which was a hand-written request repeating what Hajji Wakil had just explained.

The deputy browsed the letter, pulled a pen from his black vest packet, and wrote to the district ten commander, "The bearer of this letter is a ranking member of the Taliban movement, my friend and dear brother, and a person of discretion and integrity whose cousin, due to incorrect intelligence, is in your captivity. I order you to release him immediately along with his property, which was confiscated at the time of arrest."

He pulled out a wooden seal from another pocket, rubbed his ink pen against it, licked the bottom of the paper, and stamped the letter.

"Here you are," Hajji Rayeece said. "Anything you need in the future, just call me, and we will, insha'Allah, take care of it over the phone. Hajji Sahib Haqani is our leader, guru, and elder, after all. If I can't be at your service, how can I look him eye-to-eye next time when I, insha'Allah, pay a visit? It would be nice if you could stay for breakfast with us."

"Thanks, Hajji Rayeece Sahib. May Allah give you the reward of one million breakfasts. Your help means a lot to me."

Hajji Wakil shook Hajji Rayeece Sahib's hand and said good-bye.

The servant entered as Hajji Wakil was going out the door. "Breakfast is ready, sir. Shall we serve you?"

"How often must I tell you to bring water?" Hajji Rayeece snapped at him. "We need to wash our hands first."

The deputy minister sighed dramatically, upset about having to request the traditional kettle and bowl used for washing one's hands before and after each meal. The servant stood still, without any response.

"What now? Hajji Rayeece demanded. "Are you taking a picture?"

"No, no, Hajji Rayeece Sahib," the servant said. "I am counting the guests."

Hajji Rayeece shook his head. "You never learn, you the son of an idiot. Go count the shoes."

"We don't need to wash our hands," an older man said. He had been leaning on a pillow with his feet stretched out on the carpet, but he sat up now. "Everyone here washed their hands for the dawn prayers a few minutes ago. Let us start, in the name of Allah. We are starving."

Together with three other men, he took his *patu* and flattened this traditional scarf over the red Pakistani carpet. Each man took care to square the corners up nicely. One of the young boys brought twenty-four naan and threw two naan in front of each guest. Three big aluminum bowls filled with french fries came next. The fries were swimming in corn oil. The young boy then brought three big trays filled with deep-fried eggs. The guests split into groups and stared at Hajji Rayeece, waiting for him to start.

"In the name of God," said Hajji Rayeece, and everyone attacked the food.

"How is the food, brothers?" Hajji Rayeece asked.

"It is delicious," everyone said. "May God reward you."

"Do you know why the food is so delicious?" Hajji Rayeece asked his guests.

"Because we eat this food with honesty to you and the Islamic Emirates," the older man said. "Also our hearts are clean, and I see this clean conscience among us."

"This is true," Hajji Rayeece replied. "But more so, the oil and the eggs come from a company that is managed and owned by Haqani Sahib. This oil is produced at his personal plant in Sharja, and the eggs are from his farm in the Swat valley."

"Masha'Allah," another man praised God.

"I ordered our logistics department to cancel all previous contracts and renew them with Haqani Sahib's company," Hajji Rayeece said, continuing his thought. "The farm in the Swat valley is managed by our brothers, so I assure you there is a 100 percent Islamic environment on the farm. The oil has no impurities, unlike the other haraam oils used by the Rabbani administration. God knows what impurities that oil may have had. I heard from Haqani Sahib that the old oil may have had pig fat in it."

Hajji Rayeece's guests muttered among themselves at the very thought.

"That's right," Hajji Rayeece said, "but you may enjoy this food. Everything is, insha'Allah, 100 percent halal."

In less than fifteen minutes, the food was devoured, after which Hajji Rayeece held a short prayer. Then he called for one of the boys to bring them tea. When the tea was finished, everyone except for Mullah Satar and Mullah Baary got up to leave. Blessings were offered to Hajji Rayeece as the men went out the door. When they were gone, Hajji Rayeece turned to Mullah Baary.

"What brings you here, other than to visit your best friend?"

"I came, sir, to congratulate Mullah Satar on his new appointment as the governor of Hazarjuft."

"Yes," Hajji Rayeece said. "He will, insha'Allah, be a good governor in promoting virtue and preventing vice. I gave him a brand-new pickup truck, but he is not happy. He wants one of those big cars with a black monster hanging on its tail. What do they call it? Corozeeng?"

"I only need the corozeeng temporarily," Mullah Satar replied, "because I have females traveling with me. How can I take them in the back of my Datsun truck?"

"What females?" Hajji Rayeece said with a raised eyebrow.

"My fiancée's father is a mullah from Peshawar. His family arrived last week to attend my *nikah* ceremony with some elders. He wanted to keep our marriage simple and among his closest relatives."

Shocked by this news, Mullah Baary wondered why Mullah Satar had failed to tell him about it, thinking there had to be something more to this story. Maybe his best friend was lying simply to get a new corozeeng.

"Mahsha'Allah," Hajji Rayeece was saying to Mullah Satar. "Your father-in-law must be a good Muslim. Do you know that music and celebration and wasting money are all haraam? However, you should have at least told me. You are here every day, and I did not see that joy in your face."

Hajji Rayeece stood up, stuck his head out the window, and pointed a finger toward a parking lot full of brand-new Land Cruisers to the side of the building.

"Go choose any of those corozeengs parked under the trees and let me know. The pickup truck and driver are yours, but make sure to send the corozeeng and its driver to the provincial governor of Helmand once you arrive safe and sound with your bride to your new home."

"Thank you for the new vehicle," Mullah Satar told Hajji Rayeece Sahib. "And now, with your permission, we are leaving."

Both Mullah Satar and Mullah Baary bowed on their way out the door.

CHAPTER 4

"WHAT IS THE STORY of your marriage?" Mullah Baary asked Mullah Satar the minute the two had stepped out of Hajji Rayeece's office. "And why did you never share this with me before?"

"Let us go sit outside under the mulberry tree," Mullah Satar told his friend, "and I will explain everything to you."

The two young men made their way down the darkened hall, stepping around all the broken furniture as they went. Outside, Mullah Satar took his patu off his shoulder and placed it on the ground under the tree, and the two sat on it.

"You know my story," he went on. "I was a little boy when I lost my parents and grew up alone, so I have always wanted to have a family, to have children and a wife who cooks for me and washes my clothes. And when I die, I want her to come to my grave and pray for me. I have no relatives, no one who can find a wife for me or have his daughter or sister marry me. I am not going to Hazarjuft without a bride."

"But you just said you already have one," Mullah Baary said, picking his teeth with a leaf barb.

"I couldn't tell Hajji Rayeece what I have just told you. I made up a story to get a corozeeng, but as I told you, I am going to find a woman and take her with me. And this should happen today!"

"Half of all Kabuli women are not fit to be the wives of Muslims like us," Mullah Baary warned his friend. "If not for their fear of the Taliban, they would be going to school and shopping and walking the streets without their burqas, watching TV, and even working in offices alongside men. But there is one family in my area of duty that I have an eye on. They have a daughter, and it looks like they are not very bad people. We will leave it for God to judge what they have done in the past, but so far they are okay."

"Tell me more about the daughter," Mullah Satar said.

"There is a woman with a blue burqa," Mullah Baary told him. "She leaves home every morning around eleven with a tray of dough on her head. A young boy always comes along to escort her, and she takes the loaves of dough to a women's bakery across from their apartment. One day, I—"

"Stop, stop," Mullah Satar said, cutting him off. "I don't want to hear any more about it. You are telling me they live in those Russian apartments? And they are using the women's bakery built by infidels? And yet you want me to marry a woman like that? How well do you know them?"

"I stopped the woman the first day I saw her. She was carrying a large wooden tray with both hands, so her hands were showing from underneath her burqa, which is very appealing to every man. Of course, what a sin!"

Mullah Satar shook his head as Mullah Baary continued his story.

"I gave her three lashes on each hand and told her to carry the tray on her head with her hands under the burqa. She cried to me and said, 'Brother Talib, I did not know this was against sharia. It is not my fault, because no one taught me! Please don't beat me. I won't do it anymore.' I asked her who the boy was and she told me it was her little brother." Mullah Baary smiled now at the memory. "I tell you, she must be very pretty, because the boy was a handsome young man."

"How do you know she is not married?" asked Mullah Satar.

"Because there are twelve apartments in that six-story building, but eleven of them are empty, and only one old man comes and goes from the door downstairs. Those apartments are only used by street dogs now. I have heard many of the residents were killed in crossfire, and those who survived have moved to safer places. But this family is newly arrived there. I know this because I have seen the little boy out collecting cardboard and pieces of burlap to use for covering the missing windows."

"So you are telling me these are good Muslims."

"From what I see, Mullah Satar, but only Allah knows about the unseen. He knows better than all of us."

"You told me she leaves home around eleven each morning, and it is nine thirty now. Let us go see them."

Mullah Satar pulled a satellite phone from his pocket and called his driver. A minute later, the driver and pickup truck appeared from around the ministry compound. Mullah Satar sat in the front seat. Mullah Baary jumped into the back with two bearded and black-turbaned bodyguards. The guards were armed with Kalashnikovs and had magazines of ammunition draped around their shoulders and waists.

Passing along the bumpy roads, Mullah Baary saw no one walking except for religious police. Taliban soldiers wearing black turbans sped through the streets in pickup trucks shouting "Allahu akbar!" and playing Mullah Babak's religious songs on loudspeakers.

When Mullah Satar's Datsun arrived in front of the women's bakery, Mullah Baary and two guards jumped out of the truck bed. Mullah Satar remained seated in the car, making what he considered to be an important phone call on his satellite phone.

Inside the bakery, all the women had stopped in their tracks, fearing what was about to happen. Aziza, a Pashtun woman in her early thirties, whispered to her small son, "Let's go home. Your sister is there all alone."

Sakina, the heavily built, red-faced Hazara widow who ran the bakery, urged Aziza to calm down. "If you are not a thief, don't be scared of the king," she said. "They know who they are looking for. Certainly not your twelve-year-old daughter. Even if she does interest them, I have heard the Taliban will bring elders first and offer money to marry a girl. If that doesn't work, they will do it at gunpoint. It is your choice, but they get what they want either way. Certainly if you rush home now you will only arouse their suspicions. They will think you are someone cooperating with the Northern Alliance."

Aziza took off her burqa and sat down again.

"Forgive me, Aunt Sakina, but I was in shock for a moment, and as a mother, I am worried. They are right when they say, 'The one who is stung by a snake is scared of a black and white rope.' Have you forgotten all about the general's daughter and what happened to her?"

"Of course I heard about her. The whole world knows the grief of Shahid Shabnam's story. Thank God these Taliban are not nearly as bad as those gunmen and *glam jams*. And may God forgive me for calling those criminals and adulterers mujahideen. The real mujahideen were wiped out by the Russians long ago. Before, the holy men rode donkeys. Now, with all the money pouring into their pockets, they own villas and dozens of Land Cruisers. This is not jihad. The true jihad has been forgotten. These Taliban won't even come into my bakery to buy bread, because we are women. And if not for the United Nations, they would have already closed my bakery."

"Give them time." Aziza said. "They need the support of the international community and are only waiting until the Americans and Europeans open their embassies. Then, once it is done, they will close every bakery run by a woman. Just give them a few more months."

"I listen to BBC news every night on the radio," Hafiza, another woman, said, "and even the Americans are arguing that the Taliban are a spontaneous movement of the people. That because of all the injustice and factional fighting and increased poppy cultivation, the Taliban is needed as a solution."

"You are right, Hafiza," Aziza said. "The burden of justice always falls upon women. The West is so focused on fighting drug trafficking and poppy cultivation, they will turn a blind eye to the Taliban torturing women."

"The Taliban," Hafiza said as if the word was a curse. "Yes, the former mujahideen gunmen raped and kidnapped little girls and boys, but at least they allowed women to go to work and attend school. Now, with the Taliban, we can't even leave our homes. What kind of justice is this? What is this purity they pretend to bring us if it means being locked up in jail?"

Curious and angry as much as she was worried, Hafiza had another look out the window and saw the Talib men still gathered near the front of the bakery. She cursed under her breath and sat back with the other women. "Look at Laalla," she went on. "Eighteen years old and playing violin in university concerts. Now, since losing her sister and fiancé, she comes in here every day and stares at the floor. Or she unfolds that letter of hers and stares at it while waiting for her bread to be baked."

"Are you saying Laalla is the sister of the famous Shahid Shabnam?" Sakina said.

"Yes," Aziza said. "That is the older sister."

"Ah," Sakina said. "I had no idea that was her."

"Yes, and I have always wanted to write a book about her story, but she has begged me not to do it," said Aziza.

"We should make her do it anyway," Hafiza said. "The world needs to know how we women are being abused."

"No, please. Don't ever talk to Laalla about the past and her sister. She refuses to discuss it. After all these years, it still sprinkles salt on her wounds. In fact, speaking of Laalla, she is usually here by eleven every day, and it's almost noon. Perhaps she has seen these Taliban and decided to stay home."

"Ah, your bread is done," Hafiza said, interrupting the conversation.

"Good," Aziza said. "On the way back to my apartment, I will stop by and warn Laalla about what is going on down in the street. That is, if she doesn't know already."

Aziza folded up the pieces of flat bread and hid them under her burqa. Her little son took the empty dough tray, and the two of them went out of the bakery.

Inside, Aunt Sakina and the other women went back to talking of life. Aunt Sakina sipped her green tea and crushed the hard candy under her teeth and occasionally peeked out at the men gathered in the street.

Mullah Satar, who remained sitting in his truck, had lost all hope of his future bride coming out of her apartment any time soon. With impatience, he watched as Aziza left the bakery with her son. Then he grew angry as she disappeared up the stairs of the apartment building where he thought his future bride must be hiding. Unable to restrain himself any longer, Mullah Satar jumped out of the truck and waved for Mullah Baary to follow him across the street to the building entrance.

By that point, Aziza had reached the sixth floor and was calling into Laalla's apartment from out in the hallway.

"It's me, Aziza. Is anyone home?"

Laalla pulled back the blanket and greeted her.

"Salaam, welcome. Please come in."

As usual, she was not very talkative, but Shah Jaan stepped out into the hallway and offered a more gracious welcome. "Please, come in, come in."

"No, thank you. I was only on my way home but wanted to warn you. Several Taliban have been sitting outside the bakery.

Forgive me. Perhaps it is none of my business, but Aunt Sakina was worried too."

"It's okay," Shah Jaan said. "This is not only a problem with girls these days. One of the young Taliban has offered to buy our little son Mirwais ice cream several times and to take him back to his barracks."

"Yes, yes," Aziza said. "We all have to live with these fears now." She looked at Laalla, who stared back at her sullenly. "Well, I have to leave now," Aiziza said. "I just wanted to warn you of the situation."

Shah Jaan thanked her again and held back the curtain as she went out into the hallway. Once Laalla heard Aziza starting down the stairs, she turned to her mother. "Mom, you should have not told her about Mirwais. The news will be all over Aunt Sakina's bakery by tomorrow, and next thing you know Dad will be hearing about it in the mosque. What do you want to do? Give him a heart attack?"

Shah Jaan appeared ready to cry over being upbraided, so Laalla hugged her and tried to take the sting out of her previous words. "Look at it this way, Mom. God has saved our honor. The women at the bakery will think I didn't go to bake my bread today for fear of the Taliban. Little do they know we don't have flour to make a loaf of bread."

Shah Jaan, still nearly in tears, shook her head. "Your father has been waiting since six o'clock behind the UN door to get a sack of flour, and it's now noon. My children are starving. If there is a God"—Shah Jaan looked to the heavens—"can you please drop us a piece of bread?"

While Laalla and Shah Jaan sat upstairs talking, Mullah Satar's patience came to an end. "I have had enough of waiting for this woman in the blue burqa to appear downstairs!" he almost shouted.

"Let's go knock on the door and talk to her father," Mullah Baary said. "We don't need to sit here outside and wait for her.

If her father is a real Muslim, he should agree. Otherwise, I know what to do with him."

"But I want to do it the right way," Mullah Satar said. "And I am hungry anyway. So let's go get some lunch for them. Maybe Kabob and warm bread. This will make us look good and not like those criminal *topakian*." *Topakian* was the Pashto nickname for looters and warriors during the mujahideen era, men who would take women away from her fathers without nikah.

Mullah Satar waved to his driver. The truck did a U-turn from in front of the bakery. Mullah Baary jumped into the back. Mullah Satar climbed into the cab as before and gave his driver directions to a restaurant around the corner. They had started to pull away when Mullah Baary knocked on the window from the back of the truck. The driver stopped again.

"What?" Mullah Satar asked him.

"The old man! Your future father-in-law! I just saw him entering the corridor of his apartment."

"This is good," Mullah Satar said. "Now we know for sure that her father will be at home."

Mullah Baary jumped out of the truck and came around to the door. "Listen, brother. The restaurant is packed with Taliban. They know us, and I don't want them to think we are taking food to a stranger's home. Just give the money to the driver, tell him what to bring, and we will wait here."

Mullah Satar agreed and sent his driver away with the money. Then he and Mullah Satar went back to stand in the shade of the building.

Upstairs, Laalla was assuring her mother that God was always opening another door, that he only took something from you to give you more, that surely a great future awaited their family, and that they should all be thankful for what they had. Her lecture finished, Laalla looked up to see General Qassim coming in the door. There was a transparent plastic bag in his hand, and inside the bag was something greasy wrapped in a newspaper. Without another look, Laalla knew her father had come home empty-handed from the UN facility.

Not realizing this, Shah Jaan was already shouting for Mirwais to come and help Laalla bring the flour sack from downstairs.

"Go," Shah Jaan added when Mirwais appeared from the back. "As you can see, your father is very tired."

The general sat on the floor with his back leaning against the wall. "Yes, I was so tired I left the sack of flour at the store next to the UN depot. I'll go back to get it this afternoon, after I take a rest."

"Dad, what's in the bag?" Mirwais asked, excited about the prospect of food.

"You like sweets, don't you?" the general said with a smile. "Here, look what Daddy brought you. Some halva and warm bread."

General Qassim sat there with tears trickling down into his gray beard.

While the others were distracted with bringing plates to the living room and dividing up the halva and warm bread, Laalla whispered to her father, "I know you did not get our rations today. You just said that for the benefit of the kids. So what happened?"

General Qassim sighed and looked out the empty windows. "After the dawn prayers, I was leaving for the UN food center, but the religious police stopped me in front of the mosque, saying my beard was not long enough. They were sure I had trimmed it and of course reminded me how this was a great sin against the Taliban sharia law." The General looked at his daughter and back out the window. "For this, as an old man, I only received five lashes on my back." He sighed and went on. "From there I went to the UN food center, but while I stood in front, another group of religious police came with cables and whips and started beating everyone. Men and women, young and old. They were shouting, 'Where are your cowardly men?

They send their wives to beg from the UN infidels. You should ask God for your daily bread!' A woman old enough to be their mother became very angry at this point and pulled her burqa away to show them her face, yelling, 'Beat me! Kill me, you bastards! My husband and three of my sons died in the jihad against the Russians. They were fighting for their motherland, for Islam. They were fighting for the honor of their sisters and mothers. I feed seven orphans, and you cowards go and beat the wives of warlords. Our martyrs were wrong in what they did. They should have stayed alive to fight cowards like you, the real enemies of Islam. You are the real enemies of mankind.'"

General Qassim sighed deeply again and continued. "Then she took her shoes off and threw them at the police and spat in the face of one of the men. Their commander, an older man with a bushy beard and a white turban, told his men, 'Arrest her. She is an agent with the Northern Alliance.' So four young men tied the old woman with their turbans and dragged her to the back of the pickup truck. The truck drove away with her still shouting, 'Kill me! Kill me, you godless bastards. If you had mothers and sisters, you would know respect for others' mothers and sisters. You fatherless, motherless pigs! Kill me, you Pakistani slaves!'"

"So what happened, Father? How is it that they denied you our sack of flour?"

General Qassim drank from a glass of water and continued. "While I watched the scene from a corner, one of the young religious police came up and asked to see my UN coupon. When he saw your and your mother's photos on it, he pulled out a metal whip made from a bicycle chain and started beating me on my legs and back and shoulders. 'That was for offering your wife and daughter to the UN officials for a sack of flour and a can of oil,' he said and started beating me again. Finally he told me, 'I declare you clean from your sins.' After that, he took my coupon and went away. When the UN food center opened, I showed the clerk my *tazkera* and told him I had lost my coupon. I asked if he could please look in their records for my name, but the man apologized and told me he could not give out rations, under the circumstances, unless I brought a written letter from our mosque and also had it endorsed by the religious police, certifying the number of children and adults in our household."

Shah Jaan, having come back from the other room, heard her husband's last words and cried up to the heavens. "My God. That means we have to take new photos for the new coupon, and we need twenty Pakistani rupees per person for that. Can you tell me where will we get the money?"

"No," the general said, trying to reassure her. "The man at the food center told me that they have waived the photo requirements for women. All he needs is a letter from our mosque and an endorsement by the religious police certifying the number of dependents in our household. I will go to the mosque this evening, since the food center has closed for the day. I will still need to have my own photo taken, though."

"For twenty rupees, which we don't have," Shah Jaan said.

"I don't know, Shah Jaan. I am lost. I will ask someone in the mosque to lend me the money. I already went there once to get this letter signed; only one of the senior imam's sons was leading the prayer. His father was off getting married. Can you imagine it? Most young men can't afford to have one wife, and this man was taking his third bride today."

"What business is that of ours?" Shah Jaan said.

"You are right, as always, Shah Jaan. In any case, as I was leaving, the young imam had two boys bring me Halva and bread. It was a gift to the poor on the occasion of his father's wedding. I was told to bring a dish to the evening prayer and there would be more food available."

"Mirwais," Shah Jaan said to her son. "I hear people talking in the hallway. Go see who is there."

"Is anyone home!" a man's voice shouted out in Pashto before Mirwais could start for the door and instantly everyone froze with fear.

"Yes. I am coming!" General Qassim called out. "Please wait."

The general started to get up, but Laalla grabbed his hand.

"Stay here," she whispered. "We'll send Mirwais to tell them that you are sick and lying in bed. Go see what they want," she said to Mirwais in the same whispered voice.

Starting for the door, Mirwais smelled the kabob aroma and was immediately swept away by old memories and dreams. He had once promised his little sister that when he became a pilot, the whole family would eat kabob every day, even for breakfast.

When he pulled the blanket back, he saw two Taliban men, one the same man who regularly patrolled their block, a man Mirwais had seen beating women and men who violated sharia law, and also the same man who had asked Mirwais to go with him to his barracks for an ice cream. This was a man Mirwais had reason to fear, but now that he had bags of kabob and Pepsi in his hands, Mirwais completely forgot his previous feelings. He even forgot to greet the men and be courteous and invite them in.

"Tell your father we brought food and wish to eat lunch with him," Mullah Baary said.

Hearing those words, the rest of General Qassim's family breathed a sigh of relief from the back of the apartment.

"Everything is okay," Laalla told her father. "Please go talk to them."

Mirwais came running back in. "They brought lots of kabob and cans of cold Pepsi!" he told his little sister, and the two of them began jumping up and down on the floor.

The general quieted his two youngest children, put on his white prayer cap, and went to the front door.

"I think you have mistakenly come to the wrong apartment," he told the two young men as he pulled back the blanket. "There is only us on this corridor, but you may check—"

"Hajji Sahib," Mullah Satar said, cutting him off, "we wanted to take a couple of minutes of your time and eat with you."

Concerned now by what the mullah had said, General Qassim bowed and waved nervously at his home. "You are welcome any time. This is your home, but please wait a minute while I prepare a place for us to sit."

The general ducked into the small room where Laalla and her sisters were waiting with renewed dread. "Laalla, it is the religious policeman, and another one is with him. perhaps his superior, but they brought food and want me to eat with them."

Laalla suspected the reason for the visit but disguised her feelings and went about gathering some blankets to use as cushions for their guests. "Mirwais, please come help Dad," she told her little brother.

Together with Mirwais, the general placed the blankets on the floor in the tiny hallway, after which the general told his guests to come in. Mullahs Satar and Baary dropped the bags of food on the floor. Mirwais stood there staring at them.

"Welcome to the hut of the poor," General Qassim said. "May God bring you all the time."

"May Allah bring you happiness," the mullahs replied.

"Mirwais, take this food and tell your mother to prepare it," the general said. "And don't forget to wash the vegetables in chlorine."

The general sat cross-legged with his head down, considering all the possible reasons these two mullahs might have come to see him. *The apartment or my daughter*, he thought at last. Rumors were circulating around the mosque that the Taliban were out buying properties everywhere in Kabul. *Perhaps they have come to make me an offer. If that is the case, I will accept it immediately. Anything to feed my family. But if they want my daughter, of that I am not so sure.*

While the general considered these things, Mirwais came with water and clean napkins for the guests to wash their hands, then a *distar khan*, a traditional long piece of cloth used as a one-piece placemat. This was followed by the food, which had been placed on a tray with three small plates, three glasses for Pepsi, and flat bread cut into small, square pieces.

Mullah Satar, who had expected them to open the greasy newspaper and attack the food while sitting on the carpet, found the preparation for lunch very neat and nothing like the usual Taliban standards.

These people must be very clean, he thought to himself happily, *just like the home of Hajji Matin in Pakistan, and now I will marry a woman who knows how to take care of a house and cook delicious food.*

"Please make yourself at home," General Qassim told them. "Start in the name of Allah, and enjoy. We're a little short on dishes. Our house has been looted twice in the past. Thanks to the Taliban Islamic police, as you see, we are safe in hour homes without a lock and even without doors or windows. Alhamdulillah, we are very happy. The water fountain, as you see, is just next to the bakery. We have fresh water all the time. We couldn't ask God for more."

Mullah Baary was furious at hearing these words. "You have water," he said. "You have the bakery next door and the mosque is just around the corner. God gave you all the happiness in the world, and still you are complaining about a shortage in dishes. Food tastes a lot better when friends eat from one bowl and plate."

"You are right," said General Qassim. "And of course I did not mean it in that way."

"And worse," Mullah Baary went on, "you wash God-grown natural vegetables with a poisonous powder that was given to you by the infidel United Nations! Don't use that haraam product anymore!"

"Of course, you are absolutely right," the general said again. "But if I may ask, what brings you to the hut of the poor? How have you respectful and high-ranking people come to a poor man like me?"

Mullah Satar popped open a Pepsi and sucked the whole can out. He let out a loud burp and stared absently at the general. "Let's enjoy the food for now, and we, insha'Allah, will talk about it over a good cup of green tea."

Hearing this in the next room, Shah Jaan worried out loud that they had no tea or even sugar.

Laalla, calm as always, went to the next room where little Mina and Mirwais sat eating their chicken. Each of them had a can of Pepsi opened in front of them and another unopened one sitting beside it.

"This Taliban is very rich," Mirwais said to his older sister. "I have seen him many times driving around in a blue Datsun with his guards and all their guns."

"Say 'Uncle Taliban,'" little Mina told him. "Dad said you always call adults aunts and uncles."

"Take this thermos to the bakery," Laalla told Mirwais, "and explain to Aunt Sakina that we have guests. Ask if she can fill it with tea for us. And remember to ask for green tea. And also bring some sugar. If she asks about our guests, tell her—tell her you don't know. No, tell her they are friends of our father."

"Okay," Mirwais said. "But make sure Mina doesn't eat my chicken kabob."

"Greedy," Mina said without anger. "God gave us enough food for a million years."

Mirwais quickly ran down the stairs and across the street and entered the bakery, explaining to Aunt Sakina exactly what Laalla had told him to say. While Aunt Sakina made the tea and poured it into the thermos, Mirwais stood looking out the window.

"Here you are," Aunt Sakina said when she was done. "Blessings to you and your guests."

"Thanks," Mirwais said and left with his pockets filled with sugar cubes.

Aunt Sakina watched him rush back upstairs and turned to Aziza with a knowing look. "Nowadays this black camel sleeps at everyone's doorstep," Sakina said.

All the women in the bakery nodded among themselves, having seen the two men go up to the general's apartment.

Back upstairs, Mirwais rushed into the apartment and took the thermos to Shah Jaan. While his mother poured the tea into cups, Laalla asked Mirwais what Aunt Sakina had said.

"Nothing."

"Nothing?"

"She made the tea and I thanked her."

"Well, who was there?" Laalla asked him.

"Aunt Hafiza and Aunt Aziza and—"

"Aunt Aziza?"

"Yes, and other women."

Ah, Laalla thought herself. *Aziza finished her baking and should have been home an hour ago. So that is it. They all saw the Taliban and are sitting there full of gossip.*

"Mirwais jaan," the general called loudly. "Come take the dishes away and bring water to wash the guests' hands."

Mirwais hurried out with the water and clean napkins.

"Where is the tea?" the general asked him.

"I will bring it in a minute, dear father," Mirwais said. He went off and returned a moment later with the tea. Mullah Satar was speaking as Mirwais put down the cups.

"Hajji Sahib. I ... we are here today to start a new friendship."

General Qassim felt a jolt of anxiety rush through his body. "I have always been friends with good people," he said in a trembling voice. "But I don't understand. What exactly can I do for you honorable people?"

"Hajji Sahib, we are Taliban," Mullah Baary said. "We are village people. We don't know much about city culture. So let me be blunt with you. Hajji district governor wants to marry your daughter. This is why we are here."

General Qassim remained silent. His mind was swirling with memories of Shabnam and worries over poor Laalla. The last thing he wanted was to see his eldest daughter married to one of these thugs. The thought of it made him feel as if his chest was about to explode.

"What are you thinking?" Mullah Baary asked. "Don't tell me you have no authority over your own daughter."

"The only one who has authority over our lives and destiny is the great Allah the merciful, who created the earth and heavens and all creatures. Of course, as a father … as a father …" The general sat trembling for a moment and thinking desperately of how to escape.   "But it is in line with the Islamic sharia as well," he said, "that I talk to my wife, who has breastfed my daughter."

"You ask your wife for permission about something that is being discussed between men?" Mullah Baary said. "And here I thought you were a wise man." He smacked his right hand hard against the concrete floor and continued.

"You have heard our decision, and we will do it no matter what you say!"

Noticing that the general was trembling in his silence, Mullah Satar made an effort at peace. "It is fine," he said. "If it makes you happy, tell your wife that this is your decision, but we don't have much time. Have your daughter pack up right away. We are coming tomorrow after the morning prayers and will have tea with you again."

"We have lived in this neighborhood for a long time," General Qassim told them, with tears in his eyes now. "For as long as my kids can remember. All the neighbors know us. This will not be good for our name and honor. Besides, it is tradition here that when you ask for a girl's hand, you first send women to talk to women many times, and then when it is finalized, elders and friends gather as a symbolic visit. It is against dignity and honor for a girl to get married in such a short time. Please at least bring a few elders with you tomorrow."

"All these traditions are from a non-Islamic culture," Mullah Baary said. "We are Pashtun. We don't send our wives and mothers to someone's home to talk about brides. Besides, what neighbors? I know most of them, and I swear to God, if it were not for fear of the Taliban, they would—"

Again, Mullah Satar cut off his more fanatical friend and offered an olive branch. "Hajji Sahib is right. We will bring some elders from the mosque with us tomorrow. I have no relatives, no females here. Otherwise, I would have sent them to honor you and your name." Mullah Satar got up, and Mullah Baary followed him.

"We will see you, insha'Allah, tomorrow."

They left the apartment, and the general rushed to hug Laalla. "My daughter, my mother, my hope, my princess," he said. "I don't understand why. Why us? Why my daughter? My Laalla …"

Laalla was stoic as usual and shed no tears as everyone fretted around her. The family had not been there but a few minutes when there were more voices at the door.

Shah Jaan! Laalla! Mirwais! We are here. Can we come in?"

"So much for keeping it a secret," Shah Jaan said over her shoulder as she went to answer the door. She found Aziza with Aunt Sakina and Hafiza standing on the other side of the blanket. "Come in, come in," she said and waved the women into the living room.

Laalla faced them quietly.

"I assume you all know," Shah Jaan said.

"We don't mean to interfere," Hafiza said, "but we saw the mullahs and feared the worst."

"Yes," Shah Jaan said. "It is the worst, and we are lost. We don't know what to do."

Hafiza turned to Laalla. "On issues like this, I never advise. It is a matter of partnership and sharing your life with someone. You must decide all by yourself."

"Dear Hafiza," Laalla said. "You speak as if we lived in the past. In some fantasy world. Women's rights? Human rights? Life partnerships? Decisions about the future? Don't you know? While the world has moved on toward a new century, we are being pushed back into the dark ages."

"I know, I know," Aziza said. "But listen to me. Since they are coming tomorrow, no matter what, let me send my husband to be with your father. He should not be alone as the only man in the house. Besides, we are Pashtun, like these men, so they are more likely to respect our opinions. God forbid that these men be rude to uncle and dishonor him. You have to remember they have no family background. They've grown up in orphanages and on the streets. They know nothing of families and traditions."

Before the three women left, it was agreed that they would take this course of action, if for no other reason than to get rid of them in a gracious manner so the family could get back to discussing their impending fate in private.

CHAPTER 5

THAT NIGHT, WHEN LAALLA lay down to sleep, she overheard Mina and Mirwais whispering to each other at the far end of the room. Laalla turned to look at Sahar, who as usual was curled up on her bed in silence.

"Listen to them," Laalla whispered. "They are so full of happiness from having a full dinner with Pepsi and candy."

Sahar looked once at Laalla and turned the other way. Laalla sighed and went back to listening to her young brother and sister.

"When I become a pilot," Mirwais was telling Mina, "I will travel all over and enjoy all the good foods of the world."

"I want to be a teacher," Mina said, "and teach my students everything I learned from Dad."

"People should love each other," Mirwais said, "and not harm others, and people should stop killing and bombing each other and stop kidnapping girls and boys and looting people's houses."

"Ssshh," Sahar said. "It's time to go to sleep."

The two young children were silent for a few moments and then started whispering to each other again. "I want to build schools everywhere," Mina said to her older brother, "so when

I stand on top of a mountain, I can see schools everywhere I look."

"That's a nice dream," Mirwais said. "But where do you plan to get the money for all that?"

"I don't know. I guess I will marry an uncle Talib or an uncle mullah. They have money and cars and houses and everything."

"Yeah, right," Mirwais said. "You think they would let you teach in a school? They have no education themselves!"

"I would talk to him and persuade him that education is a good thing, and he would allow it because he loves me. Remember Dad said that with love and education, you can turn even tigers into your friends."

Mirwais turned to his older sister Sahar. "What do you want to be when you grow up?"

"I just want to have a bedroom to myself, where I can get a good night's sleep without listening to you and all your nonsense. Now it's time for bed."

Laalla, too, was listening to her siblings' conversation, but with joyfulness, not exasperation. She could not remember them ever being so happy. Usually they went to bed with a glum good night and nothing more.

What a miracle, she thought. *Suddenly they have hope for their future. They're thinking how they might change the world and the lives of others. Everything has changed for them, and all this because of a cold dinner and a couple cans of soda.*

Laalla lay awake until almost midnight thinking about a million things, when she suddenly realized her father wasn't snoring. He always did, and she always heard him, but on this night there was no sound. Worried over his health, Laalla got up to check and found her mother praying on her mat.

"Laalla," her father said when she entered the room, "please bring me a glass of water."

Laalla brought the water as asked. "Thank God you are okay," she said, "and only sleepless like me."

"My daughter," Shah Jaan said, breaking from her prayer, "Your father is awake. Let's talk. They are coming tomorrow."

"There is nothing to discuss," Laalla said. "Let's see what Aziza's husband has to say to them. He is a Pashtun and the son of a prominent elder. Maybe they will listen to him. Otherwise, what can we do?"

Shah Jaan stared.

"Little or nothing," Laalla said, concluding the thought. "Now go to sleep, Mom, and we'll see what happens in the morning."

Laalla went to check on Mirwais and Mina next.

"Good-bye, my angel," she whispered, kissing Mina's forehead. "May God be with you."

When she readjusted Mina's blanket, she found that her little sister had fallen asleep with two cans of Pepsi at her side. Seeing Sahar was still awake, she showed her the sodas with a smile. Then she kissed Mirwais on the forehead and went back to her own bed.

Thinking about the words Laalla had just spoken and fearing Laalla might do what Shabnam had done to herself, Sahar sat up on her blankets.

"Are you okay, my sister?" she asked.

"Are you up worrying too?" Laalla said. "Go to sleep, I am fine."

Sahar lay there pretending to be asleep when in fact she was watching and worrying over her older sister. When Laalla finally seemed to have fallen asleep, Sahar fell asleep too.

Several times in the night, Laalla woke and considered her fate. If she married this Taliban without love in her heart, it was a sin. If she jumped from the balcony to avoid her fate, it was a sin. Behind all that was her family's fate. As the wife of an important Talib, they would be provided with everything they needed. And she would never have to fear for their safety again.

Or at least as long as the Taliban were in power. Laalla decided to get on her prayer mat and pray.

O almighty God, she said in her heart. *Please forgive me for what I am about to do. I know you created us to be probed and tested in our faith, and as a human being, I have suffered and resisted all temptation so far, but I cannot take this burden of life anymore. You promised that hell belongs in the afterlife, so why am I being burned in fire today? Forgive me, but I can't marry this Talib. If I say yes during nikah and don't believe it in my heart, it is a sin, for which you have warned of harsh punishment. Besides, this man can never be a replacement for my darling Farid.*

Unable to concentrate on her prayers, Laalla remembered how her grandmother had told her when she was a child, "If you pray and ask God to help you with planning an important decision, God will send angels to your dreams to advise you."

Laalla went back to her bed and took a letter from under her blankets. It was a letter that she had read every day since Farid had been killed, but in the darkness she was unable to read it, so she unfolded it and held it to her chest and went back to thinking about her sinful decision.

There is no way out, she told herself. *If I sacrifice my life to rescue my family by marrying a man I have never seen, a man I don't love in my heart, then that is a sin. If I commit suicide, then that is equally a sin.*

Laalla's thought drifted back to the happy conversation her siblings had been having a few hours earlier. They had been happy for the first time in as long as she could remember, and simply because they had gone to bed with full stomachs.

Laalla lay there thinking, torn by what she had planned. Everyone was asleep now. There was no one to stop her from jumping from the balcony, yet she couldn't bring herself to do it.

Finally, she fell asleep. Laalla's mind was filled with dreams until dawn. The loudspeakers in the mosques went off. The Imams called out for morning prayers. Laalla heard a car honking and peeked out the window. A freshly washed white car garnished with red tulips and red ribbons was parked in front of their apartment building. Her father's chauffeur, Glulam, was in the same uniform he had worn to take Laalla to Kabul University every day. He opened the door, and a beautiful young bride got off the car, dressed in the very same white wedding dress that Laalla and Farid had picked out for their wedding from a catalogue.

"Shabnam, is that you?" Laalla shouted from the window.

The bride waved and showed Laalla a bunch of tulips in her hands.

"Come downstairs!" she shouted up at Laalla. "These are for you!"

Laalla ran downstairs to hug Shabnam. "Where have you been all these years?"

"I live in block 105. I don't come to visit you, because I don't want to see Mirwais and Mina in misery. Last night I came here because they were so happy, and I will come again, bakhair, to visit them. I only hope they will always be as happy as they were last night."

"But block 105," Laalla said, feeling confused. "It was hit by rockets and collapsed into ruin."

"No, we fixed it, and it is like a palace now," Shabnam said and smiled. "Laalla, why don't you say hello to Ghullam. He is my chauffeur, just like in the old days. After his recovery from the hospital, I took him with me."

"Ghullam, we miss you!" Laalla said. "Dad will be so happy to see you again. Shabnam, please, let's go upstairs to see Mom and Dad."

"I see Daddy all the time on his way to the mosque, but no, I have to go now. These flowers are for your wedding, and I will come to visit you again. Kiss Dad, Mom, Mirwais, Sahar, and little Mina for me."

Shabnam quickly got into the white car, and it started driving away.

"Wait, wait!" Laalla shouted after her. "Whose wedding? Tell me which wedding! Are you speaking of Farid? Have you seen him lately? Does he also live with you in block 105? Wait, wait! Don't go away! I need to talk to you, Shabnam! Is Farid coming back to marry me?"

"Laalla, Laalla, wake up! Wake up!"

Laalla opened her eyes to find her father sitting next to her. His hand was on her shoulder. It was the early hours before dawn. The Imams were calling out for morning prayers over the loudspeakers at the mosque.

"It is time for your prayers," the General was saying. "The mullahs will be coming back very soon now."

Laalla sat up in a sweat. "Dad, it's okay. I'm okay now. I was having a bad dream. But no, maybe it was a good dream. Yes, it was a good dream. God may turn it to our happiness yet."

"Just relax," the general whispered. "Your mom will put the blankets in the wardrobe. They are coming very soon, after the prayers."

The general went away, and Laalla lay back down. She was alone with her memories and her decision. She would accept the marriage. Her dream and the conversation between Mirwais and Mina had changed her heart.

After the dawn prayers, Aziza and her husband, Dr. Nazir, appeared at General Qassim's door. Their little son was also with them. They had brought pound cake, chocolate cookies, Pakistani biscuits, breakfast dishes, three packs of milk, green tea leaves, sugar, and fresh bread. Aziza helped Shah Jaan to prepare the breakfast.

"When we left for home last evening, there were two Taliban with Kalashnikovs keeping your house under surveillance. Just now we saw them again. They are still out there, the same two guys."

"I saw them too, Aziza jaan," General Qassim said. "When I was coming back from the mosque last night. So you must know. A Talib is coming to take Laalla for his bride, and no doubt they fear we will escape to Pakistan or something. And believe me, if I had some way to do it, I would. I only hope they won't beat me for missing my prayers in the mosque this morning."

"No, General Sahib," Dr. Nazir said. "You had a valid reason to have your prayers at home this morning. Besides, everyone at the mosque knows that you show up for all five prayers every single day."

"Please don't call him general in front of these Taliban," Aziza told her husband. "It will open another can of worms."

Soon after, Mullah Satar arrived at the door with his entourage.

"Assalamu Alaikum," Dr. Nazir said. "Come in, please, and honor us."

A lean Kandahari of average height with an oily face came in first. His long black hair showed from underneath his white turban. Mullah Satar and Mullah Baary came in next, followed by a younger man with no turban. He wore an arakhcheen, a traditional Kandahari cap, on his head, embroidered with blue and white beads. He also had a Kalashnikov in his hands. Mullah Satar's eyes were anointed black with collyrium.

All of them sat on the double-folded blankets. Mullah Baary was staring at Dr. Nazir. "Who are you?" he asked. "You were not here last time. I can tell by your tongue and look that you are Pashtun."

"My name is Nazir. I am from the Maroof district of Kandahar, and I'm the son of Hajji Abdullah and the grandson of Hajji Mohammad. My father and older brother were killed in the jihad against the Russians."

"As God is my witness, I have never heard these names before," Mullah Baary said with his usual rudeness. "Where is the owner of the household?" he added.

The gunman with the beaded cap whispered into Mullah Satar's ear but loud enough so everyone could hear it, "If the bastard has escaped, just give the word, and I will kill the whole family."

"He is in the other room." Dr. Nazir said, making no secret of the disgust he felt for these men. A man spoke his father's name with pride and dignity and was accustomed to receiving respect in return, not such rude comments and insulting words, and especially not for the family of one's future wife.

"How did they find you?" the man with the Kalashnikov asked. "And what are you doing in his home?"

Before Dr. Nazir could respond, General Qassim entered the room. "Assalamu Alaikum, welcome!" General Qassim said.

Out of respect for the general, first the man with the white turban and black hair stood up and then Dr. Nazir, Mullah Satar, and Mullah Baary. The gunman remained seated and only extended his hand.

The man in the white turban started reciting from the holy Koran and then offered a short prayer for the owner of the household, his wife and children, and his neighbors and relatives.

Mullah Satar, who had been sitting quietly through the prayers, said, "Hajji Sahib, we have come again as promised."

The general looked at the gunman, who continued to stare with his unfriendly look. The general looked back at Mullah Satar. His mouth had gone dry. "Welcome. May God bring you all the time," he said in a shaky voice.

Mirwais and Dr. Nazir's son came to lay out a white distar khan and napkins that Aziza had brought with her that morning. This was soon followed by the breakfast that Shah Jaan had helped Aziza to prepare.

"Please start, in the name of God," General Qassim told his guests. Dr. Nazir poured milk into everyone's cup. The general passed the cream in a small saucer and asked all the guests to try the cake.

The man in the white turban who had recited the holy Koran was very polite and made a good impression on General Qassim and Dr. Nazir.

After the breakfast was finished, the general called for Mirwais to come take the dishes.

"Hajji Sahib," Dr. Nazir said, "the children took breakfast out to Mullah Sahib's driver and guards. Please help me and we will remove the dishes."

Dr. Nazir had asked the general to join him because he knew the Taliban would be enraged if a man who was not related by blood had seen the general's wife and daughters unaccompanied, especially since one of the daughters was Mullah Satar's future wife. Thankfully, he remembered just in time not to call his friend General in front of the Taliban.

Once the general and Dr. Nazir left the room, the man with the white turban snapped at the gunman. "Commander! We are representing the Islamic movement of the Taliban here. You should watch what you are saying!"

"People call me Commander Crazy," the gunman said. "I am not hungry for his breakfast. I am here to take the bride with us. I will change my name and shave this beard before I leave here empty-handed. Or I will kill the entire family. He thinks that he can fool us with his hospitality."

"For the last time, I'm telling you to be quiet and let me talk!"

"Mawlawi Sahib is right," Mullah Satar said to the gunman. "We are not here to make enemies. We want to build a friendship. They are good people. That's why we want a relationship with them!"

"If you don't want to fight, then why did you ask me to watch the house all night?" the young gunman asked them. "And why am I here?"

"Who told you to watch the house all night?" the man with the white turban asked.

"Mullah Satar told me."

"This is not the right place for these arguments," Mullah Satar said. "I have anointed my eyes with black as a sign of blessing and happiness. Now let me be in happiness. And, Mawlawi Sahib, I will explain my reasons to you later."

When the general and Dr. Nazir came back, the man with the white turban recited a few more verses from the holy Koran. This was followed by a short prayer in Pashto. Then he switched to Dari. "I will speak in Farsi," he said, "so our mothers and sisters who are in the house can benefit from the instruction of God through the holy words of the Koran."

"Hajji Sahib, first of all, it's an Islamic tradition to have eaten in your home and to have enjoyed your hospitality; I should thank you and our mothers and sisters, who must have awakened earlier than usual to prepare this breakfast for us. Secondly, and according to the Sunnat of the Prophet Mohammad, peace be upon him, I want to introduce myself and my friends by all our full names, as this is a requirement of sharia. Then I will ask you kindly to introduce yourself and this gentleman, who has been such a good host. In this way, we will comply with sharia and make sure that we are in the right place and meeting with the person we intended to meet."

The general nodded and was very touched by the politeness of this man.

"My name is Mawlawi Abdul Karim from Kandahar," the man in the white turban said. "I have studied in Mullah Yaqub Akhundzadah's madrassa and have never left my country. May the almighty Allah help me always to be in my country and in the service of my fellow citizens. Next to me is Mullah Abdul Satar, whom you met yesterday. Next to him is Mullah Abdul Baary, who was here yesterday as well. This gentleman is Mullah Zabet, a first lieutenant in the police. He is the head of the religious police in this district. Now, if you'll kindly introduce yourself and this gentleman briefly."

Dr. Nazir, fearing the general might absentmindedly introduce himself as a general, jumped ahead of General Qassim.

"My name is Dr. Nazir, and as I previously said, I am from the Maroof district of Kandahar and very privileged to have become a part of this noble family by marrying Hajji Sahib's niece. My uncle's name is Mr. Qassim. He used to be an administrator in the eye clinic in Darullaman where I was practicing as a doctor and—"

Mawlawi, who was an intelligent man and knew that the doctor was lying, held his hand up.

"Masha'Allah, this is good enough. Let me say this in Farsi so my mothers and sisters hear this in the other room. It is my duty as a Muslim, and it is our Prophet's Sunnat, to preach the words of God and his messenger wherever the opportunity comes. Not necessarily in the mosque, but in gatherings of happiness like this one or, Allah forbid, during solemn events. Almighty Allah created human beings in different colors and races with different looks and with different languages, like a big garden full of colored flowers and beautiful birds, and each breed sings a different melody. It would not have been difficult for the creator of the earth and the heavens to make all human beings from one race and one language. We Afghans are lucky to have the privilege of living in this large, colorful garden with different flowers and different birds."

Mawlawi now looked at General Qassim and told him, "Hajji Sahib! The reason we are here today is to ask you if you and your wife, the mother of your daughter, the woman who breastfed her, would please ask your daughter if she agrees to choose Mullah Abdul Satar as her husband and her life partner."

Commander Crazy pinched Mullah Baary's back and whispered to him, "I have never been insulted this way before.

What the hell is he talking about? Let me pull the trigger and tell him, 'We want your daughter.' It is that simple. A Pashtun begging for women is not a man."

Mawlawi gave Commander Crazy a fierce look and continued, "Hajji Sahib, this is not the nikah process yet, but I always make sure that everything is according to sharia. Since they have not met each other, I want to make sure that there is no factor of fear or force, financial need, or extortion involved."

The general bowed out of respect and got up to go to the other room. There were tears in his eyes, but his wife smiled and offered him comfort.

"It is okay, my husband. We have been talking about it ever since Aziza jaan came here this morning, and Laalla will accept. She is happy and believes this is the will of God."

"Yes, Father. I thought about it all night and made my decision this morning."

The general returned to the men and sat down. "They agree!" he told Mawlawi.

"I want her to agree, not her mother or sister," Mawlawi said.

"Yes, my daughter agrees," General Qassim assured him.

"You're saying she agrees," Mawlawi asked one more time.

"Yes, she told me that she agrees."

Mawlawi asked all the men present in the room if they had heard Mr. Qassim's testimony, and everyone said yes. Mawlawi then grinned widely and said yes again directly to Mullah Satar. Mullah Satar turned red in embarrassment and was even a bit angry about being embarrassed in this way, but he was very happy too.

Mawlawi then started the nikah process. The general shuttled questions and agreements back and forth between the bride and groom, as Laalla was forbidden by Taliban rule to be in the same room.

After the religious process, Mawlawi went on to the social aspect of the marriage, and with that he congratulated the bride and groom.

"I now declare you husband and wife. A Pashtun marrying a Tajik means Allah will strengthen the ties between two flowers that are from different breeds in the beautiful garden that we call Afghanistan." He turned to Mullah Satar with a smile. "Mullah Sahib, it is your Islamic duty to treat your in-laws like your own father and mother. If you don't have the time to visit your in-laws, you must allow your wife to visit them any time she wants. May Allah give you sons and daughters who will serve Islam and their country. Remember, my brothers and sisters, almighty Allah says that the more you educate yourself, the closer you come to him. Education is the Islamic duty of every Muslim man and woman. An educated mother can raise good children to be healthy and useful to society. The most wealth a child can inherit from his parents is education, so you two, with the help of Allah, must put all your effort toward your children's education. Our brothers and sisters have suffered from war and its tragic consequences for almost two decades. We have seen so many enemies dressed as friends. In order to fight our enemies effectively, we need first to identify them and then attack them all at once. So we have identified our enemy. It is not Communism or socialism. It is not Russia or Pakistan or even America or China. It is *jahaalat*," Mawlawi explained. *Jahaalat* is the Islamic term for ignorance and lack of knowledge and education.

"What nonsense is this bastard talking about?" Mullah Zabet whispered to Mullah Baary. "I swear he is an infidel himself. Or he's an American agent in disguise."

"I don't know," Mullah Baary said. "I never heard these words when I was in Pakistan."

Laalla, who had already made the decision to sacrifice her life in exchange for a better life for her family, found herself feeling invigorated by Mawlawi's comments. Hope began to trickle into her heart.

"My brothers and sisters," Mawlawi continued, "the first message from Allah, the Almighty, to his Prophet Mohammad, peace be upon him, was that he should read. Read in the name of Allah! And may Allah bless you all! Now I have to go to a funeral."

Mawlawi said good-bye to everyone, and Dr. Nazir escorted him down to the first floor. When he returned, he heard Mullah Baary speaking to Mullah Satar.

"It is getting late, but if the district governor leaves Kabul at noon today, he will arrive in Garmsere by Saturday."

The general, who had been hoping his daughter would live closer by, felt great shock and sadness and looked at Dr. Nazir for some kind of hope.

In the other room, Shah Jaan was fuming at Aziza. "No. No, I won't let this happen."

She was about to grow loud, but Laalla restrained her. "Mother, please. Do we have any choice now? Do we have any options? No. God wanted it this way, and God's will be done."

"Mullah Sahib," Dr. Nazir told the new husband, "perhaps you will allow the family spend a bit of time with their daughter before she goes. Maybe until Friday. There are many more relatives and family members she needs to see."

"I told you that he needs to leave Kabul today." Mullah Baary said before Mullah Satar could speak, "People say that if you listen to women, they will be like Satan and derail you from the right way. We cannot postpone our trip just because she wants to see her relatives."

"If that's the case," Dr. Nazir said, "then please give the new bride a couple of hours to pack."

"It is around eleven o'clock now. We will be back at four and ready to leave." Mullah Baary said.

Mullah Satar unwrapped his patu and gave a plastic bag full of Pakistani rupees to Dr. Nazir. "This is a small gift from me to the family of Hajji Sahib."

He said good-bye to the general and started down the stairs with Mullah Baary and Commander Crazy.

"Couldn't you have found a good Pashtun family," Commander Crazy said, "rather than marrying into this bunch of infidels? I want to put two guards in front lest they try to escape."

"We don't need to watch them," Mullah Satar said. "They know they cannot escape or hide."

"If they fly, I will pull on their legs," Mullah Baary said outside the apartment. "If they run, I will pull on their ears."

Inside the apartment, Laalla's mother and her three siblings were hugging their sister and sobbing over her imminent departure.

"This Mawlawi sounded like a good man," General Qassim said. "Let's see how long he will live before he is thrown in jail or killed."

"The district governor himself is not a bad man either," Dr. Nazir said. "It looks like he has a good heart and is as good as a Talib can be. Look how polite he was. He thought it was insulting to give the money to the general, so he gave it to me."

"Thank God he is not like those other two Taliban," Aziza said. "With those two around, we will have to hide all the young girls in our neighborhood."

Dr. Nazir had opened the plastic bag and was counting the bundles of rupees. He quickly figured there were roughly five thousand dollars.

"As your father's adviser and right hand," Aziza said to Laalla, "should my husband help General Sahib plan how to use the money?"

"I can't think right now," Laalla said. "I am sorry. Besides, the future is not in our hands. If you need to, talk to my father about it."

"Here is my advice," said Dr. Nazir. "I can help your father find a used taxi for no more than three thousand dollars. I will also help find people to fix your doors and windows, because winter is coming. That is another thousand dollars. And the last thousand dollars Shah Jaan will keep for a rainy day. What do you think, Laalla?"

"I think that's a good idea," Laalla said, resigned. "At least I know that they won't freeze to death this winter."

CHAPTER 6

A LITTLE AFTER THREE thirty, Mullah Satar arrived carrying two plastic bags. Dr. Nazir pulled back the gray blanket for him, and Mullah Satar sat down on the folded blankets.

"Here," he said, handing the plastic bags to Dr. Nazir. "These are clothes for my wife to wear, according to our traditions."

Dr. Nazir took the clothes into the other room, and the general took this moment to speak in private with Mullah Satar. Sitting next to his new son-in-law, he grabbed for his hand and cried, "Let me kiss your hands and feet. Please don't spare mercy for her. She is my hope, my life and my oldest daughter. Please, let her at least come to my funeral when I die. I know this is the last time I will see her. But please, treat her with respect."

He bowed down to Mullah Satar's feet, expecting kindness, but Mullah Satar's demeanor had changed. He was not the same person he had been that morning in front of Mawlawi Abdul Karim.

"Only almighty Allah knows who dies when and where," he told the general in a dismissive tone. "But make sure you go to the other room and stay with your daughter, because that man is not related to my wife. This is against my religion, and

I don't want him to see my wife's face anymore. She is the wife of a Pashtun now."

The general rushed to the other room in fear. "Dr. Nazir, go back and sit with the mullah. Hurry. He is enflamed that you will see my daughter's face."

"Mullah Governor," Dr. Nazir said, hoping to apologize, "I am also a Pashtun and considered a member of this family. Your new bride is like a sister to me, like my own daughter."

"Leave this conversation," Mullah Satar said, "and tell my wife it is time to go."

Dr. Nazir went back and found everyone in the other room crying. The clothes Mullah Satar had brought Laalla were lying before her. There was a black Pakistani suit with a long, black blouse and black trousers, a pair of red socks, a pair of green plastic sandals, a dark green burqa, a thin yellow wristwatch with a green plastic band, and two red shawls. Laalla quickly put them on and then hugged her parents and kissed their hands, and then she hugged her siblings and Aziza. Aziza held the holy Koran with her hands on top of the door so that Laalla could pass three times under the holy book before taking a long trip.

Laalla said good-bye to her mother and Aziza and her siblings one last time.

"It is not appropriate for you to come out," General Qassim told his wife and children. "It will only provoke the Mullah's anger."

When Laalla finally appeared, Mullah Satar quickly dragged his new wife down the stairs by the hand. General Qassim escorted Mullah Satar to his new blue Land Cruiser. Four armed guards were parked behind the Land Cruiser in the Mullah's Datsun. As a sign of respect, according to the Taliban's mythology, the guards turned their backs to the mullah's bride as she came out of the apartment. Laalla sat in the backseat and became almost entirely invisible behind the dark, tinted windows.

The general went to sit in front of the building entrance, unable to stand another moment under the weight of his grief. Shah Jaan had started down the stairs but had passed out on her way. Across the street, Aunt Sakina and a handful of women watched discreetly from inside the bakery as Mina and Mirwais came to the vehicle door with glasses of water in their hands. Little Mina pulled herself up to the vehicle window to kiss her sister one last time, but Mullah Satar shouted at her, "Go! People are watching you!"

The mullah's Land Cruiser rolled away, followed by the Datsun pickup. Mina and Mirwais tossed water behind the car. The women from the bakery came out and also threw water behind the truck for good luck. Mullah Satar showed no emotion as the car drove away from the Russian apartment complex. The general held his scarf to his face and cried. Aziza helped Shah Jaan back up to her apartment. Aunt Sakina and five other women came running upstairs from the bakery. The little apartment was crowded with everyone crying over the swift farewell.

Mullah Satar's vehicles made their way out of the complex using shortcuts, driving on sidewalks and broken curbs and through a dusty park that had been Laalla's playground as a child. They passed by an abandoned market that had once been part of a modern shopping center. Laalla noticed the sign for the beauty salon where she had once had her hair done. It had been crossed over with a big X in black paint now.

In front of block 18, in the third Macroyan, she saw a crowd of people—old men, young men and children—running in front of their Land Cruiser. The mullah's driver stopped when they came to an old, gray truck made in Russia. The truck had a crane mounted on its back, and the body of a young man was suspended from the crane's cable. The man appeared to have been in his early twenties and was dressed in a blue Kandahari dress with white embroidery and a red Mazari cap. There was a gold wedding ring on his left hand. A religious police officer was shouting into a loudspeaker.

"Look at this body! If anyone betrays the Islamic Emirates of Afghanistan, this is what his destiny will be."

The driver pulled around the crane and headed south out of the city toward Kandahar. As they came upon the monument to lost soldiers, Laalla saw two amputated feet and two amputated hands hanging from the old cable car wires overhead. As they passed to the south of the next traffic circle, a gathering of women and children passed down the street with their belongings. One of the women kept walking as her scarf slipped from her face. She held a baby in her arms and was trying to hold the other end of her scarf with her teeth. Mullah Satar, who had been watching this from behind the black tinted windows, could not stand this insult to decency any longer and told the driver to stop the vehicle right away. He got out of the car and made a show by throwing his shoe at the woman. She tried to run away, but the mullah broke the antenna from his new SUV and caught up with her, beating her head and legs as he did. Another young girl came running up toward the woman but tripped on a hole in the worn asphalt, and the chicken she had been holding ran away. The young girl lay there with a bloodied knee, crying.

Satisfied with himself, Mullah Satar got back into the car.

"Let's go," he told the driver, "before I wipe all these infidels from the face of the earth."

"Hajji District Governor," the driver said. "These people are Massud's and Rabanni's people coming from the north. I am sure they are going to the old Russian embassy. We have a concentration camp for them. I don't see many men. It looks like their men have, insha'Allah, either died or fallen into the hands of Taliban fighters."

Leaving the city, the two vehicles made their way over a bumpy dirt path, which was the main road connecting Kabul to Kandahar. They passed what had once been a ski area, but, absent snow, it was now littered with burned out oil tankers, armored Russian tanks, rusted containers pocked with holes, and even burned planes and helicopters.

Laalla's eyes took in the landscape from behind her netted burqa. It was almost sunset, Laalla's favorite time of day, but the mullah's bodyguards had pulled their pickup truck around in front of the Land Cruiser, and she could hardly see through all the dust rising off of their wheels. The netted burqa over her face only made it that much more difficult to see.

They drove all night and pulled to a stop in front of a mosque around six the next morning. A loud generator was running next to the front door. A single lightbulb hung from the mosque's minaret.

"It's prayer time," Mullah Satar said to his driver. "Let's pray here, and maybe they will have a place for us to rest for a couple of hours."

"Good idea, Mr. District Governor. It's a good sign that we made it in time for the morning prayer."

The mullah had ignored Laalla throughout the journey as if there were no one in the vehicle but him and the driver, and Laalla had been too fearful through the night to tell him she was greatly thirsty.

Once the driver had left, she whispered to Mullah Satar before he too got out, "Please, can I have a sip of water?"

"Wait!" he said. "Don't you see there are men all around us? I'll bring you water after the prayers."

Some time later, Mullah Satar returned with a clay pitcher of water. "Here," he said.

Laalla brought the pitcher under her burqa and took a couple of sips, then dabbed some on her face.

"This is the city of Ghazni," Mullah Satar said in a kinder tone. "I asked the people in the mosque and was told there is a hotel downtown. They also have rooms for females. You must be tired too. We will rest a few hours and then continue on our journey, insha'Allah. The guards will stay here in the mosque. I gave them money to eat breakfast."

When Mullah Satar's driver returned, the mullah gave him instructions on how to find the Maiwand Hotel. After several diversions through the city, they came to a mud brick building. There was a two-foot-high mud platform that served as a porch in front. A rough canopy held up by cracked oak posts stood over that. Bamboo bird cages hung from the canopy. A dozen pickup trucks and three new SUVs were parked around the hotel.

"Go ask them to make a female room ready," the mullah told the driver.

The driver got out and approached an old man sitting in front. He had a beard that was dyed red with henna and was facing Mecca after morning prayer, his hands slowly turning his wooden prayer beads.

"The female room is in the back of the hotel," the old man told the driver. "Go around this way."

The driver took the key from the old man and handed it to Mullah Satar. Then the driver turned his face while the mullah's bride got out of the car. Laalla followed Mullah Satar to the back of the hotel. There was a yellow padlock hanging on a green wooden door. Mullah Satar unlocked it, and they went into the room. The room had a wooden bed on each side. The beds were covered with clean white sheets and two neatly folded blankets. It had been dark as they entered, but someone turned on a generator, and the lights suddenly came on. One wooden door inside led to a toilet, the other to a bathroom with a concrete tub and a corner for ablution. A half-filled green plastic bucket sat next to the floor drain. There were no plumbing fixtures.

"You can take off your burqa now," Mullah Satar told Laalla.

She complied, and Mullah Satar saw his wife for the first time, his heart burning with desire at the sight of her beautiful eyes. Her innocent black eyes, framed underneath with blue rings, could not challenge the mullah's sharp and lusty eyes;

Laalla looked down. The fingers of her hands were intertwined in front her. Mullah Satar caressed her tiny black eyebrows and long eyelashes.

"Stay here," he told her. "I'll bring you food."

As Mullah Satar left the room, Laalla heard him lock the door from the outside. Laalla went to soak her legs and hands in the bucket of water and then used one of the red shawls Mullah Satar had bought her to dry herself.

When Mullah Satar returned twenty minutes later, he was followed by a little boy. Laalla turned around toward the wall so the little boy would not see her face. The mullah was carrying a one-liter bottle of Pepsi and a glass. The little boy placed two trays on the floor and left.

"Eat this food," the Mullah told Laalla. "I will be back in a while."

"Perhaps you could find me some aspirin?" Laalla said. "I have a bad headache."

"Let me see what I can find," the Mullah said. He left, and Laalla sat there trying to read his personality. He could be so kind in one moment and so inhuman in the next.

Having neither enough information nor the energy to find the answers, Laalla sat down in front of the food. There was a greasy beef stew in a small bowl, green peas in another bowl, three slices of cold roast beef and Kabuli rice on a plate, some onion rings and French fries on a smaller plate, and pieces of flat bread with chicken kabob on the tray itself.

Laalla remembered again how happy her little brother and sister had been two nights ago with the sudden abundance of food, and she smiled. Then she thought of how impossible it was for her to love a man like this, and anguish stabbed into her heart. There was no running away, but neither was there any hope of falling in love with him.

She ate some of the bread and drank nearly the entire bottle of Pepsi, leaving some in case the mullah found her some medicine. He came back a short while later with two strips of Prostamol and a bottle of multivitamin syrup.

"This is what they had in the hotel. The strip of pills is for your headache, and this bottle will be good for your thirst when we travel." He looked down at her tray. "Why don't you eat? If you are waiting for me, I already ate with the driver."

"I am not hungry," Laalla said and stood up from the dishes. Mullah Satar removed the turban from his head and unfolded his hair. It fell down past his shoulders. He then grabbed Laalla from behind and pulled her onto the bed.

"Please," she said. "We have a long trip ahead, and I am tired and full of sweat."

The mullah grabbed both wrists tightly, and Laalla tried to pull away.

"Please," she said again. "I am your married wife. I am yours, but can't we wait until we get to our new home?" Once again Laalla tried to release her hands, but he would not let her go.

"Are you defying your husband?" he said and pulled more tightly on her wrists. When Laalla pushed at the Mullah, he slapped her across the face. "You daughter of a whore!" he hissed. "I know you are not a virgin. I know you could read the bottle of medicine. God only knows how many boyfriends you had in school. You are only reluctant because of the sins of your past."

"If I can read the labels on a bottle," Laalla said, "then I can also read Quran, and this is not how a Muslim should treat a woman."

Mullah Satar slapped her on the face again.

"You are not just any woman; you are my wife. I am your owner, and you must do what I tell you to do." The mullah took out his pistol. "I will kill you and all of your family and the bastard Mullah Baary, who told me to marry this daughter of a whore if you don't do—"

"Then kill me!" Laalla said, interrupting him. "But for God's sake and the sake of his prophets, stop insulting me and my parents! We are human beings, after all!"

Mullah set his gun aside and threw Laalla on the bed.

Once he had satisfied himself, he fell over and pushed his wife away with one knee. She fell from the bed.

"Go sleep on that bed," he told Laalla.

Broken in spirit and hardly able to move, she used the wooden bed frame to help herself up from the floor and walked to the other bed, holding her back.

Mullah Satar rested for a few minutes and stood up. "God saved you. If you had not been a virgin, I would have emptied this whole magazine into your head." He left the room and reattached the padlock on his way out.

CHAPTER 7

LAALLA PULLED THE COARSE blanket over herself and curled up on the bed. She was exhausted and could not think anymore, not about her sisters or brother or mother and father for whom she had sacrificed her life.

Sleep came finally, but it was a restless sleep and filled with troubled dreams. Laalla saw herself standing outside the hotel with her back against the mud walls. It was before sunset, and the sky was smoky. The smoke was rising from the cemetery and floated toward the hotel.

A group of musicians with drums and saxophones passed by, but it was utterly silent, and Laalla could not hear a thing. The musicians were followed by Hafiza and Aziza, the ladies from the bakery. A crowd of children and other women came along. They were followed by a couple dressed in Western wedding clothes. The man wore a dark suit. The bride wore a white dress. Everyone in the wedding procession looked familiar to Laalla, but their faces were somber. There were no smiles. Even the children walked as if in a funeral ceremony.

As Laalla watched, she could see the contraction and expansion of the trumpeters' cheeks, but she could not hear a sound. Everyone passed by, staring at Laalla with their grim faces.

Farther away, soldiers stood, looking like mujahideen, some with round *pakool* hats, some with turbans. Some were dressed as regular soldiers. Some of them were heavily armed with modern rifles. Some were barefoot and held shovels and long sticks in their hands. Among them were foreigners who came with the smoke from the cemetery. Others were climbing out of the torched Russian tanks and armored vehicles and army trucks that were scattered around the hotel. The men bore green and white flags and signs that said "Allahu Akbar" and were shooting their guns into the air. Laalla saw the smoke from the rifles, but again there was no sound. It was cold, and she held her arms to her body and witnessed this scene, wanting to escape but unable to move.

From the foothills, an army of black-turbaned young men waving white flags and signs that said "Allahu Akbar" approached the first group. This group, too, had foreigners among them, all heavily armed like the first group. The numbers in the crowd had multiplied exponentially. Laalla could see that the two groups were shooting at each other in the eerie silence.

Finally, the two groups merged. Laalla saw an explosion. She stood against the wall, enveloped in a silent battle of artillery and huge explosions.

Then a new army of soldiers in green uniforms emerged. One group of soldiers passed close by to Laalla, and a soldier looked at her with a strange and threatening expression. Afraid, she ran toward the cemetery. The soldier left his battalion and followed her. She thought to hide in a ditch, but as she stepped down into it, she found it was full of human skulls. With her heart pounding, she ran toward a burned out Russian tank. Then she desperately tried to climb into the back of a burned out military truck. Finally, she tried hiding inside a burned and rusty old container, but the soldier had followed her. The young soldier stared at Laalla and looked very angry. He took off his hat, took Laalla's hand, and pushed her onto the floor of the container just as the mullah had done. Laalla lay there in fear and silence.

The soldier disappeared, and Aunt Sakina, the big, red-faced Hazara baker, stood next to Laalla in the container. She placed a blanket on her and began to sprinkle Laalla's face from a bowl of water. "If any woman with sin puts water on herself with this Quran bowl, God will forgive her sin," she said. "This is not your fault, Laalla. You are still our angel, and you are in our hearts and prayers. I know you did this to save the lives of your parents and siblings. You did the right thing by not killing yourself like Shabnam, although you will suffer for the rest of your life."

Laalla felt the water on her face and opened her eyes to find that she was still on the wooden bed in the hotel, and it was the mullah who was sprinkling water on her face from a tin cup.

"Are you okay, Khadija?" the mullah asked. "I have been trying to wake you up for the past ten minutes. You were cold, so I put an extra blanket on you."

Laalla sat up and pulled the extra blanket around her shoulders.

"You were crying in your sleep, so you must have been attacked by ghosts. When we arrive in Kandahar, I will have a cleric recite the holy Koran over you to remove the ghost from your body." He paused for a moment and stared at his wife. "I have two buckets of water here for you, one hot and one cold. Go wash yourself so we can continue our journey."

Mullah Satar started for the door. "Oh," he said, before going out, "I am calling you Khadija because I have only heard your name once and cannot remember it. But Khadija is a very appropriate name for a clean woman like you. Khadija was the name of the wife of the Prophet Mohammad, peace be upon him." The mullah left the room and put the padlock back on the door.

When he returned thirty minutes later, he brought with him a small, tin tea pot, a piece of fresh naan, and a small tray holding a pack of milk and two boiled eggs. Laalla was on a prayer matt facing Mecca when the door opened, and the Mullah beamed at her with pride. He sat and watched her happily until her prayers were done.

"You did not eat earlier this morning. Eat these eggs, and I will come back for you soon."

He left and again put the padlock on the door. Laalla ate the eggs and had a cup of tea with her vitamins and Prostamol. Then she tied a red scarf on her head and pulled on her red socks. She had a terrible headache but was ready to go.

The mullah returned and said that she should take special care not to talk in the presence of men and to make sure that no part of her hands or feet were visible. He then led her outside. The mullah's Land Cruiser was parked close to the hotel room. The driver was standing in front of the vehicle, looking away. Laalla hurried into the backseat. Then the mullah called to his driver, who came around and climbed behind the wheel without looking at Laalla.

It was around noon on Thursday when they left Ghazni and headed for Kandahar. Outside the town, they went by the lake where the Russians had been fond of depositing prisoners from ten thousand feet. The two cars made their way along a meandering dirt road. There had once been an asphalt highway going south, but after two decades of war, little was left of it, and the dirt road crisscrossed back and forth across the wasted highway.

They did not stop to rest except briefly at roadside restaurants, or to get out at prayer time, or to allow one of the men from the pickup truck to take over as the mullah's driver. In this manner, they arrived in Kandahar at around two on Friday afternoon.

Close to the airport, about five miles outside the city, the mullah ordered his driver to stop the car and bring food for his wife. As the mullah jumped out from his side of the Land Cruiser, he noticed a tall, handsome man in a white Kandahari outfit standing along the roadside and went over to greet him. After touching his shoulder, the Mullah bowed down to kiss the man's hand, and the two engaged in conversation. Laalla watched this interaction intently from behind the tinted window

When the driver returned with the food, the mullah personally passed it to Laalla. There were cubes of lamb kabob and flat bread wrapped together in an English-language Pakistani newspaper along with two cans of Pepsi. As Laalla unwrapped the Kabob lunch package, she noticed an article in the newspaper on how Saudi Arabia and Kuwait had joined Pakistan in recognizing the Taliban in Afghanistan. Another article noted that the Taliban were pressing the northern provincial capital of Mazar-e-Sharif, and it was expected the city would fall any day now. Reading further, Laalla noticed the Pakistan and China and all the central Asian republics were discussing strategies for how to integrate the people of the region through a network of land communications and Euro-Asian continental bridges. If these bridges were built, the article noted, unprecedented economic momentum would be generated.

My enemy has too many friends, Laalla thought to herself.

She ate her lunch while the mullah outside spoke to the man in the white Kandahari outfit.

"So listen to me," Hajji Tareq was saying to the mullah, "we can both call the minister of the interior. Or maybe it's better if you call him yourself. I don't know him that well, but I do know the minister of foreign affairs and will tell him that we need you in the border city of Spin Boldak. I'm sure your minister won't say no. And if you become the governor of Spin Boldak, I will, insha'Allah, make you a millionaire in less than two months—I mean a dollar millionaire." Hajji Tareq smiled and went on. "You see, I have two hundred Land Cruisers I need to send to Pakistan next week alone, for which I will have to pay someone a bribe, which is haraam. But with you as governor,

I can pay my good friend a commission instead. And there is much more that we could do together."

"It will be my pleasure to help a friend who has helped me so much."

"Good," Hajji Tareq said. "So let's go to my home, and we'll call your minister from there. Then tomorrow you can go to Spin Boldak with me, and the district governor there can move to Garmsere."

"I can't go to your home. I have my female with me."

"What? Don't tell me you got married!"

"Yes."

"Congratulations! You grew up in our family, so my home is your home, and of course you can spend the night with us. By the way, my daughters and wife are here from America. My sister-in-law, Nang's wife, is also here."

"How is Nang doing?" Mullah Satar asked him.

"I'll tell you more later, but life is not easy in America. Nang was sentenced to fifteen years and has only served three and a half so far, and my cousin Ahmad was killed by his enemies. They chopped off his head in his car."

Laalla was so absorbed in reading the newspaper that she failed to notice the mullah returning to the car. An awkward moment followed as Laalla quickly folded up the newspaper and pretended to eat under her burqa again as the mullah climbed in and looked over the seat.

"Our plan has changed," he said. "We are following my friend in this white corozeeng up there to his home in the city."

Laalla listened, as usual, and said nothing in return.

"Hajji District Governor!" the driver said. "The stoning of a woman and an evil man is taking place at four o'clock at the Eid Gah mosque. We have to witness this. To witness events like this is good for every Muslim man and woman; it teaches them lessons."

"I told you to follow the white car and not to talk too much!" the mullah snapped at him.

The driver started away, and Laalla continued her clandestine reading of the articles in the folded up newspaper. There was nothing new to see outside—just the same dusty roads, the same damaged houses and burned out vehicles and tanks and rusty containers.

As they passed through downtown and came close to the famous Eid Gah Mosque, they saw that religious police with black turbans were stopping every car and instructing people to pull over to witness the stoning. The white Lexus SUV belonging to Hajji Tareq pulled onto a dirt road leading to the mosque. The mullah's Land Cruiser and pickup truck followed.

Thousands of people were gathered in and around the front yard of the mosque. There were young boys sitting in the trees and standing on rooftops or on the tops of trucks and SUVs in order to witness the event.

Laalla felt fear growing into a knot inside her chest.

"We'd better stay here and not get out," the mullah told his driver.

Two Taliban with Kalashnikovs and the driver of Hajji Tareq's Lexus came to Mullah Satar's window. The mullah rolled it down.

"Our brother here tells me you have a female inside," one of the Taliban said to Mullah Satar.

Mullah Satar nodded that he did.

"Fine, then we will help you to move closer to the scene so you can watch the stoning from inside your car."

The Mullah thanked the man for his consideration, and the driver followed as the gunmen made a path through the crowd.

"I have not paid attention," the mullah said to his driver. "Can anyone see into the back seat of our car from the outside?"

"No, sir. These windows were originally black, and I made sure to put another layer of black tinting on top. It is like a mud wall painted black."

Satisfied that his wife was not visible to anyone walking by, the mullah leaned back to observe the spectacle around him. Tractors had come from the countryside pulling trailers, and men overflowed from both the trailers and the tractors themselves. Row upon row of SUVs and trucks and Mercedes surrounded the mosque. Between all the vehicles, the aisles were packed with men. Closer in, rickshaws and bicycles and motorcycles were packed together, and young boys wandered through the crowd selling bottled water, Miranda, and Pepsi from tin buckets filled with ice.

Double white lines made with lime powder marked the perimeter of the ceremony itself, and in front of these lines the religious police had allowed two rows of prominent men to sit. All these arrangements had been made the day before once people started to appear after their morning prayers.

Beyond all the parked vehicles, nearby shop owners had erected tents and had pastries and sweets on display for sale. The city mayor had requested that everyone do what they could to help quench the thirst of the growing and restless crowd. Passenger buses had been instructed to bring people free of charge from the different districts of the city.

Finally, the religious police brought the condemned couple to the mosque in the flatbed of a truck. Space was made so that relatives of the condemned pair would have a clear view of Taliban justice. There were a number of small children among them.

The condemned woman was lowered into a pit dug into the earth and buried until only her chest and head were above ground. She was dressed in a sky-blue burqa. The woman's stepson and lover was taken to a spot about twenty paces away, blindfolded, and turned to face the Muslim cleric who was their judge. Laalla tried not to watch from behind the tinted windows, but the mullah had his radio tuned to a live broadcast of the event.

Outside in the glaring sun, the cleric spoke briefly about the process for stoning adulterers in the sharia. Then, following tradition, he stooped to pick up the first stone. There were two piles, one for the woman and one for her lover.

Once the first stone had been thrown at the woman, a group of Taliban fighters quickly stepped forward and launched a torrent of stones at both the man and the woman. Each of the stones was big enough to fill the palm of a man's hand. Neither the man nor the woman cried out.

The man appeared to be dead after a few minutes, but the killing of the woman took much longer. Finally, an old man from among the crowd stepped forward to confront the judge. "It is against the sharia for us to throw stones at her while she is dead."

Other men spoke up and expressed the same opinion. "And only a blood-related man can check her to see if she is really dead," one of them said.

The judge considered this and decided that her seven-year-old son should be the one to check. The young boy stepped forward and turned to the judge crying.   "My mother is alive! My mother is alive!"

At the sound of the boy's cry, Laalla turned to look, but she turned away again as one of the Taliban fighters picked up a large rock and smashed it down on the woman's head. Finally, the woman was pronounced dead.

At the conclusion of the stoning, Mullah Satar told his driver to wait until most of the crowd had left. He and the driver agreed with satisfaction that the execution by the Taliban had represented justice, but out on the streets and sidewalks, the giddy excitement that had prevailed in advance of the stoning had turned to a state of gloom. The thousands of people heading back toward their homes and businesses went along like statues now, their heads held down.

Laalla remembered her father saying, "If we go to Kandahar sometime for vacation, you will see the fun-loving Kandaharis, always with smiles on their faces, with their tape recorders and loudspeakers tied to the backs of their bicycles and horse-drawn carriages garnished with flowers like a Buddhist temple. They are very friendly with animals. They walk the streets with their dogs and have cages with birds in their outdoor tea houses, where they play cards and chat until all hours. They are very hospitable and protective of their guests, regardless of whether they are Afghan or foreign. Guests and foreigners never get robbed or dragged into an argument there, because everyone protects them in Kandahar."

Laalla wanted to ask her husband if this was the same Kandahar, but then she remembered that she was not allowed to talk in the presence of their driver.

It makes sense, though, Laalla thought bitterly. *Look what happened to our beautiful Kabul. Ten years ago, I hoped to establish the first female orchestra in Afghanistan. Now I am a slave to a man who doesn't know the first thing about his own religion. He's just an illiterate man who never had a family and doesn't even know the name of the woman he married. How could I ever love this man? He married me literally at gunpoint, taking advantage of my family's desperate need for a piece of bread.* Laalla clenched her jaw and thought, *If someone had to be stoned, it should have been us.*

CHAPTER 8

HAJJI TAREQ WAS THE name of the tall, handsome businessman Mullah Satar had run into on the streets of Kandahar, but his American friends and business partners knew him as Tommy. In addition to his younger brother Nang, who was in an American prison, Tommy had an older brother named Hajji Matin, who was a well-known drug dealer in the city of Quetta, Pakistan.

Back in 1979, after their wealthy father had been arrested and killed by the Communist government, Hajji Matin had moved his wife and children and two younger brothers from Kandahar to Pakistan. There, Hajji Matin had worked with one of the conservative mujahideen groups for a short time but quickly had become a wealthy drug dealer in the province of Baluchistan, gaining a great deal of respect from Thailand to central Asia to Iran and Colombia for his exploits in the drug business. At the pinnacle of his power, he could transfer millions of dollars from one dealer to another, anywhere in the world, with just one phone call.

With his wealth, Hajji Matin had been able to send Tommy and Nang to establish a business network in the United States. As a front, Tommy and Nang had invested in two fried chicken restaurants called Three Amigos, one of them in downtown Flushing, New York and the other in Albany. That had been in 1986, but within a few years Nang was indicted on a slew of narcotics and money laundering charges. He was finally arrested in 1994 and sentenced to fifteen years by a federal court.

Tommy had spent much of his time over the past year and a half taking care of the family drug businesses in Kandahar and Quetta and on the day Mullah Satar arrived, he already had two business associates staying with him as guests: Rick White, an American, also known as Duck, and Gustavo Gonzales, a Latin American who went by the name of Master. Master was famous for his heroin recipe and had been brought to Afghanistan from Bogotá to train Tommy's men and help them set up three heroin manufacturing plants in the Kandahar and Helmand provinces. Duck was a highly educated man and at one time had served in the federal government. Then he had moved to Bogotá with his girlfriend, and his priorities had completely changed. When asked, Duck could talk politely and intelligently about international affairs, but talking politely about international affairs was not what had brought him to Afghanistan.

As Mullah Satar and Laalla drove behind Tommy's car, Laalla gazed out at the neighboring houses, thinking what fine homes they were. They were like palaces to her. She had never seen anything like them in her life.

A few blocks farther into this prestigious neighborhood, Tommy's Lexus came to a halt in front of two large, yellow metal gates, and two doormen wearing red overcoats with yellow trim and black turbans opened the giant gates. The white Lexus went through, followed by the mullah's Land Cruiser and finally the pickup with the mullah's gunmen. At the end of a long driveway, the Lexus stopped in front of a huge, three-story house. Tommy got out of his car and came back to speak to the mullah's driver.

"Pull to the left, then make a sharp right and follow the concrete driveway. You'll see the house for women in the back."

The mullah started to say something but Tommy cut him off. "Dear Satar, there are only members of my family here. My wife and daughters always go with my driver into the city. It's okay." Tommy called to a little boy standing in front of the gate watering the flowers with a garden hose. "Come here! Sit in the front seat and show the driver the way to the women's quarters. Send the driver back here to park, but stay and take our guest inside. Tell them that she is the wife of Mullah Satar and tell them to call me."

The Land Cruiser went away with Laalla. Tommy walked with Mullah Satar over to the main house. It was located in a beautiful garden with tall pine trees along the perimeter. The pine trees surrounded a beautiful lawn bordered by flowers. Four crescent-shaped steps made of red marble led up to a white marble porch at the front of the house. Curved planters anchored either side of the marble steps and were filled with purple flowers. A huge glass chandelier hung in the arched ceiling above the open front porch.

"To your right is the guest toilet, bathroom, and ablution area," Tommy told Mullah Satar. "To your left is the mosque. Go freshen up. You will find hot water." Tommy looked at the big clock hanging on the wall next to the mosque door. "In thirty minutes we will have evening prayers." Tommy left Mullah Satar and disappeared into the other wing of the house.

At the same time, the garden boy was leading Laalla back to the women's house. At another yellow metal gate, the boy pushed the doorbell three times. A skinny young woman with dark skin opened the door. She had no head scarf and was wearing a white apron. "Who is this?" she said. "And what do you want? Didn't I tell you not to bring your relatives here without Bibi's permission?"

She slammed the door, but the little boy immediately started knocking again. "This is Hajji Sahib's guest!" he shouted.

The skinny young woman opened the door again. "Who is this stranger?" she asked, almost hissing.

"Hajji Sahib said this is the wife of his special guest, and he wants Bibi to call him on the guest room phone."

The woman sighed and told Laalla to come in. Laalla did as she was told in silence and on the other side of the gate found a garden. It was smaller than the garden surrounding the entrance to the main house, but it was flush with flowers and green lawns and equally beautiful.

Three middle-aged women were sitting on the lawn in red and blue striped outdoor chairs. The chairs were gathered around a white plastic table. The striped umbrella in the middle of the table was unopened.

A stocky woman in her early fifties was lying on a lounge chair that had the same red and blue striped cushions. The woman's brown hair was highlighted with blonde streaks. Her white feet were fat and had red nail polish on the toes to match the lipstick smeared generously on her thick lips. She was using her right hand and a white pillow to prop up her chin.

"Bibi, this is Hajji Sahib's guest," the skinny maid in the white apron called out to the fat woman and pointed at Laalla.

"Since when is he bringing strange women to my house?" asked Bibi.

"I mean, her husband is in the men's house and she was sent here by your husband," the maid said.

"How can I be sure she is not the husband if she doesn't show me her face?" Bibi laughed loudly at her own joke and revealed four gold crowns in the process.

Laalla pulled her burqa up quickly to show her face but made no eye contact with Bibi. "Salaam. My name ... My name is ... Khadija. Yes, my name is Khadija." Laalla spoke in broken Pashto with a Dari accent. Her dry and chipped lips barely moved. She felt completely disoriented, but her beauty distinguished her from these other women.

An older woman with a white apron came out from the kitchen. "Hajji Sahib is on the phone and needs to talk with you."

Bibi gave another look at Laalla's face and got up to walk toward the kitchen, dragging her noisy slippers on the white marble porch as she did.

"Hello," she said into the handset.

"Yes, wait a minute," Tommy said and put his palm over the phone. Two men had just entered the reception room next to the mosque where he was sitting on a couch, and he told them to wait outside for a minute. He had just received an important call from Mullah Omar, the Taliban leader.

"Nice try!" Bibi said, having heard her husband's lie. "You can fool your friends, but you can't fool me. And don't tell me this little bitch is another buyer from Russia and not your girlfriend. Because by looking at her—"

Tommy cut her off. "No, listen to me. I'm telling you. She is the wife of Satar, Hajji Matin's servant in Pakistan. Remember the orphan boy we adopted?"

"It can't be true!" Bibi said loudly and then whispered into the phone, "I mean, I believe you, but not about Satar. This girl is very pretty and looks intelligent. She doesn't look like any Afghan woman I know. God forbid she is an agent of the G-men and trying to use him."

"You are an intelligent woman too, Bibi, but way too paranoid. The FBI and drug enforcement agencies aren't coming here. They've never been here. This is Afghanistan, not Mexico or LA. As long as we operate within the country, we're safe. Now, be nice to her. We need Satar's help. He has been appointed as the governor of Spin Boldak district, so get ready. I'm about to show you some real money."

"Satar? Governor?" Bibi said. "He can't even read or write!"

"Who can around here?" Tommy said and laughed. "But he respects us, just like in the old days. When he recognized me, he kissed my hands. We should use him before these Taliban turn him into something else. Now go and show his wife your best hospitality."

This whole time, Laalla had been standing with her head down, waiting for the next command. The two women out in the garden were drinking tea and hardly noticed her. Two homely teenage girls with short, black hair were playing badminton out on the lawn. One of them wore an orange jumpsuit, the other a blue one. They both had on white tennis shoes and were speaking to each other in English.

"It's around ten a.m. in New York," one of the two ladies called out to the children in Pashto. "Bring your father's satellite phone so I can call Nang in New York. It's visiting time at Sing Sing."

Just then, Bibi came back with a big smile on her face. "Khadija, are you still standing there? Oh my God, please come sit down! You are our guest! Come sit, and please take off your burqa! Make yourself at home!"

Laalla started to sit directly on the marble floor.

"No, no," Bibi said. "Please sit here on the chair next to me. We need to talk. I didn't know that you were Satar's wife. He is like my son. So, you are our new bride?"

The skinny maid brought freshly squeezed carrot juice, and the two teenage girls left their game of badminton to take a glass of the juice.

"Our bride?" one of them said in English and made a face at her. "Over my dead body. Whose bride is she, anyway?"

"Easy, baby, easy," Bibi said in her own version of English. "Making no problems, okay? This person is important to us." She took a glass of juice and offered it to Laalla.

"Please, enjoy," she said.

Laalla took the glass with both hands and looked absently at Bibi, still in shock over the stoning of the man and woman and thinking now about her distant family.

"Drink!" Bibi said. "This juice is freshly made.

Just as Laalla was putting the glass to her lips, the voice of an imam came over the loudspeaker, calling everyone to the evening prayer. Laalla waited, but none of the three women or the girls or the maids moved to go pray. No one started for the washroom or got out their prayer mats.

CHAPTER 9

WHEN THE MEN WERE done with their prayers, the imam offered his usual sermon to those in attendance. The group mostly was made up of Taliban, including those who had come from far-off villages to witness the stoning. Business associates of Tommy made up the rest.

"Having a non-Muslim in your house," the imam warned, "or a Muslim who stays in your house and is not praying five times a day, is haraam. Allah will punish you in this world and in the afterlife for feeding people like this. It is true that I saw some of the guests in the guest house not attending to their afternoon prayers."

Tommy got up and left the mosque with Mullah Satar. "Your guards will go to the room that is prepared for them," Tommy said to Mullah Satar. "You will stay with me in the reception room so we can eat together. Then we will call the minister of foreign affairs about your new appointment. But now I must sit down and make some important calls. I will see you in fifteen minutes."

Mullah Satar went back into the mosque. Tommy went out to sit on a wooden bench under a large mulberry tree and pulled a cigarette out of the pack of Marlboro Lights in his pocket. After lighting it, he called out to his guard, who was standing at a distance, "Go tell our imam to come here and see me right now."

"Yes sir, I will go tell our imam to come here and see you right away."

Tommy's most trusted guard always repeated his orders, because on the day Tommy had first promoted him from being a gardener, Tommy had instructed him to do this. The last thing Tommy wanted was any miscommunication.

While Tommy puffed on his Marlboro, the imam appeared. He was in his late sixties and came shuffling along quickly.

"Hajji Sahib, I am here."

"You are a good man," Tommy told him, "and your father was my father's imam. I respect you, but I don't want you to make enemies for me. You are here to pray for me and my family so everyone else will follow you."

The old man began shaking at the tone of Tommy's voice. "Sir, I am getting older. I do not remember saying anything wrong. My father and my grandfather ate your food and made their living thanks to your father's and grandfather's generosity. How could I forget to pray for you? In every prayer, I mention your name and Nang's name. We pray for him to be released from the infidels' jail!"

Tommy took a long drag on his Marlboro before continuing. "You know that I am dealing with all kinds of people here. And that foreigners are helping the Taliban movement to, insha'Allah, take over all of Afghanistan. Even the world. So right now I have two Americans staying in my guest house, and most of the other people in the guest house know this. Why did you say having non-Muslims in my household is haraam?"

"I don't remember saying that, sir. As I asked, please forgive me, because I am getting older and often forget things."

"That's okay," Tommy said and studied the man. "How is your family? How is your grandson? Is he recovering okay?"

"Everything is, Alhamdulillah, fine, with God's help and your support." The old man lowered his head now as sign of respect.

"Take these hundred thousand rupees," Tommy said, "and send your grandson to Quetta for treatment." He handed the imam the equivalent of $2,000 in Pakistani notes.

When the Imam saw this large amount of money, he bowed down at Tommy's feet.

"Stop it," Tommy said and lifted the imam back up on his feet. "You are like a father to me, and I will really be punished by God if you keep bowing at my feet like this."

The imam bowed and groveled his way out of Tommy's presence, and Tommy went back to scheming about his new plans.

Out in the women's quarters, Laalla was nursing her carrot juice, her eyes on the floor or sometimes up at the sky, but she did not cooperate as Bibi tried to extract as much useful information from her as she could.

"I know your language is not Pashto," Bibi said. "But don't be shy. You can speak Farsi with us if it is more comfortable for you."

Laalla nodded but still did not speak. Her index finger ran nervously along the rim of her juice glass. Bibi studied Laalla's every movement.

"My name is Bibi," she went on. "This is Nergis, my brother-in-law's wife. This is Malalai, Nergis's sister, and these are my two daughters, Malalai and Sheila."

"Mom! I'm not Malalai. I'm Michelle."

"And I'm not what you said. I'm Shelly!"

"They were born in Pakistan but grew up in America," Bibi said as if to explain their lack of respect. "Anyway, they don't speak Farsi. Only English and a bit of Pashto."

"Dinner is ready, Bibi," the skinny young maid called out.

"Bring the food to us here at the table," Bibi said. "The weather is nice."

"As you wish, Bibi," the young maid said.

"May I use your washroom?" Laalla asked Bibi.

"Of course, of course. Nergis, go show Khadija the bathroom."

Nergis got up, clearly annoyed at being asked to help. Laalla got up and was careful to pull up her sports socks before following Nergis.

Nergis started downstairs from the porch, thinking to show Laalla the toilet used by the maids, but Bibi interrupted her. "No, no. Take her to my bathroom."

Nergis did as she was asked and came back to the porch.

"Why are you letting this dirty woman use our bathroom?" Nergis asked Bibi.

"Ssshh," Bibi said. "This is not an ordinary Afghan with the standards of a typical Taliban woman. But I am trying to figure out why she has married Satar."

"Either she is a spy," said Malalai, "or from a family of the Northern Alliance, abducted by Satar."

"Either way," Bibi said. "She is hiding her identity from us by acting primitively."

"I sure she making marriage to Satar for money," said Nergis in the English that she and Bibi had learned while working in the fried chicken stand in Albany, NY.

Inside, Laalla wandered around the huge bathroom in a state of awe. There was a Jacuzzi with a frameless, half-inch-thick glass enclosure and a separate shower in the corner with the same opulent glass. Two pink bathrobes embroidered with gold hung on a porcelain hanger next to the shower. A round, purple vanity with a glass bowl sat against the opposite wall.

Laalla stopped to look at herself in the mirror hanging over the vanity, not sure what to think of her appearance anymore. She had not seen a mirror since the third time their home had been looted by gunmen, one day before the Taliban took over Kabul, which was almost three months ago now.

She opened the cabinet and saw a body lotion jar from Winn Casino and Resort and some shower gel from Jumaira Beach Hotel in Dubai, among others. She closed the cabinet and sat on the floor, wondering who these people were and what game they were playing.

"I have to find out," she said to herself and stood up. The words of her father came to her as she stared into the mirror. *There are ups and downs in life, but the beauty is that nothing lasts forever. Life keeps going forward, so have hope and don't let your problems overcome you.*

As the memory of her father faded away, Laalla was about to go and ask Bibi for permission to use the shower but stopped herself. *You have gotten so weak; you don't even have the confidence to wash yourself without asking others for permission.*

"It's ridiculous," she said out loud and climbed in to take a warm shower. Even so, she used her red scarf to dry off rather than using one of Bibi's towels. She also thought about rubbing under her eyes with the aging cream in the cabinet but decided against it.

After rinsing the red scarf and squeezing it mostly dry, Laalla put her red socks and green plastic sandals back on, draped the red scarf over her head, and went back out to the porch. Her beauty sparkled, and Michelle and Shelly glared at her jealously.

"We are waiting for you," Bibi said in Farsi and wished her a healthy bath, which was a gesture of politeness among Kabulis.

On the table sat a large plate of Kabuli rice, three different kabobs with salad, stuffed fried flat bread, a big bowl of soup, fried eggplant, okra, and yogurt. At the sight of the food, a thousand thoughts about her family flashed through Laalla's mind. Were they starving? No, they had money now. Would they spend it carefully? She hoped so and imagined them with the windows repaired and a taxi and the thousand dollars left over. But what if someone broke into the house? But no. That was the only good thing about the Taliban. There were no longer any thieves or robbery.

"Your scarf is wet," Bibi said, breaking Laalla from her thoughts. Her eyes had been on the table and came up.

"I'm sorry. I used the shower without permission but didn't want to use your towels as well, so I dried off with my head scarf."

"I told you," Bibi said. "Please treat this home like your own."

"Nergis!" she called out, and Nergis rushed off to the bathroom—without an attitude, this time. She came back with a white towel and handed it to Laalla.

"Here, take this towel, and we'll have the maid put your scarf in the washing machine."

The maid came to take the scarf away, and Laalla wrapped the towel around her head.

"Now eat!" Bibi said. "We've all been waiting for you."

Laalla poured two big ladles of the fresh-cut noodle soup into her bowl and grew lost in thought. Bibi was watching her.

"Khadija, are you okay?" Bibi said. "Eat your soup. Then I need to talk to you."

Laalla ate the full bowl of soup, which was the first good meal she had eaten in recent memory.

"Try this Kabuli," Bibi said, "and the lamb kabob, and this *bolani* is also good. The green stuffing is from this garden."

Laalla thanked her and placed three spoonful of yogurt with the bolani onto her plate. She sipped from a can of Pepsi while eating and tried to act primitive, aware that Bibi was watching her every move. She did not want Bibi to know she had attended a university or that she was the daughter of a former general. Laalla did not want anyone here knowing the first thing about her. She felt certain if they did it would only work to her disadvantage.

CHAPTER 10

TOMMY TOOK THE LAST puff of his cigarette, dropped the butt, and rubbed it into the ground with the heel of his shoe. He got up from the bench and walked to the reception room, where Mullah Satar was lying on his back on a couch, snoring. He was covered from head to toe with his patu.

I don't blame him, Tommy thought. *He must be very tired after driving all the way here from Kabul.* He picked up the intercom phone from the wall and told the maid in the kitchen to keep dinner warm for one of his guests and to send it over as soon as he called.

He left the room and entered the ablution area, took a key out of his pocket, and opened the door leading to the garage. From inside the garage, he buzzed a switch three times. The door opened, and his business partner, Rick White, appeared from behind the door. Rick was over six feet high, imposing in girth, and had a red beard. He was dressed in a white Kandahari outfit and had a round netted hat on his head.

"Hey, Tommy," he said in English.

"How you been?" Tommy said. "Any news?"

"This freaking goddamned Internet wasted ten hours of my time. The IT guy just left."

"I told that bastard to wait for me," Tommy said. "Damn it. I wanted to make sure he understood the importance of keeping his mouth shut. I don't want him to share what we're doing here with anyone, and I especially don't want anyone knowing he was sent here from Pakistan by Baboo."

"What do you mean?" Duck said. "I thought we were safe in this Taliban kingdom."

"It's not us, Duck. It's our Pakistani partner, Baboo. We don't want anyone knowing he's our contact outside of Afghanistan."

Tommy started out through a small door cut into the larger garage door. "Let me send someone after him," Tommy told Duck. "I need to catch him before he gets away."

Tommy found his main guard eating on the front porch with the two other guards and Tommy's driver. "Go get that Pakistani guy you brought here this morning to fix our telephone. And take one of these guys with you," he added.

Both the guard and driver got up right away. "Okay, sir," the guard said. "We are leaving now to bring back the Pakistani guy who was here to fix the phone."

"Send him upstairs," Tommy added. "And ask him if he's had dinner first. If he hasn't, feed him. Then send him upstairs to the guest room."

Tommy went back in the way he had come out and then walked up a narrow stairway to an apartment above the garage. There was a small square foyer, a sizable living room, two bedrooms, a shared bath, and an extra toilet.

In the living room, Duck and Master sat on two couches separated by a large coffee table. There was a lamp on the table. Duck had a remote control in his hand and was aimlessly clicking through the five hundred channels provided by the satellite dish. A seventeen-inch Sony TV sat on the floor. There were a dozen or so crushed, empty Heineken cans next to the TV.

"Wassup, maestro?" Tommy said to Gustavo.

Master took a last sip from his Heineken and let out a burp. A bit of foam was dripping down his fat chin. "Can't complain, bro," he said. "It's work, but man, I can't wait to go back to Dubai."

"How's the TV?" Tommy asked Duck.

Duck opened the door of a large fridge and tossed a can of Heineken to Tommy. Tommy caught the can and set it on a table.

"No, thanks. I can't drink yet. I have to go see my guests downstairs. I want to introduce you to this guy Mullah Satar later on. Maybe tomorrow."

Duck popped open another Heineken for himself, and Master took Tommy's beer.

"If the mullah finds out we drink," Tommy said, "we'll be in a lot of trouble. We could lose his future cooperation, which is very important to us."

"What does he drink?" Duck asked.

"Opium juice" Master said and laughed.

"No, the Mullah doesn't even smoke cigarettes," Tommy said. He looked at his partners, partly amused, partly perturbed. "You guys are something else. You know what goes on in this city. The religious police are going from door to door. People are being beaten for watching TV. Hell, they send people to jail for having an audio cassette. If they caught us with all this stuff, we'd be lucky if we didn't get hanged."

"I'll take stoning," Duck said with a laugh.

"What are they, nuts?" Master said. "No, bro. This country is not my kind of place. Anyone comes to my house, I can blow his freaking head off and nobody will say a thing." He appeared to think for a moment. "Hey Tommy!" he said. "Is Dubai like you guys? Are they Muslims or are they Jews?"

"Yeah, they're Muslims, Maestro."

"Man! They're cool. Why can't you guys be like them?"

"What?" Tommy said. "You want me to explain the whole history of Afghanistan to you? We've got fanatics, and they play nasty games, so watch it before they start playing nasty games with us."

"Speaking of nasty games," Duck said, "when this goddamned system was up, the first message I received from my source was that UNOCAL is here in town."

"You're surprised?" Tommy said. "BRIDAS from Argentina has been here for months. I know their chairman, Bulgheroni, has been meeting with both Mullah Omar and the Northern Alliance. He's probably spent half of central Asia's fuel jetting between Argentina, DC, and Pakistan. And I know for a fact he's already invited a Taliban delegation to Buenos Aires. UNOCAL is trying to get one to DC. All they need now is a blessing from Prince Turki himself."

"Who's Prince Turki?" Master said.

"Only the chief of Saudi intelligence," Duck said.

"What do the Saudis have to do with it?"

"Don't be dumb," Tommy said. "They're all in this together. Saudi is the Taliban's religious mentor, and Pakistan is their godfather. These oil companies don't care who wins around here, as long as they keep things nice and peaceful."

"Jesus, let's hope not," Duck said. "I mean, we only make money when everything is messed up, right? If there is a central government, we'll have the FBI around with their noses up our asses before you know it."

"That's why I don't pay taxes," Master said and laughed. "It's not my tax money that goes to FBI missions."

"You are a rotten little Bogota kingpin," Tommy said. He glanced at the surveillance camera and saw his guard and driver coming back without the computer technician. The guard knocked on the door, which was unlocked. Tommy stuck his head around the corner and called out, "Come in, it's open."

The guard came upstairs.

"Sir, when we went behind the guest house, there were many vehicles and gunmen—"

"Wait a minute," Tommy said, cutting him off. "What kind of gunmen? Official Taliban, private people, or what?"

"No sir, they were all religious police. Hajji Maalem's people from the police headquarters. As we arrived, they were carrying a body out on a stretcher. One police officer asked me what I was doing there, and I told him you were planning to have a *qari* to recite the holy Koran for the month of Ramadan and I was there to check the availability of a room and see if it was an appropriate place for your guests to stay for a whole month."

"Good job," Tommy said proudly and translated what the guard had said for Duck and Master. "This is how you train your guys."

"Then what happened?" he asked his guard.

"He told me a Pakistani engineer just got killed and asked me why you wouldn't have your guests stay in your own villa, so I told him that you already had many guests coming to stay for Ramadan from the villages and needed to find a quiet place for these extra guests."

Tommy laughed loudly and translated the rest for Duck and Master. "Good job," he told his guard again. "I know you're a smart man, and that's why I trust you. Now, go to see if the guest in the reception room is awake, and let the kitchen help know to send him food."

The guard repeated his order as always and left.

"Wow, that old man is good," Tommy said, shaking his head. "Damn good."

"Who, the guard?" Master said.

"No," Tommy said. "Our friend Baboo. He just trashed the IT guy."

"Just makes our job that much easier," Duck said.

"Yeah, it does," Tommy said, "but it also tells me how well connected he is here. To be honest, I've been thinking about this since this morning but couldn't quite come up with the right plan. And here Baboo had already done it from two thousand miles away. And not to protect our secret, even though it's his secret too. He did it because he wanted to show me his power. That he had men working right here, in the heart of the Taliban's city."

"Two birds with one shot," Master said and laughed. "He's my kind of guy."

"Yeah, when I met this guy in Karachi, I knew he was no dummy."

The guard called through the intercom on line two. "Sir, our guest, the district governor, is up. I brought him food. He is asking for you, sir."

"Tell him I will be there shortly," Tommy said. He turned to Duck and Master. "We can't meet him up here tonight. I'll introduce you guys to him tomorrow. Remember, if you need anything, call me on line one. Don't use the satellite phone. And no booze or drugs before you meet him."

"See you, bro," Master said.

"Good night, guys" Tommy said.

In the reception room, Mullah Satar was sitting on a handwoven Mazari silk rug eating the late dinner that had been saved for him.

"I didn't want to wake you up," Tommy said. "I could tell you were tired by your snoring."

Mullah Satar stood up out of respect and half bowed.

"No, no," Tommy said. "Don't bother. You shouldn't interrupt your dinner to greet someone. That is against the sharia."

The mullah sat back down and ate silently. His eyes were on his plate.

"While you finish your dinner, I will pray two *rukaat* of *nafal* for the Taliban's success," Tommy said.

The mullah finished his food while Tommy was finishing his prayers.

"Your wife is not alone," Tommy said when he returned, "My wife, my two sisters-in-law, and my daughters are here too. I raised my daughters in America according to Islamic sharia, and no male over seven years of age is allowed to enter our female villa."

"Is it too late to call the minister?" Mullah Satar asked him.

"It may be, but I want to call someone in Pakistan who will put pressure on the minister of foreign affairs, and he will pressure your minister." Tommy grinned and dialed numbers on his satellite phone. "Mr. Baboo? This is Tommy."

"Assalamu Alaikum, my brother," Baboo said on the other end of the phone. "How is your new office? Is all the equipment set up?"

"Alhamdulillah, everything is first-class," Tommy said. "My office is all set up, thanks to you."

"That was my engineer's last job," Baboo said. "I made him retire."

"Yes, I just heard about his retirement an hour ago," Tommy said. "Thank you. I knew you'd take care of it. I always rely on your wisdom, and I called now to ask for another favor."

"Tell me. I would never spare any help to you."

"It has to do with the issue we talked about a month ago," Tommy said. "I have the right candidate for the position of district governor at the border city of Spin Boldak."

"Wait," Baboo said. "Let me get a pencil and a piece of paper."

Tommy smiled at Mullah Satar again and waited.

"Okay, go ahead. What is his name?"

"Mullah Satar. He was appointed by the minister of the interior as district governor for Hazarjuft, also called Garmser. He is sitting right here next to me. I haven't let him go to his new appointment yet. He will be here until we send him to Spin Boldak, and the current district governor of Spin Boldak, Mullah Mohammad, goes to Hazarjuft."

"I'll call you back," Baboo said.

"Okay. I'll be waiting."

"Who is this man?" Mullah Satar asked. "How can he be so powerful that he is over my minister?"

"Haven't you ever heard the saying? No matter how high a mountain is, there is always a path leading to the top. Thanks to this man, our forces are progressing dramatically. The fall of Kabul, the fall of Shamali and Herat—he is the man behind it all. We didn't want Hajji Mohammad as the governor of Spin Boldak, but we didn't have a better alternative. I promised him I would find someone we could trust, and here we are. Now let's go to sleep. It's late."

He pushed a button on his desk, and after a long buzz, his guard appeared.

"Tell your boys to bring two cots and put them in here for me and Mr. Governor," Tommy said.

His guard repeated the order and left.

Tommy usually slept at his home in the female villa, but tonight, with the mullah's wife staying there, Tommy intended to put on appearances and stay in the men's villa.

When two men came in, each carrying a navy green canvas camping cot and a thin mattress, Tommy scolded them about not positioning them the right way so that their feet would be pointing toward Mecca.

"And take these thin mattresses," he said to them. "Bring back something more suitable for my guest."

Tommy smiled again at Mullah Satar as they waited. Mullah Satar sat there, a man suddenly feeling awkward and lost in a world beyond his station.

CHAPTER 11

BIBI TRIED THROUGHOUT THE evening to loosen up Laalla with conversation, but apart from the most cursory answers, Laalla remained silent and stared down at the floor. Her mind was busy, though, trying to unravel this Taliban game. For the past two months, she had watched what little happiness remained in her country, torn apart by brutal oppression. She had watched as the women around her were increasingly treated like slaves. All laughter had gone out of Afghan society, and after she had witnessed the stoning ceremony that afternoon, all hope had gone out of her own heart.

But now, as she listened to these ignorant women, who lived in a palace and had traveled the world and still couldn't speak respectable English after living for years in America, Laalla's self-respect began to return. She had a college degree. Even Najiba, the widow working at the bakery for five loaves of bread each day, had studied to be an engineer.

Who am I to hang my head? Laalla thought. *Why should I give up hope? Even if it costs me my life, I have to find out more about this game.* Remembering her family, she reminded herself to be careful, but otherwise she had nothing to lose except the life that had already been taken from her.

"It's late," Bibi said, "and you must be tired."

Laalla looked up.

"Tell them to make Khadija's bed in the maid's room," Bibi called out to Nergis in English without waiting for an answer from Laalla. "And tell the maid she should sleep in the kitchen."

Bibi held her hand over her mouth and yawned. Laalla noticed the shiny gold teeth peeking through the fat lips.

"I'm going to bed now," Bibi said and grabbed her Virginia Slim cigarettes and lighter on the way out of the room. Laalla watched her walk away, her sandals dragging noisily on the porch as she went.

"Dad told us that he would hook up the satellite dish today," Michelle said to her sister, "but it looks like he forgot. I'm so sick and tired of watching this stupid Pakistani channel. It's all we can get here!"

Nergis, Michelle, Malalai, and Shelly all left the patio without saying a word to Laalla. After fifteen minutes, the young, skinny maid who had originally escorted Laalla to the women's quarters returned.

"I have made a place for you in my room," she said with a kindly look on her face. "And Bibi said it's okay for you to use her bathroom."

"Bibi gets up around two in the afternoon," the maid added, "so you should use the bathroom before that. The girls have their own bathroom."

Laalla stood up and grabbed her green plastic bag, which held her only belongings. It also held the English newspaper that had been wrapped around her meal earlier in the day.

Laalla followed the maid down the three steps of the patio and crossed the lawn under the mulberry tree. The maid opened a wooden door with green paint that was chipped and peeling away. A mattress lay on the floor with clean sheets, a white pillow, and two blankets. A clear plastic pitcher of water and a glass sat on a tray beside the bed. The maid also left a lantern for Laalla and a book of matches.

"Sometimes the power goes out when the weather is windy," the maid said, "and it looks like it might be a stormy night. There is a small toilet and ablution area next door, but Bibi prefers that you use her bathroom. No one is ever allowed to use her bathroom. When she goes to America, the door is locked, so she must like you a lot. I am sleeping in the kitchen. When you climb the patio, watch your step."

"Which way is Mecca?" Laalla asked, the first words to have come out of her mouth over the past two hours.

"Mecca," the maid said. "I'm not sure. It may be this way." She pointed to the garden wall.

"Which way is the sunrise?"

"This way," the maid said, pointing toward the kitchen. "There are no dogs in this house," the maid said, "so if you hear barking, don't be afraid. It must be from the men's house."

She smiled and left. Exhausted, Laalla lay down, pulled one of the blankets over her, and used the second to support her tired feet. She noticed the door was cracked open and went over to close it properly, but the door did not fit the frame, so she moved an old, rusty metal trunk against it.

She went back to bed, but instead of sleep, she found her mind filled with thoughts. Mostly they were about the hypocrisy she was witnessing. Her father had been beaten for having a toothbrush in his pocket a few days earlier, and look at the opulence surrounding her. In Kabul men were encouraged to divorce their wives if they didn't pray five times a day. Here, they didn't know which way Mecca was.

She looked at the plastic wristwatch her husband had given her as a bridal gift. It was half past one in the morning. She found her bag, unwrapped the paper from the leftover bread, kissed the bread twice, rubbed it against her forehead, and placed it on the tray next to the water pitcher.

"Four days ago, my father was desperately looking for this much bread to feed his starving children. I am not going to throw it away. Perhaps there are more starving generals in this city."

She started to read an interview in the English paper. It was with the new foreign minister, Wakil Ahmed Mutawakel. "These are our traditions," he said in the interview. "We do not agree with human rights as defined by the Western countries."

You certainly don't, Laalla thought. *But let's face it. You don't agree with anyone's notion of human rights.*

Just then the lights went off. Laalla wanted to turn the lantern on but was unable to find the matchbook. She heard the wind blowing hard outside. She closed her eyes and was soon asleep.

Around six in the morning, the speaker sounded in the private mosque of Tommy's residence. Mullah Satar and Tommy, like every other guest in the compound, went for ablutions and their morning prayers. After the prayer, the imam started in with his usual sermon.

"Last night, I talked to you about the importance of praying five times a day and the duty of the host in making sure his guests are praying while they reside on his premises. We all know that Hajji Sahib has provided us with a mosque, water, electricity, and my salary for a good cause so we can have our regular prayers. Thus, it is our responsibility to make sure we don't miss a single prayer while we are here. However, this does not apply to guests from other faiths. The Almighty says, 'Let everyone deal with their religion in their own way.' So as the vanguard of all religions, it is right for Muslims to let Christians and Jews worship God as they see fit."

Tommy smiled and went back to the reception room, having heard what he wanted to hear. *And for two thousand dollars,* he thought to himself. *The imam almost ruined my reputation with his stupid comments yesterday.*

"My men will serve you breakfast out on the porch," Tommy told Mullah Satar. "That is, if you don't want to sleep again. I need to nap for another hour or two. Then we'll talk."

Tommy disappeared into his residence, but Mullah Satar wasn't sure what to do with himself. He was hungry. He was tired. He also had a hunger to see his wife. In the end, he decided to rest again and soon fell asleep.

In the women's residence, Laalla had gotten up with the call to prayer. All the other women were still asleep, so she had prayed alone.

When she was done, she went into the kitchen and found the maid still sleeping. She used Bibi's shower to bathe again, made her bed, took the piece of bread that she had saved, and went outside to walk along a little stream that flowed from behind the men's villa. The stream passed through a stone arch cut in the brick wall. Beyond it was a garden. Laalla pulled the bread into small pieces with her tiny fingers and threw them one by one into the stream.

Around nine, the doorbell buzzed a number of times, and the skinny young maid finally went to open the door. The garden boy had brought fresh bread from the bakery along with some milk and cream. Laalla was still sitting next to the stream remembering the two lovers who had been stoned the day before when she heard a voice behind her.

"When the power went off last night, I came to check on you," the young maid told Laalla. "But you had something heavy against the door. I tried to push the door but could not. You must have been very tired. I hope you had a good sleep."

"I did, thank you," Laalla said.

"Here," the maid said. "I brought you breakfast."

"Thank you again," Laalla said. "Let's take it to the porch and eat together."

The maid was unaccustomed to such an act of friendship but returned to the porch with Laalla and helped her to spread out the meal on the table.

"What is your name?" Laalla asked the maid, sitting down.

"Parwin," she said. "The older maid is my sister. My only sister. Her name is Runa. There is no one else in our lives now. Just us the two of us."

"And where is Runa?" Laalla asked. "Why doesn't she eat with us too?"

"She has a bad headache," Parwin said.

"So where is she resting?"

"She is in the room next to Bibi. Bibi respects my sister and treats her like a mother." As Laalla ate in silence, Parwin went on. "Runa said that when she first saw you, she knew you didn't deserve to be the wife a Talib."

Parwin paused, expecting Laalla to say something or ask a question, but Laalla kept eating in silence.

"We have been working in Bibi's household for the past fourteen years. In Pakistan first. Now we have been here in Afghanistan for over a year."

Laalla nodded and sipped at her tea and waited for Parwin to go on.

"I saw the English newspaper you were reading last night. My sister was a—"

"That was not my newspaper," Laalla said, cutting her off. "Mullah Satar bought me kabob and bread yesterday, and it came wrapped in the paper. The bread was leftover, and I took it to feed the birds this morning. Then I saw there were no birds here, so I threw it into the water."

Parwin watched Laalla, knowing she had touched on a sensitive area.

"My sister, Runa jaan, finished her schooling in America. She was dean of a girl's high school here before we moved to Pakistan during the Soviet invasion. I speak Russian, too, and was with my husband in Kiev for almost four years. I went to a university and studied contemporary art from 1979 to 1982."

Laalla remembering how her father had dreamed of her studying violin in Kiev, and she was greatly interested in Parwin now. "How did you end up here, working as a maid for them?"

"I was a young child when Runa jaan received a scholarship from a student exchange program. She went to high school in America to finish her last year of schooling there. Since she was one of the top students, she received a scholarship from a university."

Laalla was suddenly holding back tears.

"What?" Parwin asked.

Laalla shook her head and wiped the tears away with her napkin. "I had a teacher. His son went to study in America. Your story brings back many sad and happy memories. When was it that your sister came back to Afghanistan?" Laalla asked, wiping at her tears.

"In 1977, one year before the Taraki coup. She was expecting to get married. Then her fiancé disappeared in the spring of 1978, days after the coup."   Laalla smiled through the tears a bit.   "You are telling the story of Nawid and Zainab," she said.

"It was the story of many people back then," Parwin said. "We lost so many members of our family."

"Yes, I know," Laalla said. "Did Runa jaan ever marry?"

"No. After her fiancé disappeared, she was always waiting and hoping that he would reappear."

"And where were you at that time?" Laalla asked her.

"I was a student in the twelfth grade. A young man from the provincial politburo wanted to marry me. He was also the chief of police for our city and was after me for almost six months. He came to my school with his guards and cars. He brought high-ranking Communists like the governor of Kandahar to our house to talk to my mother. He was a very handsome man and looked good in his uniform, but I didn't want him. Each time I thought of the martyrs in our family, and the bloodshed his party had caused our peaceful country, I hated him. Especially when I learned that he was one of Hafizullah Amin's men, who had killed thousands of young students. But then he began to threaten Runa jaan, saying he would accuse her of cooperating with Hezb-e-Islami, and I finally agreed to marry him. That was in the winter of 1978."

"Was he nice to you?" Laalla asked.

"Very much so," Parwin said. "I can't begin to explain it in words."

"Did he respect you?"

"Not only that. He worshipped me."

"Then what happened? Where is he now?"

"I will tell you everything. But first, let me make a cup of coffee. How about you? Would you like a cup as well?"

"No, thank you," Laalla said.

"Okay, I will make you a cup of fresh green tea," Parwin said. "We are friends now, and I know you must have gone through many of your own hardships in this life."

Laalla smiled and looked away. Parwin headed for the kitchen but stopped to check on Runa along the way. She found her awake now but still with a headache. "Did you want coffee anyway?"

"Yes," Runa said. "Black. And I heard voices. Have you been talking with that Kabuli girl?"

"Yes, she's very nice."

"That's fine, but be careful not to say anything about Bibi and Hajji."

"Sister, I am not a kid. I'm thirty-five years old."

"I know. I also know that once you start talking about your past, no one can stop you."

"I'm not that stupid," Parwin said. She made coffee for her sister and herself and brought a pot of green tea out for Laalla.

"Here," she said and poured some tea into Laalla's cup. "I used to be a chain smoker like Bibi but gave it up when the

Taliban came to Kandahar last year. That's when I started drinking a lot of coffee."

While she sipped at her cup, Laalla studied her. "You were talking about your Communist husband."

"Yes, his love for me transformed my hate for the Russians. After our marriage, we went to the Soviet Union, where he continued his training at the police academy. He also helped me to get a scholarship from the College of Contemporary Arts in Ukraine. Then we returned to Afghanistan in 1982 with our one-year-old son, Lemar, but at that point the Soviet invasion had changed everything. It was during Karmal's era. My husband had no job and was constantly under surveillance. One night, my husband's friends in the government came to our home and told him to leave by the next day or he would be put in jail. So we packed and left for Pakistan the next morning with our son. Runa jaan and my mother came with us. We had little money and took nothing except some clothes. My husband Torialai soon learned that most of his friends were already in Scandinavian countries seeking asylum. Those still in Pakistan were working with the mujahideen. Can you believe it?" Parwin said. "They claimed their membership in the Communist party had been a falsehood all along."

Parwin shook her head and sipped her coffee.

"Thanks to our education, Runa jaan and I were both able to find good jobs. She worked for one of the European NGOs in a refugee camp as a women's affairs consultant. I found a job as a nurse with a Kuwaiti Red Crescent hospital in Quetta. Life was good, except Torialai had started to receive threats from Hezb-e-Islami about being a Communist spy. I was working in the hospital when I got a call from our Afghan neighbor. Her mother was hospitalized with us, so this neighbor had my number. When she called me that day, saying my mother was not feeling well, I knew something wasn't right. If my mother was not feeling well, my husband would have brought her to the hospital. I immediately took a rickshaw home, with my mind cooking up all kinds of awful scenarios, but I could never have imagined what I was about to find."

Parwin paused in tears, and Laalla waited while she brushed them away with her napkin.

"When my rickshaw turned down our narrow alley, I saw it was packed with a mob. My thought was, 'It's really true. My mother has had a heart attack.' I got off the rickshaw and pushed my way through the crowd. People were saying, 'This is the wife,' and 'This is the mother.' When I entered our front yard, I saw that Runa jaan and my mother were all right, and I knew. My heart went black. A body was lying on a wooden bench in the middle of the yard covered with a white sheet, and I knew it was my husband. My mother and sister came rushing to me, crying and trying to hug me, but I held them away with my hands and shouted, 'Where is Lemar?' My mother fell to her knees in grief. 'Don't you see?' she said. 'He is in his father's arms.' I passed out and cannot remember anything else about that day."

"I'm so sorry," Laalla said.

Parwin dabbed at her red eyes and nodded, acknowledging the sincerity of her words. "That was last time I saw Torialai and Lemar," she went on. "When I opened my eyes, I had an IV in my arm. Later that day, Runa jaan explained the whole story. Torialai had taken Lemar to get my son's birthday cake. They were coming to the hospital to surprise me, but as he opened the front door to leave, two gunmen on a motorcycle sped up and started firing. Torialai tried to protect our son, but they both were killed.

"Very quickly, rumors spread through the city that we were Communist spies. The Kuwaiti hospital fired me. The Europeans gave Runa three months' severance pay and a letter of appreciation. Runa jaan knew the mother of Hajji Sahib, Bibi's mother-in-law."

Parwin lowered her voice and leaned forward. "Just between us, we are close relatives, and Bibi's older brother-in-law, Hajji

Matin, moved us all to his house in Quetta. My mother passed away in their household, and step by step our status changed from being their guests to what we are today. Maids. We served for twelve years in her brother's household in Pakistan, and two years now with him here in Kandahar."

Parwin sighed and stood up. She wiped again at her eyes and held her shoulders up proudly. "I have to go to the kitchen now and prepare breakfast for Hajji Sahib's guests. He must have some foreigners in the guest house. I can tell by the breakfast he ordered."

Laalla started to say something, but Parwin cut her off. "I know you have a story to tell too. Perhaps you will share it with me later on. Just don't tell Bibi or Runa jaan what I have shared with you."

Laalla nodded, and Parwin carried their dishes back into the kitchen. Laalla went back to her room and rested. Parwin came an hour later.

"Thank you for telling me your story," Laalla said. "Your courage and patience are just what I needed to hear right now. And because you shared your story with me, I will share a little of mine with you. I graduated from Kabul University with a major in English literature and received violin training from Ustaad Mohammad Hussein. It was my father's dream to send me to Kiev for further training. That is why I had tears in my eyes when I heard that part of your story."

"Then how did you end up being Satar's wife?" Parwin asked. "Why would you marry this uneducated servant of Hajji Matin?"

"So you know him?" Laalla said.

"Of course. He grew up in front of my eyes, sweeping the front yard and watering flowers, just like this little garden boy who brought you here yesterday."

Laalla shook her head and explained how she had fallen into the hands of the mullah. "I would have died first, if not for my family."

"Listen," Parwin said. "I know Satar, and he is very manageable. A bit of love and attention, and you'll have him wrapped around your finger. But more importantly, this whole Taliban movement is a game. Most of the people involved, like Satar, were picked from refugee camps and from the streets of Pakistan. They've never had anything—family, love, education. They don't know what happiness is. The leadership is another story. Look around you. These people live like they're from the West. Watching TV all night. Sleeping in until the afternoon. Bibi pretends to be a big supporter of the Taliban. Her best friend, an Afghan American woman, is lobbying for the Taliban in the US Congress. Her best friends are Afghan women married to Americans."

"It is so new to me, Parwin," Laalla said. "I don't know what to think anymore. I haven't had time to gather my thoughts."

"I'll tell you what to think," Parwin said. "For almost two decades now, we have been a culture where carrying a gun and killing are the greatest honors a man can have. Until we rid ourselves of such ignorance and illiteracy, what can we expect?"

"Thank you," Laalla said. "You remind me that it has not always been this way."

"No," Parwin agreed. "As hard as it is to remember sometimes, it has not always been this way."

CHAPTER 12

Mullah Satar was sitting on the grass under a tree when his satellite phone rang.

"Salaam alaikum," he said.

"Wa alaikum u salaam," the voice on the line said. "Who is this?"

"Who do you wish to talk to?" the mullah asked.

"I wish to speak with Mullah Satar, the district governor. I am from Hajji Rayeece's office in Kabul."

"Okay, I am Mullah Satar."

"Hold on. Hajji Rayeece wants to speak with you."

There was a rustling sound and Hajji Rayeece came on.

"I have decided that you will go to Spin Boldak instead," Hajji Rayeece said, "and Mullah Mohammad will go to Hazarjuft in your place."

"It doesn't make any difference to me," Mullah Satar said. "I'll go wherever you appoint me."

"By the way," the deputy minister said, "you are connected to some big shots down there. I did not know this."

"It is only because Hajji Tareq is my godbrother. I am staying with him now. He is a good Muslim, and his brother is in jail in America because he started jihad against the infidels there."

The deputy laughed. "Okay. I'd like to meet this man. He is very powerful, and I've heard good things about him. But I want you to stay there for another day or two and wait for my telephone call. I don't want you to go to Spin Boldak and start a confrontation with Mullah Mohammad. There are also people who want Mullah Mohammad to stay in Spin Boldak. So wait for my call."

Hajji Rayeece hung up. The mullah went to give Tommy the news, but the door to the reception room was closed. Tommy's guard was sitting next to the door in a chair.

"Hajji Sahib is sleeping," he told Mullah Satar. "I can't bother him until he opens the door."

"This is important," Mullah Satar said. "I need to talk with him right away."

"I told you I can't bother him," Tommy's guard said and stood up. "If it was so important, he would have said so himself."

"Tell him it's me, Mullah Satar."

"I know who you are. You were his servant for many years. Now go and don't talk loudly or you'll disturb him from his sleep."

The mullah cursed under his breath and went back to sit on a bench under the tree. Having heard the conversation, Tommy opened the door and spoke quietly to his guard.

"I'm going back upstairs. When I call you, bring the mullah to me."

"Okay, sir. When you call, I will bring the man upstairs to you."

Tommy walked through the ablution room, unlocked the door leading to the garage, opened the door leading to the narrow stairs, and walked up them into the foyer. Crushed cans of beer and an empty bottle of Johnny Walker lay on the floor. The TV was on. Tommy called down to the kitchen on line two. "Prepare an American breakfast for three and a naan and two fried eggs for our guest as well."

"Right away, Hajji Sahib," Parwin told him.

"Is Bibi awake?" Tommy asked.

"Not yet, sir."

There was a pause. "Is there anything I should let her know?"

Tommy hung up without answering Parwin, went to sit on the couch, and turned on the news channel. They were announcing the fall of Jabul Saraj, Masood's stronghold in the north. It was expected the Taliban would have control of the entire country in a matter of weeks now. General Ameerzai, a former head of the Pakistani ISI, would be on in a moment to share his analysis. Stay tuned. They'd be back right after a commercial.

"Hey guys!" Tommy shouted. "Get up! The world is on fire, and you're sleeping right through it!"

Duck emerged sleepily from his bedroom.

"Whoo haaa," he said and sat down on the couch.

"What kind of a prayer have you got going on around here anyway? That goddamn old man has the voice of a Tarzan. I hear him screaming all night and day. I was just falling asleep when that SOB started up again.

Tommy smiled. "I'm telling you," Tommy said. "If these people were the least bit civilized, we wouldn't exist. Thanks to people like my imam, the masses get the dark ages, and we get a twenty-first century paradise." Tommy smiled even more broadly. "This is a good one. I gave the imam some money last night, and you should have heard him change his tone at the dawn prayer. You guys are no longer infidels. You're helping the Taliban movement to defeat the infidels and take over the country. That's what he said after the dawn prayer."

"The last thing I want is to sit behind that idiot and listen to his nonsense," Duck said. "Especially at six in the morning."

"Pashtun, Tajik, Communists, Taliban," Master said, stumbling out from the back room. "Tajik, Pashtun, ethnic cleansing. Screw 'em all and their grab for power. All I want is for you to shut that goddamn imam of yours up. Man, is that guy is ever loud. The next time I hear him shouting at six in the morning, I'm going to blow his fucking head off."

Tommy pushed the wireless attendant button on the table, and his personal guard came.

"Clean up these empty bottles and cans and bring the mullah to me. Tell him I'm waiting."

"I will clean up these empty bottles and cans, sir, and tell your guest you are waiting for him upstairs."

He quickly cleaned the room and left. The intercom rang.

"Breakfast is ready, sir. If you could please send the garden boy to pick it up."

Tommy hung up without answering. Duck went off to shower. Master disappeared into his bedroom. The guard came in a minute later with Mullah Satar behind him. Tommy took the mullah to a small room with Afghan mattresses and pillows. Tommy asked his guard to send the garden boy to bring the breakfast.

"I received a call from Hajji Rayeece," Mullah Satar told Tommy. "He said that my appointment to Spin Boldak is approved, but I should wait a day or two until the current district governor has moved out. He will call to let me know when it is okay to go to my post."

"I told you we could do it," Tommy said and stood up. "I'll be right back."

Tommy went out into the hallway, closed the door behind him, and knocked on the bathroom door.

"Hey Duck. I have the guy here. Put your clothes on. Don't come out in your shorts." Tommy went to knock on Master's door. "Maestro, are you alive?"

"I've been up all night, man. I'm trying to get some sleep before your guy starts yelling at infidels again."

"Get up. I want you to meet the guy I was talking about last night. You'll love him. He's the future doorman at the Pakistani border, where you almost got killed last week."

Duck came out of the bathroom dressed in a local kameez and shalwar. He was combing his beard.

"You look like a Nuristani," Tommy said.

"Is that good or bad?"

"No, no. It's cool. Nuristanis are considered Pashtun nowadays."

"Anything to keep the wheels rolling," Master said. "I'll even wear my Taliban outfit, as long as he accepts me without a beard."

"Don't worry," Tommy said. "I will introduce you in such a way that he'll worship you. I have to go sit with him. You guys come join us once you're ready."

Tommy went back into the room with Mullah Satar. The guard came in after him with two trays of breakfast.

"I have two more trays coming, sir."

He went back downstairs and returned with the other trays. The mullah was served his fried eggs and flat bread. Tommy poured a cup of coffee.

"Start with the name of Allah," Mullah Satar said. "What are you waiting for?"

"I have two important friends of the Taliban I want you to meet. They were sent by Baboo, the powerful man I called last night. Usually these people stay in the governor's house, but this time I told them to stay with me, since they don't want to be seen by the journalists."

"Why?"

"Our brothers have made good progress toward the north. They pushed the Northern Alliance back to the mountains, and we are rushing like lions toward Mazar-e-Sharif. All of this is because of the help of American Muslims like these two men."

Duck entered the room, followed by Master. "Salaam alaikum," Duck and Master said simultaneously.

Mullah Satar stood politely and greeted both men with a two-handed shake. "Waalaikum salaam, jazakallah, jazakallah," he said.

Tommy stood up as well to show the mullah that his guests were respected people. Then they all sat cross-legged on the floor cushions together. Tommy pushed one tray each over to his American guests and took the metal plate cover off. There were scrambled eggs, freshly squeezed orange juice, cheese, butter, coffee, and homemade chocolate chip cookies. Tommy poured coffee for each of them. The mullah was gazing at his breakfast with his head down.

"Why is his head down?" Duck asked in English. "And how was our greeting? Did we do it the right way?"

"Don't worry," Tommy said. "He doesn't know any better. This idiot is illiterate and doesn't even know what he just said to you in Arabic."

"Mullah Sahib," Tommy said, gesturing toward Duck first, then Master. "I wanted you to get acquainted with Mr. Ahmad and Belal. Of course, these are their new names after God shed the light of wisdom into their hearts and they converted to Islam."

The mullah recited more words in Arabic that he had memorized without knowing their meaning: We all came from God, and will return to him ...

"They will be crossing the border often, insha'Allah, through Spin Boldak," Tommy said. "They are helping the Taliban movement just for the happiness of God. The Northern Alliance is getting lots of money from the Russians from the proceeds of precious stones—precious stones that should be the property of the Muslim people of Afghanistan."

"And the people of Pakistan," the mullah interrupted. "Mawalan Rayhan always said that if we take over the mountains of Panjsher, with the sale of the emeralds, we can buy enough weaponry and ammunition to liberate Kashmir and Palestine."

"But our Taliban have no source of income other than with the help of God," Tommy continued. "So we need ammunition, weapons, trucks, fuel, and hundreds of other expenses to defeat our enemy. These two friends are taking white powder out through Spin Boldak to sell it for us and to bring money to the Taliban so we can pay our expenses."

"Are they selling the powder to Muslims?" Mullah Satar asked.

"Of course not," said Tommy. "God forbid. If they did that, I would kill them before you right now. They take the powder to the Americans and other enemies of Kashmir and Pakistan, like the Hindus. They are able to kill two birds with one stone. We get our money, and these infidels get addicted."

"Jazakallah," said the mullah. "May God give you rewards."

"You can stay in the reception room next to the mosque for as long as you are here," Tommy said. "But I have to take these friends to an important jirga in Helmand province. We will be back tomorrow."

"I will be here waiting for a call from Hajji Rayeece and his permission to leave for Spin Boldak."

When Mullah Satar had finished his breakfast, he shook hands again with Master and Duck and left the room. After the noon prayer, Tommy left with Duck and Master for the site of their new heroin production plant in Helmand. Mullah went to lie down on the same couch where he'd spent the previous night. He was dozing off when his satellite phone rang.

"Assalamu alaikum, Hajji Rayeece Sahib," he said.

"Waalaikum salaam," Hajji Rayeece said. "I wanted to tell you that you should leave for your new post right away. Governor Mohammad left for Pakistan as soon as he heard about his transfer to Hazarjuft district."

"I will leave in an hour," Mullah Satar assured his boss.

"Just give me a call once you are there," Hajji Rayeece told him.

Mullah Satar called for his guards and driver and made arrangements for their departure. The Land Cruiser was to be moved closer to the women's residence. The garden boy was to call for his wife. They would be leaving for Spin Boldak in less than an hour.

The garden boy pushed the door buzzer three times before Parwin opened the door.

"Mullah Sahib said for his guest to come. The car is waiting. They will be leaving soon."

Parwin went to her room, where Laalla was sleeping. Knowing she had not slept well for many nights, Parwin was reluctant to wake her.

"I'm sorry," Parwin said when Laalla finally opened her eyes, "But your husband is waiting."

Laalla got up and prepared to face her duty. "It is better to have things behind us than to be dreading what lies ahead," Laalla said, but to herself she was thinking, *Let's see what's next among the things I never wanted to know.* She wrapped the red scarf around her head, pulled on her burqa, and placed her few belongings into the plastic bag.

Parwin hugged her before she went out the door. "I wish you were here for another day."

"Yes, I wish I could linger, but thank you again for your stories."

Laalla climbed into the backseat. The driver backed up the car to where Mullah Satar was standing on the marble porch of the men's villa. He had been watching the car and driver intently and hopped into the front seat.

The two uniformed doormen opened the gate, and the mullah's vehicle left Tommy's residence. The pickup truck and gunmen followed close behind them. Just outside the gates, men, women, and children waited with empty aluminum bowls and plastic containers. When Mullah Satar's vehicle passed by, all these people extended their hands a little further. Some of the younger children ran alongside the Land Cruiser as it sped up and drove away. The mullah and Laalla had soon left the city of Kandahar behind for Spin Boldak and the Mullah's new post as the district governor.

CHAPTER 13

TOMMY'S LAND CRUISER MADE its way toward the city of Herat over what was left of an old highway running northwest from Kandahar. The highway had been built by the Russians back in the seventies, but after so many years of neglect, it had become a potholed mess. There were long stretches where the highway was simply missing.

Before the city of Gereshk, Tommy's driver turned onto a narrow dirt road and headed south. Dust rose up in their wake, but for all that the dirt road lacked, it was a marked improvement over the highway.

Some ten miles later, they clipped the northwest corner of the Nahre Sararj desert, passed soon after through the provincial capital of Laskar Gah, and then crossed the Helmand River and arrived in a small village to the south of Laskar Gah before evening prayers.

The imam in charge of the mosque, Hajji Mullah Sahib, owed his lucrative monthly salary, if not his life, to Tommy's generosity, and made a not-so-veiled reference to this fact after completing the prayers.

"We will now hold an elder jirga," he told everyone gathered around him, "at which we will finalize the long-standing issue between our two Muslim brothers Hajji Nazar Mohammad and Hajji Abullah. Afterward, you are all invited to a barbecue next door, which has been set up in honor of our elder Hajji Sahib Tareq. This brother, who came to visit us from Kandahar, has devoted his life and family to keeping the flag of Islam flying in foreign countries. He has two guests in his company, who are new believers of Islam, so I want you to keep your emotions under control during our jirga and to exercise the utmost Islamic behavior in order to show the real face of Islam to our new believers and Muslim brothers, who now, with the blessing of Allah, have joined the true soldiers of God."

The speech concluded, everyone rose and raced with each other to where three lambs were being barbecued outside. The smoke from the barbecue had drawn every villager for miles around, whether they were welcome or not. Young and old, men and women, widows and mothers breastfeeding their infants, they all sat in line with their tin bowls in hand, admonishing the people next to them to sit calmly before the imam sent everyone home empty handed.

"There is enough food for everyone!" one of the elders shouted at the crowd. "Pushing and shoving each other and making noise will only upset Hajji Rayeece Sahib and Hajji Mullah Sahib!"

Inside the imam's tent, dinner was being served strictly for the most prominent village elders and businessmen. Tommy sat at the top of a thirty-foot-long green distar khan lying on the floor. Master and Duck sat on either side of him. The imam sat next to Duck. The poor waited outside, hoping to receive whatever was left over after the guests of honor had been served their rice and kabob with naan. Once this was done and everyone in the tent had finished sucking the last juice from the bones, the imam asked Tommy to say a prayer.

"The fact that we all sit around one distar khan and eat with full stomachs," Tommy said, his hands held up in the air, a long chain of wooden prayer beads in his right hand, "should not to be taken for granted. This is a gift from the Almighty, who has promised in his holy book that he is merciful to all those who follow the path the Prophet, peace be upon him, has laid out for them. What we enjoy today is only a fraction of the Almighty's immeasurable treasure, which we alone as Muslims are privileged to enjoy. Our real reward comes in the afterlife. The treasure of his wealth there is vast and unbounded, and only those who have followed his instructions and know this life is but an experiment will have access to it. May the Almighty give us the power and wisdom to overcome evil and to devote our lives to helping our Muslim brothers. Amen."

The imam, after praising the service of Hajji Tareq and his commitment to expanding the reign of the Islamic Emirate over the temporal world, asked his assistant, a young man, to come forward and read the history of the conflict between Hajji Nazar Mohammad and Hajji Abdullah.

"Before he reads," the imam added, "Let me remind you this conflict and animosity has already cost our community the lives of two young Muslims, and if it is not checked, God forbid, it will expand to animosity and division between two villages from the same tribe."

The imam nodded to his young assistant with the black turban, who started reading from the prewritten script in his hands.

"In the name of Allah the Almighty, conduct your affairs in mutual consultation. These are the words of the Almighty, the merciful who created the heavens and earth. My brothers! Evil comes through men's deeds alone, of which they cannot avoid the consequences. But guidance comes through Allah's mercy and revelation. With permission from our elders and guests, I will recite the dispute between Hajji Nazar Mohammad and Hajji Abdullah as follows. Laal Mohammad, the son of Hajji Abdullah, was engaged to the daughter of Hajji Nazar Mohammad some eight years ago."

One of the elders stopped the man and asked him to mention the name of Hajji Nazar Mohammad's daughter. Hajji Nazar

Mohammad protested, saying it was not right that her name be mentioned, since she was still alive. A dispute over this point went on for most of an hour, the imam emphasizing that her name must be mentioned or this jirga would not be in compliance with sharia. As precedent he cited how a girl's name was mentioned during nikah and even the name of the Prophet's wife was mentioned many times in the holy Koran. But Hajji Nazar Mohammad was very insulted by this request and warned them against mentioning his daughter's name, especially in the presence of people who were not from his family, and some not even from his own village.

"Does Hajji Nazar Mohammad have another daughter?" Tommy asked.

"No, sir. I had five sons and one daughter. Four of my sons were martyred fighting against the Russians, and the last one was killed by the cowardly son of this man." Hajji Nazar Mohammad pointed his finger at Hajji Abdullah. With that, the two men began arguing, and many of the others present were drawn in.

"Mullah Sahib and respected elders!" Tommy called out, and everyone in the jirga fell silent. "The reason it is important to mention the girl's name is to avoid any misunderstanding or confusion with Hajji Sahib's second or third daughter. For this same reason, one has to mention the name of the bride during nikah to prevent confusion and future disputes. Since he never had another daughter, I say it is okay not to speak her name out loud."

With some grumbling, all present agreed to the solution and praised Tommy's judgment and wisdom. The imam's assistant went on.

"Each time Hajji Abdullah took elders to Hajji Nazar Mohammad's house to ask him for permission to plan the wedding, Hajji Nazar Mohammad rejected it, because he had clearly put forth the condition that Hajji Abdullah should pay a *walwar* in the amount of five hundred thousand Pakistani rupees, the amount that Hajji Abdullah and his son had agreed upon at the time of engagement."

Another argument commenced between Hajji Nazar Mohammad and Hajji Abdullah, again with many of the others present joining in.

"Enough!" Tommy said, his anger boiling over. "It is in keeping with the jirga that you remain silent and agree to the consensus of the elders, unless there were any questions to be asked and clarified."

There was more grumbling between the two principal parties, but the imam's assistant continued anyway.

"Two months ago, Laal Mohammad, the son of Hajji Abdullah, bought a gift, a red shawl, for his fiancée. He decided to give it to her in person when she came to the river to get water. The couple was sitting—"

"Stop! Stop!" one of the elders shouted. "They were not a couple yet. They can be considered a couple only after nikah before witnesses."

Everyone agreed that the word *couple* should be removed, and the imam's assistant read the recitation again with this correction.

"Laal Mohammad and his fiancée, the daughter of Hajji Nazar Mohammad, were talking about their future life and wedding plans while keeping a good distance between them so they were out of one another's reach. Aminullah, the son of Hajji Nazar Mohammad, arrived on the scene. He happened to be armed with a Makarov gun and used it to kill Laal Mohammad. His sister screamed and ran home, followed by her brother, who fired a couple of shots at her as well, but she managed to reach home unharmed. Aminullah escaped from the village but was killed three days later in Kandahar by an anonymous gunman, allegedly a friend of Laal Mohammad as retaliation for his friend's murder. We have witnesses that Aminullah threw a glass full of acid on his sister's face on the day of the incident before he managed to escape to Kandahar.

Witnesses say that she lost her right eye completely and can barely see with her left eye."

"He was a coward!" a young man shouted from the back of the room. "If she were my sister, I would have killed her on the spot!"

"If she were my daughter," an old man said loudly, "I would have stoned her to death."

Another man asked the imam to remove the acid part of the recitation, since it was a family matter, and a heated argument over that point went on for some time. Finally, Tommy managed to bring everyone into agreement, saying it was only fair to remove the story of the acid injury, since it could be interpreted as punishment for a wrongdoing on the female's part, and this would hurt the family pride.

The jirga went on for a good six hours, marred again and again by the same squabbling. Three young men were finally asked to leave the room because of their belligerent behavior. In the end, Hajji Nazar Mohammad accepted that he would not pursue any claim or dispute whatsoever. He agreed to stay away from Hajji Abdullah for the rest of his life and mourn the death of his young son with his blind daughter and aging wife. Hajji Abdullah claimed that he wouldn't allow his son's fiancée to marry any other person but his older son, who was in his early fifties and already had three wives and nine sons and daughters at home. He wanted his older son to marry his brother's fiancée. After six hours of debate, Tommy reached a verdict acceptable to the majority of the jirga attendees. It read as follows:

"Taaj Mohammad, the older son of Hajji Abdullah, will marry Hajji Nazar Mohammad's only daughter, and will pay a walwar in the amount of five hundred thousand Pakistani rupees, which is payable right away in front of the jirga attendees. Both of them, Hajji Nazar Mohammed and Hajji Abdullah, are committed to having a normal relationship, and both of them will forget and forgive the animosity of the past."

Tommy reached into his pocket and gave the new groom five hundred thousand Pakistani rupees, the equivalent of ten thousand US dollars, which the groom passed on to Hajji Nazar Mohammad, and in this way the dispute between the two villages came to an end.

The following morning after the dawn prayers, the imam joined Tommy, Duck, and Master on a trip to their new heroin plant in the Musa Qala district of Helmand province. They drove Tommy's black armored 4Runner back up to the highway, crossed what was left of that pocked, asphalt road and headed north through a dry, barren country. A silver Lexus SUV and two green pickups had joined them at the highway, and one of the pickups went out ahead of everyone else, kicking up dust, two gunmen seated in the back. The silver Lexus and other pickup had fallen in behind Tommy's 4Runner.

In time, they came to a river and followed it north, surrounded by rich farmland. When the river split into two tributaries, they took the left fork. The valley steadily narrowed around the river, but the terrain had been the same all along the riverbanks: miles and miles of poppy fields, red and white and coral in color, with the dry, barren hills above and all around them.

"Amazing," Duck said to Tommy. "We've been driving for a few hours, and I ain't seen nothing but poppies growing. Makes you wonder what these bastards would be cultivating if it wasn't for opium."

"Cotton," Tommy said. "That's what they grew before the Soviet invasion. Helmand had the best cotton in this part of the world, except for maybe Turkmenistan, which, as a Soviet state, never exported to the West.

"I'm serious," Tommy said. "The Germans, Brits, even the Americans came in here showing the farmers how to build irrigation systems and shit. My father used to call cotton white gold. A gift of God. The West got clothes. We got cooking oil from the seeds and used the husks for everything from feeding our cows to cooking to heating our houses."

"Hard to imagine the Americans coming around this place playing the nice uncle," Duck said.

"Are you kidding?" Tommy said. "The city of Laskar Gah was nicknamed Little America in the fifties and sixties. It was the most modern city around. The Americans had big engineering outfits building infrastructure all over the place. Even had their families living here."

"So what happened?" Master asked.

"What happened. War, you idiot. What do you think happened? And the only way to defeat a superpower like the Soviets was to get a bunch of barefoot peasants ginned up on religion. That's how we got all these zealots, and in their zealotry, these idiots will do anything to whip your ass, even if it means ruining a few souls with heroin."

"Especially if it means ruining a few souls with heroin," Duck said with a laugh and a wave at all the poppy fields.

"Speaking of money," Master said. "I saw you give a whole pile of it last night to that one guy to shut him up. So what happened to the young girl?"

"The old man got the girl. The money was for her father."

"No way!" Master shouted. "What kinda frickin' justice is that? Some old geezer gets to sleep with a twenty-year-old girl? And this idiot sitting up front calls himself a judge?"

"Look, Master," Tommy said. "I explained everything to you the other night. If it was the old days, when these people still had a culture, you and I wouldn't be here breaking ground on the world's largest heroin plant, so quit complaining." He looked over at Master. "Look, I feel sorry for the girl, but I can't change things. This country is up for grabs, and like everyone who comes here, I'm taking everything I can before the party's over."

"Okay. It's cool, man! I was only asking. I'm going back to Dubai anyway. I can't wait to get back, man. This place ain't for me."

In Musa Qala, Tommy's convoy was received warmly by the district governor, the chief of police, the head of the religious police, and every former mujahideen commander who had thrown his stakes in with the Taliban. During a lunch that was served in a tent erected especially for the occasion, Tommy was introduced to two Russians. The Russians were Chechen mujahideen who had joined the Taliban in their holy jihad.

After the lunch, the imam who had come with Tommy held a short prayer praising those who had provided the lunch and hospitality.

"May Allah give us the ability to pay back a fraction of the great hospitality we have enjoyed today," he told the village elders. "You have created work for the farmers and unemployed young men of the Musa Qala district, who have been deprived of the very basic and everyday needs of life." He turned to Tommy. "With the permission of the district governor and all other worthy brothers and guests, I would like to ask you to honor us by cutting the ribbon and setting the first foundation stone with your blessed hands."

After a brief recitation from the holy Koran, Tommy gave a short speech, which was followed by speeches from the district governor and two village elders.

"I want to warn our brothers, young and old," one of the village elders said to the gathering. "Using narcotics of any kind is against Islam and the instructions of the Almighty and his Prophet, peace be upon him. We are not producing powder to use ourselves. This is the only weapon we can easily manufacture, profit from, and use to defeat our enemy. If the world chooses to drop bombs on us and kill our children and destroy our huts and land and even our livestock, then why should we care what happens to them?"

Many testimonies followed about how a man could plant wheat and watch his family starve to death, but with one field of poppies, he could feed his family for an entire year.

When all the speeches were done, Tommy, together with the imam and the district governor, held a pair of scissors and cut the ribbon. They then laid a large rock for the foundation of the new factory. The rock was decorated with green ribbon.

Finally, Tommy was given a silk turban by the district governor, which he said was from all the people of Musa Qala. Duck and Maestro each received their own pair of embroidered Kandahari kameez.

A short while before the evening prayer, Tommy's convoy gathered on the dusty road and started back toward Kandahar.

CHAPTER 14

ON THE DAY OF Laalla's departure, after sitting for some time and staring down the road toward where his daughter had disappeared, General Qassim went back up to his apartment and lay on the floor. His wife tried to rouse the general by having him install the cardboard pieces wrapped with burlap in the windows, but he would not respond. His son and two remaining daughters tried but could not get his attention beyond a pat on the head. The general had lost his first child, his oldest daughter, his princess, and what little hope he had left went out of his heart.

Late that afternoon, Mullah Baary, while on his rounds as a religious policeman of the Macroyan district, returned to visit with General Qassim and his family, and even though General Qassim was in mourning over the loss of his loved one, and even though Mullah Baary was a friend to the man who had taken away his daughter at gunpoint, and even though the general felt sure this mullah had designs on his daughter Sahar, he also felt it was his duty to be hospitable and ask the man to stay for dinner.

On that occasion, they all trod lightly around the subject of Laalla's departure, but when Mullah Baary returned the following night for dinner, General Qassim felt compelled to ask about his daughter.

"Mullah Sahib," the general asked in his grief-stricken voice, "any news from Mullah District Governor?"

"No," Mullah Baary replied. "How should I know about him? I'm just a small, local policeman. Do you think I own a satellite phone like Mullah Satar?"

"Then, if you happen to be around someone who has a satellite phone, could you please call and ask how my little daughter is doing?"

"Me? Ask a man how his wife is doing? What do you think I am, a pimp? You are a man. Act like one."

Mullah Baary went on to say that he was not like these Kabulis, that he had pride, and he could not find enough words to insult the general. Meanwhile, the general sat there with tears trickling into his gray beard.

"My apologies, Mullah Sahib," the general said, trying another approach. "I meant that I wish I were with someone who had a phone so I could call and talk with him. I did not mean to put your manhood or Mullah District Governor's manhood in question."

Mullah Baary left soon after without granting any hope in response to the general's request. The general went down and sat in the dirt pit next to the apartment where once there was a green lawn and now there was a red flag marking the spot where Shabnam had died four years earlier. Shah Jaan came down and sat with her husband.

"What do you want to do?" she asked him.

The general stared straight ahead. "There was talk outside the mosque today of what happened up in Mazar-e-Sharif just yesterday. After the Taliban had massacred nearly all the Hazara living in the city of Mazar-e-Sharif, the new governor, Mullah Hassan, had announced over a loudspeaker to those who remained, 'You have three options. Surrender and convert to Sunni Islam, leave Afghanistan and go to Iran, or stay and die.'" The general looked at his wife.

"So? We are not Hazara," she said,

"And women in the bakery said that the minister of the interior had asked all Hindus to wear yellow arm bands so they can be distinguished from Muslims."

"So? I expect nothing better of these bastards." There was silence for a moment. "So?" Shah Jaan said again.

"So I think we should leave for Pakistan."

Shah Jaan raised her eyebrows at him.

The general looked away. "Tomorrow," he said. "Why waste money on fixing up the apartment? They'll only come take away whatever improvements we make. That or arrest us." He looked back at his wife. "And you? What do you think?"

"I think if we stay here, Sahar and Mina, God forbid, will suffer either the fate of Laalla, or the fate of Shabnam."

"Then we are agreed," the general said. "For the future of our children, we must leave this place and go to Pakistan. With the money this warlord gave us, we will have something better than life in a refugee camp."

"I think it would be best for us to have a Pashtun along as an escort," Shah Jaan told her husband. "At least until we reach the border. Let's go speak with our friend Dr. Nazir."

The general agreed and went upstairs to watch the children. Shah Jaan walked with her son over to the next block and up to Dr. Nazir and Aziza's apartment.

"Shah Jaan," Dr. Nazir said after welcoming her in and hearing her concerns, "I have too much respect for you and your husband to interfere without your asking, but Aziza and I have been thinking this very thing. You and General Sahib need to get out of this country. Things are only getting worse. We are Pashtun and will somehow get along, but you have little or no future in this country at this point."

"There is more to worry about," Shah Jaan said. "The religious policeman, Mullah Baary, came to our home yesterday for dinner and again this evening, and I am afraid he is after our little Sahar."

"Shah Jaan, you should have told us this immediately. You have no time to waste. Go home and start packing. I mean it," he said and encouraged her toward the door. "Take only what you absolutely need. You cannot afford to wait another minute. I will take you to Peshawar myself. We will leave first thing in the morning. It is the least I can do for my dearest friends."

At the break of dawn, General Qassim went to his morning prayers as usual. Meanwhile, Dr. Nazir gathered Shah Jaan and her children into his car, and as soon as the prayers were over, they left Kabul together and headed east for Jalalabad. Very soon, they had climbed up into the narrow valleys of the mountains. Streams rushed alongside the road, and the mountain peaks rose high up around them.

At one point, Dr. Nazir was forced to stop and retrieve some water for his radiator from a stream down below the road. The general got out but waited by the car.

"One thing in favor of the Taliban," Dr. Nazir said, coming back up to the road. "They got rid of Commander Zardar's check post. It was at this very spot, I believe, where he used to stop all the passing cars. Did you ever hear of the dog Abdullah Shah?"

"Of course," the general said. "Zardar's two-legged dog."

"It was said they kept him in a cave with a chain around his neck and only brought him out to intimidate the captured travelers."

"Yes," the general said, looking off toward the hills. "If I should become charitable in the years to come, I will thank the Taliban for getting rid of Commander Zardar. And all his gunmen bastards."

The general looked to the mountains and felt his heart growing strong again from anger. It seemed as if the old juices of war were stirring inside him, though it was a far different kind of war he now fought, a war to save his family and perhaps his own sanity. He thought suddenly of Laalla.

"There," Dr. Nazir said, finishing up with the radiator. He smiled at the general. "I'm not sure about Zardar's two-legged dog, but I have heard the commander himself now lives comfortably with his family in England."

"Don't ever let Shah Jaan hear you say that," the general whispered. "She will be nagging me endlessly that if that bastard Zardar can make it to Europe, so can we."

"Who knows?" Dr. Nazir said. "Maybe with your money and living in a refugee camp, you will find a way. At least your children will be able to go to school. And maybe Shah Jaan will find work as a teacher or administrator with one of the NGOs."

"Yes, I suppose there will be opportunities," the general said. "Something we no longer have in the land of my forefathers."

The two men climbed back in the car, and Dr. Nazir started back on his way to Jalalabad. It was less than two hundred kilometers from Kabul to the border, but the road was a difficult one, and it was very late in the day when Dr. Nazir and what remained of General Qassim's family finally arrived at the border city. They arranged for a motel, and after dinner, Dr. Nazir was able to contact a longtime family friend and Pakistani businessman by phone in Peshawar. The next day, Mawlana Haq Nawaz met Dr. Nazir at the Pakistani border. The usual introductions were made, and from there Mawlana Haq Nawaz drove the general and his family into Pakistan.

Hajji Haq Nawaz had a guest residence at the back of his house, and he immediately showed the general these quarters when they arrived. "You see? There's a path that leads through this gate to the back of our house, so you can come and go without disturbing anyone."

They went through the gate and into a backyard with trees and a garden. The guest house was beyond the garden and opposite the house.

"You have two rooms, a kitchen, and a bathroom with a shower," Hajji Haq Nawaz said, opening the door. "This is the place where our male guests usually stay, but you and your family can use it for as long as you wish."

"How much shall we pay you for rent?" the general asked him.

Hajji Haq Nawaz held up his hands. "Please. I have no financial need to rent my house. I do this in appreciation for all the hospitality I have enjoyed during my many visits to the home of Dr. Nazir. Besides, Afghans are our brothers. We have to be there for them in their time of need."

"Then at least allow me to pay for the electricity and gas."

Again Hajji Haq Nawaz held up his hands. "We shall see. But for now, please make yourselves at home and rest. I know you have had a long and difficult journey in this world."

Both men bowed, and Hajji Haq Nawaz went back out through the garden.

CHAPTER 15

THE HOURS OF LAALLA's life in Spin Boldak passed with intolerable slowness. She spent most of the time locked up alone in the district governor's three-bedroom house. She spent most of her nights lying lifelessly beneath the barbarian advances of her husband, whose primary intent, beyond ingratiating himself, was to get his wife pregnant. As time went by and his efforts did not bear fruit, Mullah Satar began to display even more bitterly violent mood swings. For failing to give him a son, he cursed his wife with ever more vitriol. That the cause might be his own infertility was never considered. Mullah Satar would not even admit that this was a biological possibility for a man.

Apart from the mullah's bad attitude, the inside of the governor's house was a very pleasant place. There was a modern kitchen and showers and toilets in every bathroom. It was not Tommy's villa, but it was a far cry from the ransacked apartment in Kabul, and Laalla went about making herself as comfortable as she could under the circumstances.

One day, in her solitude, she grew curious about what might lay hidden in the attic and crawled up there to discover it filled with boxes. Most of the boxes were filled with agriculture reports written in English. Some had photos of Americans who had lived there, and some of those photos showed men sporting big cigars, round hunting hats, and hunting rifles. Laalla also found a biography of famous Afghan scholars, each of whom had obtained PhDs from prestigious American universities.

In reading the reports, Laalla's mind was taken back to a time before all the wars, when it appeared, from what she was reading, that Americans and Afghans had lived side by side in this house and had managed these agriculture projects together. It was the very sort of cooperation and advancement that Laalla had dreamed of taking place in her country and just the sort of thing that the senseless wars and now the brutality of the Taliban had made impossible.

But aside from the comfort of the house itself, Spin Boldak was a hot and dusty and miserable place. The summers were unbearable. The sky regularly turned dark yellow from dust storms. The town's only advantage was that it straddled the Pakistani border, so when Mullah Satar came one day and told Laalla to pack her belongings because they were moving to Musa Qala in Helmand province, she was all too happy to oblige him.

Laalla knew they had been in Spin Boldak for less than a year, because it was shortly before the month of Ramadan when they packed up the car. A week or so after their arrival in Musa Qala, Mullah Satar brought home a new bride. She was a beautiful woman but not yet twenty years old.

Her name was Qamar, and because there was absolutely no reason for Laalla to be jealous of her, the two women quickly became good friends. Laalla learned that Qamar, too, was an educated woman. She didn't have a university background, but her mother had been a teacher before the Russian invasion. Her father had been a lieutenant-colonel in the army.

Qamar told Laalla the story of how her father had helped to orchestrate an uprising against the Communist regime in Herat back in the winter of 1978. Subsequently, after spiriting his family off to the mountains of Badghis, he had joined the mujahideen. He was then killed in a firefight with the Taliban in 1995, when they first came to take over the area around Herat.

With their mother recently dead, Qamar's brother had forced his younger sister to marry Mullah Satar, basically because he needed money to pay for his mother's funeral and to feed his own children.

In time, Mullah Satar took to beating Laalla in front of Qamar for no other reason than sheer barbarism. He often told Laalla that the only reason he did not kill her outright was because he wanted her to see what a handsome son Qamar would soon bear him. Within the year, when it became clear that Qamar was also infertile, Mullah Satar took to beating both women at once.

About the time Mullah Satar first moved Laalla to Musa Qala, General Qassim took to selling vegetables from a wooden cart on the crowded streets of Peshawar. An Afghan carpenter and fellow refugee had made the wooden cart for the general. The vegetables were purchased from a produce wholesaler on the far side of the city. Every day after his morning prayers, he walked the mile or so to the wholesaler, bought what he could carry in a large burlap sack slung across his back, and carried it back to where his cart sat on the city street. His income from this enterprise was barely enough to cover the family's gas and electricity bills each month and to pay the local police to turn a blind eye to his unlicensed operation, but at least it kept the general's mind off his troubles. It kept him from dwelling too much on his sorrow over Laalla and the loss of his homeland.

Meanwhile, Shah Jaan was increasingly frustrated with her own failure to find a job. From the first moment the family had arrived in Peshawar, she had been out in search of work with an NGO or an Afghan school, but in vain. This had left her to dwell endlessly on her personal circumstances and the general's failure to provide for their family. Week after week, they steadily went through the money Mullah Satar had given them.

"You are not the only one selling vegetables on the roadsides," Shah Jaan told her husband one day. "There are hundreds of Afghans who have the same business. I wonder how they make money when you can't. They even send their kids to private schools."

Whenever Shah Jaan took to slinging barbs at the general this way, he sighed and looked off as if he could still see the snow on the mountains above Kabul, as if he still felt that brief bit of fire he had experienced when he and Dr. Nazir had stood by the roadside on their way to Jalalabad. In fact, General Qassim was still able to exhibit the admirable detachment of any old soldier, but he was simply an old man now who no longer had any will to fight.

"I have to pay 20 rupees to the police every morning," he told his wife. "That or they will throw my vegetables onto the street and tell me to clean them up. And if I failed to do so, I would then pay a 150 rupee fine for the municipal services to do it for me. Give me time. I am new at this business. I have never sold anything before in my life."

Two months after General Qassim launched his vegetable selling business, his landlord took note of his hardship and failure and introduced him to a Pakistani fruit dealer named Chaudry Sahib. Chaudry was a soft, congenial man who wore the loose cotton shirts of a barber. His ever-present smile was filled with gold and sparkling chatter, and every day he delivered fresh cartons of oranges, apples, and mangoes directly to where the general now had his cart parked beside Sher Pau Hospital. And with fresh fruit much easier than vegetables to sell on the streets, things were looking up. The general's proceeds were suddenly enough to pay for the utility bills and to provide his family with a reasonable stipend.

Given this relative bounty, the general and Shah Jaan decided to send Mirwais, Sahar, and Mina to a private school.

They had hoped of course to send them to the schools expressly set up for refugee children, but because they lacked the proper paperwork, they had been unable to obtain refugee status for their three children, and as a result, the children had been sitting around the house all day long, deprived of the companionship of their schoolmates.

Otherwise life went on more or less the same. One hot summer passed into the next, and then another hot summer came. Shah Jaan failed to find work and grew shriller and went on pecking away at her husband. Then another year flew by, and another one, until the general had become an old man in deteriorating health.

He was forced to cut back on his hours at work. His son Mirwais attempted to make up for this shortfall, but lacking skill in dealing with the police, Mirwais soon found himself being chased from street to street with the fruit cart. And in all these years, through all their tribulations, the family heard no news from their long-lost daughter Laalla.

CHAPTER 16

AT THE END OF one long, hot summer day, Shah Jaan put Mina to bed and stayed up with Sahar waiting for Mirwais and the general to arrive home from work. When it got to be eight o'clock, Shah Jaan grew concerned. By nine o'clock, she was frantic. Finally, the general and Mirwais arrived home a little before ten.

"I know you have been worried," the general said, "but there was a little too much sun where we were standing this afternoon, and my nose started to bleed, so Mirwais took me to the hospital."

"For God's sake," Shah Jaan said. "Why didn't you send someone to tell me you were all right? You never think of my feelings."

"You're right," the general said. "I should have sent someone to tell you."

"And think of your health," Shah Jaan went on. "Think of your family's future. You didn't try to get us to Europe when we had the money. Hundreds of people you helped to get visas when you were in power, but not us. You never listen to me! Shabnam's death and Laalla's disappearance are all because of your foolishness. I'm not listening to you anymore. I'm going to work in the beauty salon that Zia Gull found for me."

"If you do that," the general said, "I will kill myself. And you first. I know what people say behind the backs of these other Afghan women who work in the beauty salons."

"You are telling me what to do? You should have bought us a home. What is this? Living in someone else's house for free?"

"Mom!" Mirwais shouted. "Dad is right. I hear what people say about women who work in these shops. You should think of the family pride and not be trying to sell—"

Shah Jaan slapped him across the face. "Be quiet and don't ever talk to me that way. You are still under my control."

Sahar took the general to rest in the back room and shut the door. She came back out into the main room and stood close to her mother. Mirwais was in a corner crying.

"Mom, what is wrong with you?" Sahar said. "All the time now you are disrespectful of Dad. I have never seen a wife talk to her husband like that before."

"Yes, you know nothing," Mirwais said to his mother. "Dad's blood pressure was very high. That's why he collapsed in the street. From now on, I will be going to work for my father instead of school. He needs to stay home. And you will not be working in the beauty salon, that's for sure."

He stood up to Shah Jaan, and she slapped him in the face again.

"Is that right?" she said. "So now I have two men in my house! Well, I'll show you what I am going to do right now."

She took her shoes and moved to leave the house. Sahar ran after her.

"Mother, please don't make a scene! For God's sake, the landlord will hear and kick us out! Please, Mother! Where are you going?"

"I'm going to Zia Gull's house to ask her for work. If your father was a man, he would find a way to send us to Europe. If he won't, I'll find a way myself. This is not a life. Look at Zia Gull. The woman has a car and maids. I cannot stay with this stubborn old man and suffer from his stupidities. He is a real Talib himself, not allowing me to work simply because I'm a woman."

"Please, Mom. I promise you I'll talk to Dad. Go start working in the beauty salon tomorrow, but please don't leave now. What should I tell Mina when she gets up tomorrow morning? Please come back."

Shah Jaan sat on the floor and leaned against the wall with her eyes closed. "Okay," she said after a long moment. "I won't leave now, because of Mina. But I don't need permission from your father to work. Or from you," she added and shook her finger at Mirwais.

The next morning around ten, Shah Jaan took Mina and caught a rickshaw to the Hayaat Abad district. The day was already hot. The temperature was pushing one hundred.

The driver dropped Shah Jaan and Mina in front of Zia Gull's home, which was behind the mosque at Fourth and Main Street. Shah Jaan buzzed the door, and an older Afghan woman opened it.

"Salaam. Salaam, Shah Jaan," she said. "This must be Mina jaan. Masha'Allah. What a beautiful family! Please come in. I recognized you from the pictures Zia Gull showed me. Why didn't you bring Sahar jaan with you? She is really pretty. A knockout, as Hajji Sahib says."

The old lady led them along a path that wandered through a lush garden with many tropical flowers and plants. At the far end of the garden, the old lady opened the door to a large room, and they passed from the hundred-degree heat of Peshawar into an air-conditioned room. The room was furnished with leather furniture and gold-framed glass coffee tables. The ornate curtains were also embellished with gold.

A Hazara woman in her twenties entered the room spraying a rose-scented air freshener. Then she came back with two glasses of lemonade and two bowls of ice cream. She put red cloth napkins embroidered with *welcome* in white silk in front of both guests, placed a glass of lemonade on each napkin, and left the ice cream bowls on the black lacquered trays set on the table. During all this, the young woman did not attempt to greet the guests or make eye contact with them in any way.

Jealous, angry, and frustrated, Shah Jaan once again secretly cursed her husband, remembering how as a young girl Zia Gull had waited at the school door for Shah Jaan to give her a ride home. She had never worn a new piece of clothing. Even her wedding dress had been secondhand. Then her parents had fled to Pakistan, and now she lived like a queen while Shah Jaan lived like a refugee.

Maybe this Hajji Sahib the old woman had mentioned was a rich man from overseas. He had called Sahar a knockout after seeing her photo. Maybe he was looking for a young woman to marry. *Well, if so, I'll be the boss this time. I don't care if he is an older man. I'll force Sahar to marry him. Once in the West, she can always divorce him. That's what most of the Afghan girls do anyway.*

Her scheming was interrupted when Zia Gull walked into the room. She wore a pink bathrobe and had a white towel wrapped around her head.

What a cultureless woman, Shah Jaan thought to herself. *She greets her guests in a bathrobe.*

Zia Gull kissed Shah Jaan three times on the cheeks and kissed Mina one time. She held a pack of Marlboro Reds in one hand and a long lighter in the other.

"I have missed you so much!" she said, taking the seat across from Shah Jaan. "Welcome! I expected you to bring Sahar Jaan with you. Please bring her out of her cage! I have a lot of young friends and goddaughters her age. Now that I have lived in Pakistan off and on for twenty years, I know a lot of people from the upper social class. You shouldn't allow her to make friends with low-class refugees."

"She had to stay home with her father," Shah Jaan said. "He is getting old and grouchy. I cannot imagine how I have spent thirty years of my life with that selfish man. He has ruined our lives with his blind allegiance to the wreckage of our country."

"Shah Jaan, in a matter of weeks, if you and Sahar work with this friend of mine in the beauty salon, you will be making good money." Zia Gull lit up a cigarette. "But please take care of yourself." She exhaled the smoke toward the ceiling. "Look at yourself in the mirror. I mean, you are younger than you look. Enjoy life and let the general do his praying and sit in a corner in the mosque. Besides, if a man cannot feed his wife, he shouldn't be considered the head of the family. No money, no honey," Zia Gull added in English and let out a big laugh.

The Hazara maid came back in. "Sima is ready," she told Zia Gull. "Don't you want to get your massage?"

"Are you blind?" she yelled at the maid. "Don't you see I have guests? And you never learn. You don't serve ice cream for breakfast. Did you ask Shah Jaan if she already had breakfast?"

"I assumed they had, Zia jaan."

"How often must I remind you? Don't talk back to me."

"Thanks, but we've had breakfast already," Shah Jaan said.

"Okay," Zia Gull said. "Then bring some of the delicious melons that Commander Sahib brought from Mazar-e-Sharif.

"It's true what they say," Zia Gull continued after the maid had left. "If you are nice to a Hazara, she will expect to become your bride. If it weren't for the way she keeps this house so crystal clean, she wouldn't be here for another minute."

After talking for two hours about nothing and eating the melons for lunch, Zia Gull was preparing to leave with Shah Jaan for the beauty salon when the mosque's loudspeakers went off, calling the faithful to prayer.

"Let's wait until these Taliban go for their prayers. Whenever they see me outside at this time, they stare as if I came from the moon."

Once the streets were empty again, they went out to a white Land Cruiser, but a soiled young man with long hair and a bushy beard confronted them before they could get inside. The ribs of his tiny chest showed through his worn clothing. He leaned against the mosque's wall, smiled at the women, and spat three times in Zia Gull's direction. "Sell them!" he said. "Sell them to the Pakistanis. Sell them! The Taliban sold our homeland in the name of God. You are selling our mothers and sisters in the name of friendship. Sell them!"

As Zia Gull hurried to get Shah Jaan and little Mina into the backseat, the man stood up suddenly and laughed derisively at all three of them. Zia Gull climbed into the front seat and told the clean-cut young Pakistani man behind the wheel to hurry and get away.

"I will see you on the judgment day, you bitch!" the homeless man called out as the driver pulled into traffic.

Everyone sat in silence as they drove to the beauty salon.

"I forgot to introduce you to Khan Sahib," Zia Gull said after awhile. She turned back to look at Shah Jaan. "Sorry. I got disturbed by that heroin addict. He used to live on our money. Khan Sahib still gives him clothes and two meals a day, but lately he refuses to eat. He is being looted by refugees living in the camps. He has gone mad, I think. Whatever money he begs from people after prayer time he spends on refugees."

Shah Jaan nodded and stared out the window. They drove in silence again for a spell.

"By the way," Zia Gull said to Khan Sahib. "This is Shah Jaan, the wife of General Qassim. You saw the photos I took of them. She is the mother of Sahar, the beauty queen."

"Welcome to Pakistan," Khan Sahib said in Pashto.

"Thanks, Khan Sahib," Shah Jaan said in Dari, "but this is almost our fourth year."

Before the conversation could continue, a policeman stopped their car at the traffic circle, but when Khan lowered the black tinted window, the policeman recognized him and saluted. Khan gave him a thousand rupee note and told him, "This is your lunch."

Once they had stopped in front of the beauty salon, Khan turned to Zia Gull.

"I am leaving for Islamabad right now, so I won't be able to give you a ride back home."

"I can call my driver," Zia Gull said, "but you don't have to lie to me. I know you are going to Lahore with the new girls that bitch brought back with her from Kabul. I'm telling you again, they're all orphans from Kabul who grew up without families."

"What are you talking about? Have I ever lied to you? Besides, if I did take anyone, I would always ask you first!"

Shah Jaan got out of the car, not wanting Mina to hear any more details of the conversation.

"Yes, you always lie to me when it comes to women!" Zia Gull shouted at him. "But go ahead and try her service. I know you will come back to me like you always have in the past. I am the best supplier not only in Peshawar but in the whole of Pakistan."

Zia Gull slammed the door hard and apologized to Shah Jaan as they walked toward the building. "Sorry. I lost my temper. These Pakistanis don't know friendship, and they are smoother than soap slipping out of your hand, especially if they have money."

"I don't know what you are trying to tell me," Shah Jaan said. "But to be honest, after the comments that heroin addict made and your conversation with that man, I'm lost."

"There's nothing to hide," Zia Gull said bluntly. "If you really want to get rich, this is the only way. You are sitting on treasure and wealth, and you don't even notice it. So let's go inside, or you can go home and go on living in misery if you want!"

She lit her Marlboro and kicked the glass door of the beauty salon open. Shah Jaan reluctantly followed Zia Gull inside.

There were red leather chairs and a glass coffee table. Two middle-aged women were at work on two young girls, cutting their hair. A large air conditioner was cranking away.

"Tomorrow is our busiest day, because Thursday night is a big thing here in Peshawar. By the way," Zia Gull said to the two hairdressers, "this is Shah Jaan, the mother of Sahar, the pretty girl I showed you the picture of."

"Give me a chance to do your hair," one of the hairdressers said to Shah Jaan. "I will make you look prettier than your daughter. The flower is hiding under the bushes, as they say."

"They also say a fox eats the sweetest grape," Zia Gull said. "You girls find out for me who is going with Khan tonight. I want to know how many girls, their names, and who their supplier is." She turned to Shah Jaan. "I was supplying this fox with the prettiest girls in Pakistan, but he sneaks out with others. That's it. He's not getting any more girls from me until he falls at my feet, begs for forgiveness, and apologizes for what he has done.

"Come," she said to Shah Jaan and pulled her into the next room, where three girls and an older woman were getting their toes done.

"It looks like you have shown Sahar's photo to everyone," Shah Jaan said to Zia Gull, "and this is not fair."

"Shah Jaan, you should be proud of her. This is where she will eventually work."

"I'm sorry, but my daughter is not a prostitute."

"Oh, come. Don't get me wrong. I'm not a prostitute either. That's a different story, one I will tell you someday. She can work in the beauty salon. None of my hairdressers are prostitutes. In fact, if I found out that they were going out with men for money, I would fire them right away. Wouldn't it be stupid for a girl who could make a thousand dollars per night to work as a hairdresser? These girls are all married."

"But I thought you offered me a job here?"

"Of course you will work here. When customers come here to get their hair and nails done, you will sit here and talk to them and bring them tea and sodas, and they will tip you. We have a little kitchen in the back. My customers are very generous. They tip as much as a hundred US dollars sometimes. This way, Sahar can be trained to work as a hairdresser while you enjoy the peace of mind of being with her all the time."

After much discussion of the matter, Shah Jaan finally declined the offer and arrived home around six with little Mina. Shah Jaan had a new hairdo. Her arms were filled with groceries, and everything had been paid for by Zia Gull.

"Mom, you look great!" Sahar said. "Where did you get your hair done?"

"It's a long story, but I will tell you later. I'm tired now. Just make me a pot of tea. And where is Mirwais?"

"He came home from school and went to the mosque for evening prayer." She paused and then shouted, "Mom, you didn't even ask about Dad!"

"Oh, yes, how is he?"

Sahar started crying. "Dad is getting weaker and weaker every day. I made him a bowl of soup, but he barely ate it and now he is sleeping."

"Zia Gull is a good woman and has a good life. It may be true that her husband is a partner to money exchangers, but she showed me the beauty salon she owns, and your father and Mirwais are wrong. It may be true about other beauty salons, but her business is very prestigious."

"So I take it you are going to work for her soon."

"No, I decided not to, in order to keep your father happy."

She said this loudly so the general could hear her in the next room. A moment later, the door opened and he appeared from the back room.

"Shah Jaan," he said. "I do not hear so well these days, but you are right. It won't hurt to try and seek refugee status with the European embassies. I am still not feeling well, so I can't do it tomorrow, and then the weekend comes, but on Monday I will leave for Islamabad."

"But Sunday is the first day of Ramadan, Dad," Sahar said. "Can't we wait until after Ramadan? Mom? Dad will be thirsty and hungry waiting behind the embassy gates."

"It shouldn't be a problem," General Qassim said. "I'll leave here at four in the morning and, insha'Allah, will be back by *iftar* time. I am getting weaker, but don't forget that your father is a soldier."

"Yeah, right," Shah Jaan said. "A soldier who never shot a bullet toward the enemy."

"A soldier, nonetheless," General Qassim said.

That next Monday, General Qassim traveled to Islamabad and visited nearly every European embassy along with those of Canada and Australia, but everywhere he went, his applications were shrugged at and declined. There were no more wars. The Russians had left Afghanistan long ago. Go home, he was told. The issue of refugee status was no longer relevant.

Going home was exactly what the general wanted to do, but how could he convince his wife of this, when her head was filled now with dreams of middle-class luxury in a Western country? As he walked out of the Australian embassy and onto a quiet side street in one of Islamabad's more upscale neighborhoods, the general smelled the money and knew his wife was longing to be in a place very much like this one.

The general had not gotten halfway down the block when a white Mercedes pulled up beside him. The driver hit his power window button. He was clean-shaven, and from his features, the general assumed he was a young Afghan. A man dressed in a Pakistani outfit sat next to the driver.

"Where are you headed?" the driver asked.

"The next bus stop," the General said.

"Hop in and we'll give you a ride to the bus station."

"Thank you, but I'll walk," the general told him.

The young Afghan driver followed along and politely offered the general a ride several more times. Finally, the car stopped and the young Pakistani in the front seat jumped out and waved to the general.

"Here, Uncle," he said. "Take my seat." Seeing that the two men were determined, the general accepted the ride but insisted on sitting in the back.

The young Afghan took off his dark sunglasses out of respect for the old man and turned to face him.

"You should have sat in front. My apologies for having our backs toward you."

"A flower looks as beautiful from the back as it does from the front," the general said.

In the ensuing conversation, the two young men were able to confirm that the general was hoping to emigrate to the West with his family, and they assured him that they knew how to achieve that end.

"You don't have to pay us now," the young Afghan said. "You leave your money with any money exchanger that you trust. After you get to your final destination, you can call the money exchanger, and he will pay us. Until then, all your travel expenses are paid by the agents we have all over the world, even your possible delay in a third country."

"You've got the wrong person," the general said when they had reached the bus stop. "I had to work all week long selling vegetables in the Peshawar bazaar in order to have the two hundred rupees it took to pay for my bus fare from Peshawar. How can I possibly pay for a trip to London?"

The two young men kept insisting, but the general got out. The Afghan man held out a thousand rupee note. When the general refused to take it, the young man pushed the money into his shirt pocket.

General Qassim arrived home about eleven that night. He had fasted for more than seventeen hours and felt exhausted.

Mirwais, Mina, and Shah Jaan were already asleep, but Sahar had waited up for her father.

"Our neighbor sent us food for iftar," Sahar said. "I saved you some."

The general had no appetite, but because of Sahar, he picked at the plate of food and explained to his daughter about his failed efforts. He did not tell her about the two young men in the white Mercedes. He knew that it would get back to his wife, and his wife's head was already filled with too many false hopes.

CHAPTER 17

IN BITTERNESS RATHER THAN out of any feeling of loyalty, Shah jaan had obeyed General Qassim's wishes about going to work for Zia Gull in her beauty salon, but life only became more difficult for the family as a result, and Shah Jaan only became more embittered for having obeyed her husband. The money Mullah Satar had given them had run out long ago. The meager income from the general's fruit cart was barely enough to keep the family alive, and the children were no longer able to attend the private school.

Then, during Ramadan, General Qassim's health began to fail so thoroughly that he spent most of his days in bed just trying to breathe without a struggle. He rarely went down to work with Mirwais.

On the eve of Eid, the last day of Ramadan, while Shah Jaan was out shopping with Mina, Sahar came into the general's room and put her palm on his forehead.

"Dad," she said, "your body temperature is low. We'd better get you to the hospital."

"No, I'm okay," the general said. "No one will see me anyway at this time of iftar. Just bring me an extra blanket and turn off the lights. Perhaps if I lie here for a little while longer, I will feel better. If not, we will go to the hospital later on."

Sahar brought the extra blanket and sat beside the general. "I know what you are thinking," she said. "You wish Laalla was here."

The general patted her on the hand. "Just be a good girl. Promise me," he said.

"I promise you, Father."

"Good," he said and patted her on the hand again. "I have heard from people in the bazaar that my old deputy, Colonel Khalil—his daughters are selling their bodies because of their poverty. People call him Colonel Pimp. I would rather see us dead than to reach that point."

He took Sahar's hand, rubbed it against his face, and kissed it three times. "And please don't let your mother work in that beauty salon. Always keep your honor and respect Shabnam's blood and Laalla's sacrifice."

"I will, Father."

"Good. Then let me lie here for a while and wake me up when the mullah calls for prayers."

Sahar kissed her father's forehead, turned out the lights, and closed the door.

Some time later, Shah Jaan returned with Mina and went about preparing the special Eid meal. She looked up and saw Mirwais coming home through the backyard. At the same moment, the loudspeakers went off in the nearby mosque.

"Sahar, go wake your father," she said. "It's iftar."

Sahar did as asked but found the general still sleeping. She shook him gently through the blanket, but he did not respond.

"Mom!" Sahar shouted. "Come in here! Dad won't wake up! I think his blood pressure must be very low!"

When Shah Jaan came into the room, she knew instantly what had happened. "Your father is dead!" she cried out and fell across his body in tears.

Mirwais and Mina came rushing into the room, and the entire family wept over his body. Very soon, the landlord and his family and various neighbors arrived to console the family and to help with the burial arrangements.

"You must stop weeping now," the landlord told Mirwais at one point. "You are the man of the house now and must take care of your mother and sisters. Come with me to the mosque, and we will bring a qari to recite the holy Koran over him all night. Someone should be up all night. We should not leave the body alone until we do ablution tomorrow morning."

Shah Jaan hugged Mirwais before he left the room. "Your uncle is right. You need to be stronger than ever now. And remember to tell the mullah we have money for the whole funeral, grave, and cemetery, and the qaris and everything. I didn't tell you, but I have saved money for a day like this."

As soon as Mirwais left with the landlord, Shah Jaan took Sahar aside.

"Stay with the landlord's wife and daughters. I will be back in half an hour. If they ask for me, tell them I am in the other room praying."

"Mom, for God's sake, what is this all about? Where are you going? They aren't stupid. They'll know you're not in the next room."

"Just do as I tell you!"

"At least tell me where you are going!"

"I'm going to get money from Zia Gull. I have to. I lied to Mirwais, but I won't accept the neighbors paying for your father's funeral."

Hearing this, Sahar went running from her mother in tears. Shah Jaan went out and took a rickshaw across town to Zia Gull's home. When she rang the bell, a man in his early thirties opened the door.

"Come in, Zainab," he said. "Where are your girls?"

Shah Jaan entered the yard without responding to the man. He was drunk and smelled of whisky. Four men in white Pakistani shalwar kameez and striped black and white vests were sitting on the outdoor benches next to the flowers. They had cigarettes in their hands that smelled of hashish.

"How does she look?" one of them asked very loudly in Urdu.

"She looks like my grandmother," the man who had opened the door responded, also in Urdu.

"It's okay! Be nice to her!" one of them shouted. "Grandmothers always have granddaughters!"

The men laughed loudly at their joke.

"Zainab, where are the girls?" the man who had smelled of whiskey shouted again.

Shah Jaan went directly into the big reception room without responding and found three half-naked girls. One of them sat next to Khan Sahib. The other two sat on either side of a man wearing an Afghan outfit. Zia Gull had a drink in her hand.

"Look what I told you!" she shouted to Khan Sahib upon seeing Shah Jaan. "I knew it. I swear I knew it!" She giggled and waved for Shah Jaan to come sit with her. "Honey, I just won a one thousand-dollar bet. I bet Khan Sahib that you and Sahar would come after Ramadan, but I didn't know that you'd surprise us on Eid eve! Where is my pretty Sahar?"

Shah Jaan whispered in Zia Gull's ear, "I am here because my husband passed away an hour ago, and I have no one to help me but you and God."

"What would you like to drink?" the man wearing the embroidered Afghan outfit said loudly in Dari. "You must be the mother of Sahar."

"Ssshh!" Zia Gull said to him. "Something tragic has happened in the family."

"Tell me who it is," shouted the Afghan man, "and I will bring his head to you! No one can hurt my fellow Afghans! They call me Commander Salim, and I am a commander forever. During the Communists, during the mujahideen, and even during the Taliban."

Zia Gull warned the men again to be quiet and hurried Shah Jaan off to a nearby room.

"I am sorry to hear what has happened," Zia Gull said. "But don't worry. You have a sister in me. Sit here and relax for one minute."

Zia Gull ran off and came back with a bundle of hundred-dollar bills.

"Here," she said to Shah Jaan. "This will take care of the funeral cost, the imams, and the qaris. And I will come to see you tomorrow afternoon."

"But how can I use this?" Shah Jaan said. "It is late, and the money changers are all closed until tomorrow."

"Let's go to my room," Zia Gull told her. "I will give you Pakistani rupees instead." She led Shah Jaan through a large kitchen to a small laundry room and knocked on the door. When no one responded, she undid a set of keys pinned to the waist of her skirt and opened the door. A marble spiral staircase led down to a large furnished basement. Two men in their late thirties were sitting opposite each other on red leather sofas separated by a square glass coffee table. On the table were two dozen plastic bags as large as a hand palm with white powder. There was also a bottle of red wine and two full glasses on the table. Both of the men were smoking cigars. One of them appeared to be American or European. He was tall and thin with a short salt-and-pepper beard. He was dressed in a blue Pakistani shalwar kameez, a gray sleeveless vest, a brown pakool, and brown Pakistani leather sandals with no socks. The second man was an Afghan, shorter but also thin, with darker skin, a long mustache, and a well-trimmed black beard. He wore a starched white shalwar kameez, a white pakool, a matching vest, and black leather shoes and socks.

"No worries," Zia Gull said to the Afghan man in Dari. "She is my sister and one of us."

Zia Gull took Shah Jaan with her into the next room. There was a king-size bed against one wall. Two trays of unwashed plates and wine glasses sat on a credenza at the foot of the bed. A large stained-glass globe of the world stood on the night table next to the bed. Each continent was represented with a different color of glass, and the globe was turning slowly around on its axis, filling the darkened room with colored lights, though not enough for Zia Gull to find her way around comfortably.

Shah Jaan stood in the doorway, also struggling to see into the darkness and searching for a light switch on the wall.

"The chandelier fell and broke earlier this evening," Zia Gull said. She walked carefully around the broken chandelier and opened a large walk-in closet. "We really need these Hazara," she said to Shah Jaan. "Look at this mess."

She came back with a bundle of rupees in denominations of one hundred. "Here is fifty thousand rupees. This is a lot of money in Pakistan. Spend it on the funeral and don't worry for one minute. Your sister is here, and I won't hesitate to do anything in my power to help you."

The two women passed by the two men in the basement and went back upstairs. Zia Gull led Shah Jaan out through the kitchen to avoid the men in front and called her driver from the back porch, instructing him to give Shah Jaan a ride home and to stay with her until midnight in case she needed to use the car.

When Shah Jaan arrived home, she found Sahar sitting next to her father's body reciting the holy Koran. Little Mina had fallen asleep at his feet.

Mirwais came back from the mosque a short time later.

"Our Pakistani neighbor is a good man," he told Shah Jaan. "He brought three qaris from the mosque. I tried to tell him no, that you and I and Sahar could recite from the Koran, but he insisted that it was his duty as a Muslim and our neighbor to help as much as he could. Also, because our home is too small to accommodate all the people who will come for the funeral, he will help us to move the body to his house."

All that night, the neighbor's wife and daughters, along with Sahar, Mina, and Shah Jaan, sat up reciting the Koran, while Mirwais stayed in the men's house with three qaris, the neighbor, and his sons. Everyone from the mosque and also friends of the landlord came to pay their respects during the night and to offer their condolences to the family of the late general.

Just before sunset on the third day of the memorial, Zia Gull finally showed up with her driver and bags full of food.

"I am so sorry I could not come on the first day," she told Shah Jaan. "I will explain it to you later. But let us have dinner together."

Over the meal, she was overly nice to Mirwais and forever patting Mina on her back and shoulders, saying she was an aunt to all three children and that they would be staying in her big house and that she would pay for all of them to attend a private Afghan school.

"In fact, why don't you pack your clothes and move to my place tomorrow, Shah Jaan. I have a separate room for each of the children. We can give away your mattresses and carpets to the poor."

"You are most kind to us with these gestures," Shah Jaan said, "but we don't want to burden your already big household with four more people."

"Nonsense," Zia Gull said. "We have more room than we know what to do with."

"Aunt Zia," Mirwais said. "We will come visit you, but we're staying here. I am working and make enough money to take care of my mother and two sisters."

"I am talking to your mother," Zia Gull said. "How dare you talk to me with such rudeness? We are Afghans. We shouldn't forget our culture. You are only twelve years old. Even when your hair turns gray, you shouldn't speak this way to your elders."

"I thought he was the head of our family now," little Mina said.

"That may be true outside the home," Zia Gull said, "but inside the home, your mother is still the boss, honey."

"He never learns," Shah Jaan said. "Perhaps I should give him another slap across the face."

CHAPTER 18

THE NEXT MORNING, ZIA Gull's driver, Abdul, came to load all their belongings onto a small flatbed truck. Both daughters helped their mother carry things outside. Mirwais, who was angry with his mother's decision, refused to participate and went off early to work at his fruit stand.

In his absence, Zia Gull placed Mirwais in a room with Abdul next to the mulberry tree at the back of the house. It had a separate door to the outside, which was good for a young man feeling his independence. Since the room had no access to the main house, it was also good for keeping him away from what went on inside.

Shah Jaan was given a bedroom with Mina on the second floor, and Sahar was placed in a room with Zia's goddaughter Muska from Waziristan, who was there only until she returned to Dubai later that month. The room had two king-size beds, two separate toilets, and a large hot tub. It also had a sliding door leading out to the porch and a garden where Zia Gull entertained her frequent guests.

Once everyone was settled, Zia Gull invited Shah Jaan to relax with her on some garden chairs out on the lawn. A blue canopy provided them with shade from the sun. Zia Gull sipped her drink and explained a bit about how things worked in her home. Shah Jaan listened as a woman who had seen far too much hardship in one life and was now willing to do anything to get a piece of the easy life, however distasteful she might find the method for getting there.

"We should wait for some time," she said after hearing Zia Gull's pitch. "Even with Sahar."

Zia Gull laughed loudly. "Of course! What do you think? I have trained more than fifty girls from all walks of life and religious backgrounds. Even girls from elite and aristocratic families. Our work is a matter of sophistication. Rich men come here to relax and enjoy themselves, and we help them. There is nothing dirty about it."

Zia Gull smiled and Shah Jaan smiled back, but it was a painful smile.

For several weeks, Sahar stayed home with Zia Gull's goddaughter and spent most of her time watching Indian movies and DVDs of Afghan concerts and weddings of people in Europe and America. Shah Jaan was already busy in the kitchen and reception room preparing drinks and entertaining guests. Mina was left to play with other young children upstairs, and Mirwais, who had come to live there, remained defiant and went off to operate his fruit cart every day, refusing the fifty rupees Zia Gull offered him daily as pocket money.

Given that Mirwais was not allowed to enter the house without Zia Gull's permission, he would call out to Mina and Sahar each day when he came home from work, and they would come to stand at their windows and talk with him. In this way, Mirwais began to figure out what was going on inside the house and grew even angrier with his mother's decision.

Muska, who was already at work with Zia Gull's customers, never came back to the room she shared with Sahar until three or so in the morning. She would then sleep until two or three in the afternoon and afterward spend time with Sahar before going back to work. Some days Abdul, the driver, would take the two of them to Zia Gull's beauty salon, where the hairdressers would fix their hair and indulge the two teenage girls' fantasies of being rich and famous movie stars.

On the fortieth day after the general's death, Mirwais went with Sahar and Mina to visit their father's grave. As a last homage, Shah Jaan and Zia Gull sent enough food to feed more than forty poor people at the mosque. It was after the noon prayer, and old and young were sitting in line waiting for the food to arrive.

After Mirwais had helped to distribute the food, he took a paper plate with food out to the young heroin addict who was always sitting around outside the mosque.

"Don't bring me this food," the young heroin addict mumbled with a derisive smile at Mirwais. "It is haraam."

"It is beef with rice and some halva," Mirwais told him. "It is halal."

The heroin addict stared back at Mirwais for a long moment. "Do you consider yourself a man?" he asked Mirwais.

When Mirwais failed to answer, the addict suddenly stood up and shouted at him, "Because if you are, you shouldn't be working for a prostitute!"

Mirwais stood there trembling with the plate of food in his hands, angry, confused, and embarrassed.

"Stay away from me!" the young addict shouted again. "You are *haraami*. Your blood is spoiled from being around that whore."

Mirwais went home that day still trembling from that experience, and all that night he lay on the bed in his room, unable to eat and unable to sleep. Early in the evening, he had peeked out from behind the curtains to see an older man sitting on the lawn tuning his *rubab*. Then more musicians came. The garden grew crowded with people.

All that night, Mirwais lay on his bed or paced in the dark, listening to the metal gate opening and closing. Cars continuously came and went. Abdul was on duty and never returned to the room.

Near dawn, Mirwais heard Zia Gull and Shah Jaan out at the gate saying good-bye to the guests. Mirwais peeked out again and saw three men in military uniforms leaving the house. He lay back down on the bed and heard the sound of the big padlock being fastened to the gate.

A moment later, he heard the sound of a door being slammed, followed by a woman screaming. He jumped from the bed and peeked out to see Sahar trying to open the gate. She had the holy Koran in her hand.

"For God's sake, mother, how can you do this to me? How can you do this to your own daughter?"

When she couldn't open the gate, she started running around the garden, screaming, "Please, someone rescue me. Someone help me to keep my honor!"

Muska and Khan Sahib stood on the porch as Zia Gull and Shah Jaan chased Sahar around the lawn. Zia Gull finally caught up with Sahar and held her tightly.

"Don't be loud. Let's go inside, and I will listen to you. But if you keep crying out like this, the police will come and put your mother in jail."

"Take the Koran from her hands," she said to Shah Jaan. "I've been drinking all night and shouldn't touch it."

Shah Jaan took the Koran, kissed it three times, then rubbed it against her eyes. "I can't believe that you would embarrass me this way," she told Sahar. "You will do whatever I tell you to do, or I will send you after your father. You are not better than Muska or any other girl who was here tonight."

When Shah Jaan slapped Sahar across the face, Zia Gull took hold of her hand. "Stop. That's enough for now."

Muska came down from the porch and took Sahar by the hand. "Come. Let's go to our room and talk," she said. "No one is going to hurt my friend."

Imagining little Mina standing at her second floor window and witnessing this spectacle, Mirwais started to bang his head against the wall. He wanted so much to change things but didn't know how to do it.

Just as he was feeling utterly helpless in the world, he heard the loudspeakers in the mosque calling for the dawn prayer and decided to go to the mosque alone. After prayers, the imam spoke about the need for purity and devotion, for kindness and caring for our fellow men.

Seeing many young men in the mosque that day, the imam added, "Remember to honor your mothers and fathers. Obeying your elders and kindness are the only true ways of God."

In the early morning light, Mirwais started down toward the bazaar with the words of the imam going around and around in his head. At his fruit stand, he unlocked the doors and began to spread out the leftover fruit from the previous day. His delivery would be there soon. Other storekeepers were opening up for the day.

Mirwais took the bundle of money he had been saving for the past month. He stood there with his wad of money and his resentments and the imam's words about kindness and forgiveness going around in his head.

A man he called Uncle Qurban Ali came and offered a prayer for Mirwais's father. "I miss him and his green tea with its cardamom scent."

As a *juwali*, Uncle Ali had no stall but was always on the move, looking for shoppers who needed help with carrying their groceries to their cars or taxis. It was a job exclusive to the ethnic Hazara, and Uncle Ali wore a red scarf around his upper waist in keeping with his position. He also kept a length of jute rope over his shoulder. The deep lines creased into his hands showed that he had been handling the rough material for many years.

That morning, Uncle Ali saw Mirwais counting his money out in the open and came over with his big, cordial smile. "Mirwais jaan," he told him, "be careful with your money. Put it back in your shirt pocket. Don't you see all these beggars around you? God forbid that they should see this and steal all your money."

"Hey Hazaragai!" a Pakistani man shouted to Uncle Ali at that moment. "Come here! Help me to unload my groceries!"

Uncle Ali hurried over to help him just as a man in ragged clothes came up and asked if his daughter could sit on the empty spot next to the oranges on Mirwais's cart. The young girl had no shoes, and her feet were cold from standing on the muddy concrete sidewalk. Busy in his thoughts and feeling sorry for the man, Mirwais said yes, took off his vest with the money in it, and set it next to the pile of oranges.

The day quickly grew busy. Mirwais's delivery came, and he completely forgot about the man and his young daughter. When he had a chance to look up again, they were gone. Impulsively, Mirwais checked his vest pocket and found that all the money he had been carefully putting away for forty days was gone.

Knowing it had to be the man with the daughter, Mirwais quickly locked up his cart, called out to Uncle Ali that he would be back in a minute, and ran as fast as he could through the market stalls and throngs of shoppers along the sidewalk. People he ran into cursed him, and still Mirwais did not stop, checking inside every store as he went, looking down every blind alley. Finally, Mirwais saw the father standing with his back to him down a narrow street. The man's daughter was running joyfully around in front of him, wearing a new pair of purple tennis shoes that had a blinking red light in the back.

Mirwais came to a halt, torn between the joy of the little girl with her new shoes, the joy of a father who had been able to bring her this happiness, and the crime this man had committed against him. Mirwais was torn even more as he remembered the fleeting joys of his own childhood, such as the day Mullah Satar had brought Kabob to their home and his little sister Mina had exclaimed, "God has given us enough food for a million years," only to have those moments evaporate into such sorrow and hardship over the years.

As Mirwais stood there with these memories passing through his heart, he realized he did not want to steal away the little girl's happiness. He too wanted her to have the shoes. He was even ready to forgive her father. All he wanted was the rest of his money back, but when Mirwais started forward, the father noticed him, quickly swept his daughter up into his arms, and fled down the alley with his daughter's cheek against his as he ran.

Mirwais went after them, calling, "Wait! Wait! I will gladly buy your daughter the shoes! Just give me the rest of the money back!"

But as if the man could not hear Mirwais's words of reconciliation amid the din of the bustling city, he ran ever faster down the alley with Mirwais struggling to keep up and calling from behind that he forgave him.

At the end of the alley, there was an open concrete channel that served as a barrier to a busy boulevard running below it, and in his mad haste, the man jumped over the open channel directly down into oncoming traffic. A minivan filled with passengers slammed into him instantly. The man and his daughter were thrown farther into oncoming traffic. The minivan spun out of control and plowed into a pile of pedestrians on the sidewalk across the street.

Mirwais stopped at the edge of the channel and stared with shock and sadness at the mayhem below him. Dead people and blood were scattered everywhere. Shopkeepers were already out helping the injured. Mirwais saw the red light from a shoe blinking underneath one of the wrecked cars.

With his money still in the man's pockets, Mirwais felt drawn to go down there and retrieve it, but the police had already arrived, and anyway he did not have the heart to admit he had been involved.

With a final look at the young girl's dead body, he turned and started on his way back toward the bazaar, his mind slowly forming a plan out of his sorrows and inner convictions. He would sell his cart to Uncle Ali and go live somewhere far away from his mother and her corruption and all the madness he felt surrounding him. But when he arrived back at his cart and explained to Uncle Ali all that had happened and all that he wanted, the usually cheerful old man sadly encouraged Mirwais not to be rash.

"Mirwais jaan, I would much rather loan you the money without taking your cart. I would even be happy to have you pay me in installments. Only I have a boss and must clear things with her before making any big decisions." Uncle Ali winked and tried to cheer Mirwais up with a little shake and a smile. "Wait until you get married, and you will know what I mean."

When Uncle Ali saw there was no changing Mirwais's distraught condition, he sighed and pulled five thousand rupees out of his pocket. "Here. Take this as a loan. You can make weekly payments to me from your profits, but in the name of your father, don't sell your cart or lose sight of your goals. Go to school in your spare time. Study to be something good in this world, but without the cart, you will have nothing but to be a juwali like me, and that is not possible. It has been the Hazara's job for ages."

Seeing Mirwais was still unmoved, Uncle Ali tried another tack. "Look, why don't you take the rest of the day off. Go be a good son to your mother and a good brother to your sisters. Be at peace with God and go pray for this poor man and his daughter."

Still lost in his grief, Mirwais took the money, thanked Uncle Ali, and started down the street with no idea what he would do. His wild plans of escape had dissipated in the face of the kindly old Uncle Ali.

Lost in these thoughts, Mirwais passed by the neighborhood mosque and was confronted again by the same young heroin addict. The derisive smile came first, followed by words that were spoken softly and almost mumbled.

"Here comes the future Colonel Pimp." Then the addict was suddenly on his feet and shouting at Mirwais. "You can fool the mullahs, but you cannot fool God with your prayers!"

His shame renewed at hearing these words, Mirwais did not want to go home and wandered all day until it was sunset. Finding himself near the central bus station of Peshawar, he sat down at a café and ordered a cup of tea.

Across the street, dusty buses painted with a myriad of colors went in and out of the bus station, each of them overflowing with men, women, and children in all manners of dress. Some men had tied turbans onto their straw hats. Some were wearing white cotton caps. Few men could be seen without beards. Women wore shawls covering their whole bodies. Mirwais read the different names listed on the front of the buses with enchantment: Northwest Frontier, Swat, Miram Shah, Chetral, Banu, Khyber, Bajaur, Kohat, Hangu, Kurm Agency, and many other border towns. People were sitting on the tops of the buses with goats and chickens, caged birds, dishes, carpets, and even TVs and refrigerators. The finer Mercedes buses were going to the big cities like Karachi and Lahore and were decorated with plastic and silk flowers.

Dreaming of faraway places but still unsure of what to do, Mirwais's thoughts were disturbed by the sweet voice of a young girl.

"Will you buy this arakhcheen, my brother? Only one hundred rupees!"

The black veil wrapped about her face slipped off as she said this, revealing her beautiful dark eyes and black hair. She was no older than Sahar, and her words had been spoken in Kandahari Pashto, which was not very common in Peshawar.

The girl was holding onto a blind old man's arm. He had a cane in his right hand and looked tired and ill. His white round cotton Pakistani cap was too small for his bald head.

Mirwais looked at the Kandahari hat the girl was offering for sale. It was used but freshly washed and worked beautifully with black, red, and green beads. Mirwais tried it on and found it too large and gave it back to the girl.

"I wish I could afford it," he told her in Peshawari Pashto. "But I too am a homeless refugee." Mirwais gave the girl five rupees as consolation. She thanked him and started to move on in the crowd, but the old man stopped her.

"You must be an Afghan," he said to Mirwais.

"Yes, I am from Kabul," Mirwais said.

"What is your name, young man?"

"My name is Mirwais."

The old blind man's lips started trembling. "O Almighty," he said, "you are the owner of sky and earth! You know better than us! Whatever comes from you is acceptable.

"When mullahs and chalis lead our nation," the old man went on in a choking voice, "this is what happens, my son. Mirwais and Malalai are left begging on the streets of Peshawar."

"Don't you have a son to help you?" asked Mirwais.

"I had two proud sons like you, but four years ago in Kandahar, a father had two options. Either pay fifty thousand rupees to the Taliban or send a son to the north to fight against the Taliban's enemies. My older son volunteered, and my younger son also went as a proxy soldier for the son of a businessman. For this I received a hundred thousand rupees. I did not want the money, but my son did it anyway and sent me to Karachi to have my failing eyesight repaired with surgery. Neither of my sons returned, and I lost my eyesight anyway. Now my wife and only daughter live with me in a refugee camp, and we can't go home for fear of embarrassment.

"May God bless you, my son," the old man added and moved off through the crowd with his daughter leading him. Both Malalai's hands held his arm, and her head leaned against the old man's shoulder.

Mirwais paid for his tea and started back down the street. He did not get far before he heard a voice calling out from behind him, "I know you must be refugee like me, my brother."

Mirwais turned back and found a man in his early thirties facing him. He had not shaven for a week or two, but he looked like an educated man, not like a man who had grown up knowing destitution.

"We are all poor and needy," he went on, standing in front of Mirwais now. "But I am not asking you for money. Only if you know someone who has the blessing of God and has wealth to spare for the needy." Suddenly the man started crying. "Forgive me, brother. We arrived the day before yesterday from Mazar-e-Sharif. My wife and three daughters are sitting in front of the mosque. We have no place to sleep and nothing to eat."

He was holding a white handkerchief that had turned yellow from dirt and sweat, and he kept folding and unfolding the handkerchief neatly as he spoke, looking for a clean spot to wipe off his tears.

Faced with the man's grief and his polite manner, Mirwais also broke down in tears and gave the man ten rupees. The man thanked Mirwais profusely as Mirwais hurried back in the direction of the bus depot.

"I want a ticket to Karachi on the next available bus," he told the man behind the window.

"I need to see your ID card."

"I am a member of the Taliban. I go to madrassa, but I have no ID with me right now."

"With a Taliban ID, I could have given a 50 percent discount," the agent said.

Mirwais waved the man off and paid him in full. A few minutes later, Mirwais was hopping onto a shiny new Mercedes bus.

Inside the bus was a mixture of people representing the various social groups of Pakistan. In the front seats were businessmen with white shelwar kameez, black business suits, and ties. Some wore blue jeans and tennis shoes, and there were women who looked like Zia Gull's goddaughters wearing heavy makeup with highlighted hair, dark sunglasses, and modern Punjabi dress. There were women with black veils and men with beards, and the poor sat in the back seats.

CHAPTER 19

LOCKED BEHIND THE GATES of Mullah Satar's mud castle with nothing better to do with her time, Laalla spent interminable days and nights thinking about her family. Where had they gone, she wondered. Would she ever see them again? Yet if Laalla ever dared to mention her concerns to Mullah Satar or asked for his assistance, he only heaped more scorn upon her for doing so.

Meanwhile, Mullah Satar's disappointment with Laalla and Qamar's infertility continued to grow until at last he brought home a fourteen-year-old bride as the solution to his problems. The young girl's name was Zarghoona. She was the daughter of a local opium farmer, and Laalla and Qamar looked after her like she was their own little sister.

In time, when it became clear that Zarghoona was also infertile, Mullah Satar began to exercise his wrath on all three women at once. In his greatest moments of rage he spat on them collectively and cursed the ancestors who had brought them into this world.

Following this third failed effort to father a child, Mullah Satar rarely bothered to come home except late at night. Sometimes he dropped off large burlap sacks filled with American money. He also brought home hundreds of Ziploc bags filled with white powder, all of which was locked away in a dark room at the back of the house.

The house had a large yard and high walls that surrounded the entire property with watch towers like a castle made of mud and cabblestone. A small stream ran into the backyard through a tube made from the trunk of a large tree that had been set under the wall, and the stream led to a pool before running out beneath the trees toward the front of the house. The three women used the pond to wash themselves and to do their laundry. There was a big wooden gate that led to the outside world, but Mullah Satar always kept it locked so that the women had very little contact with whatever events might be developing outside their compound.

Shortly before the fourth Ramadan of Laalla's stay in Musa Qala, the first bombs began to fall, and they went on falling for over two months. The sound of them was faint and far away for the most part, and the bombing was eventually followed by the sound of gun battles for most of a week. After that, things grew relatively quiet.

By this time, it had been almost five years since Laalla was stolen away from her family by Mullah Satar and over a year since Mirwais had run away to Karachi. It was the second week of Ramadan and the best time of year to be in that port city. The weather could not have been more beautiful as groups of angry youths, including Mirwais, burned the American flag and the American president in effigy. CNN and the BBC had long ago canceled their regular programming, first to cover the progress of the bombing campaign in Afghanistan and then the progress of the US special forces' ground assault in and around Kandahar, the Taliban stronghold.

Meanwhile, Pakistani state TV was broadcasting bombastic speeches by President Musharaf, who showed up almost daily in his military uniform offering Pakistani support to the American effort in fighting terrorism. Private television stations, in contrast, were host to a parade of clerics and former members of the ISI, who debated the fall of the Taliban, the interests of America in the region, their unjust invasion of a sovereign country, and a possible armed reaction from the angry Muslims of Pakistan and Kashmir.

That anger had been spilling out into the streets of Karachi for over two months, much of it organized by violent groups, many of which were newly established and showcasing their agendas to the world for the first time.

On a relatively quiet evening a few weeks after the Pakistani army announced martial law and banned political gatherings, Mohammad Ibrahim, a Pashtun Afghan American, was sitting in a red plastic chair at a McDonald's outdoor eating area. He had a large order of fries and a Pepsi on the yellow table in front of him. Pakistan's version of the American hamburger sat in a red tray. It came with a special mix of curry and hot chili sauce, and Ibrahim picked it up to take a bite.

As a businessman, Mohammad Ibrahim had raised some money from Afghans living in the States, which he had transferred to one of the money exchangers in Peshawar in order to buy flour, oil, rice, blankets, tents, and lanterns for Afghans living in refugee camps in the Peshawar area. He had arrived two days earlier, but with the unrest in the streets, the money exchangers had all closed for business, and Ibrahim could not leave for Peshawar until things calmed down and the money exchangers reopened.

Just as Ibrahim was biting into his hamburger, a boy with sad eyes and a gloomy look on his face came up to greet him. "Assalamu Alaikum!"

The boy's head was shaven. There were signs of a black, silky mustache over his dry, chapped lips. He was skinny and tall and wearing a round, white Pakistani cap. He also had his arms wrapped tightly against his chest and appeared to be freezing. Between that and his sad look and oversized worn-out black Pakistani kameez, Ibrahim felt his heart breaking for the boy.

"Waalaikum salaam," he said to him, and the boy said something back in Urdu.

"Can you speak to me in Pashto?" Ibrahim asked, and all of a sudden a ray of hope and joy spread across the boy's face.

"Yes, I am an Afghan," the boy said.

"Then come and sit in this chair," Ibrahim said.

"The owner won't allow me to sit in these chairs."

"He can't say no when your uncle is here," Ibrahim said, his voice breaking, his heart close to tears. "Let me buy you food, and then we will have plenty of time to talk."

"I don't eat this food, Uncle," the boy said. "It is haraam. They cook everything in pig oil."

"Who said that?" asked Ibrahim.

"All the people in the mosque talk about it."

"So where can I find halal food?" Ibrahim asked him.

"Sharja Restaurant is five stores away," the boy said.

Ibrahim was silent for a moment, thinking. Then suddenly he stood up.

"Thanks for letting me know," he told the boy. "Let's go to Sharja Restaurant, and you will be my guest." They walked up the street together.

As Ibrahim and the boy reached a counter next to entrance of the restaurant, a chubby man of medium height with a gray beard and a shaved mustache waved to Ibrahim.

"Assalamu Alaikum," the man said and said something in Arabic.

Ibrahim, not wanting to be labeled as an Arab or a member of Al-Qaeda, said to the man, "Sorry, but I'm not an Arab."

"Oh, welcome, welcome," the old man replied in fluent English. "You must be from the UK. I guarantee you, we have the best tandoori in town."

Dozens of whole skinned chickens and lamb legs were hanging over the counter and to either side of the man's head.

"Take one of the lamb legs," the Pakistani proprietor told Ibrahim. "Look at this one. It has no fat at all. We make a special first-class *karayee* in fifteen minutes. Take a couple of chickens with it as well. All of it will take only fifteen minutes to prepare."

Ibrahim laughed at the thought. "I am hungry, but not that hungry," he told the man. "Who can eat two chickens, let alone a whole leg of lamb?"

"You look, Masha'Allah, very rich, sir," the proprietor said, shaking his head in admiration. "You must be a successful businessman. I know, sir. You can afford anything you want sir. You can buy food for these hungry refugees sitting outside, sir."

"Let us have a good cup of tea first," Ibrahim said, "and send me the menu. We will decide on what to eat later."

They entered the long and narrow restaurant. The lighting was poor, and the place had no heaters. There was a row of wooden tables down the center of the room with wooden benches on either side of them. There were also small, square tables with wooden chairs along each wall. That left two aisles running down the length of the restaurant in what looked like the cabin of a commercial jet.

All in all, the restaurant was lifeless and depressing. There were perhaps a dozen customers sitting down to have dinner, a group here, a group there, and none of them seemed to be having a good time.

The young Afghan boy told Ibrahim that one naan with a cup of tea would be enough for him; he was not hungry. But Ibrahim wanted to buy him a full dinner.

"Don't be shy," Ibrahim insisted. "Have anything you want. Or if you know of a better place, it is not too late. I will be happy to take you to any restaurant you want."

"Those chickens," the boy said, pointing to the ones hanging over the counter. "I've never had such a thing. Only once in a dream did I eat roasted chicken, and I ate and ate all night and couldn't get enough of them."

Saddened to hear these words, saddened to think this orphaned Afghan boy was out begging on the streets of Karachi, Ibrahim ordered two fried chickens from the waiter.

"What did he order?" the restaurant owner asked the waiter in Urdu.

"Two fried chickens, and he is an Afghan, not a Pakistani Briton."

Ibrahim was busy watching and taking everything in and overheard this snippet of conversation. He understood that these men were trying to figure him out.

"What is your name?" he asked, looking back at the boy.

"My name is Mirwais."

"Do you have any members of your family here with you in Karachi? Or anywhere here in Pakistan?"

"I have no one. My parents, my sisters, everyone is dead."

The tea came, and Ibrahim busied himself with stirring in some sugar.

"Can't you find a job? Maybe work in a place like this?"

"I have a job. I do fundraising for our party, for our mujahideen who go to Afghanistan to fight against the American invaders."

"Do they pay you?" Ibrahim asked Mirwais. "Do they provide you with a place to sleep?"

"My work is for the happiness of God," Mirwais said. "A soldier of God does not work for money. I eat and sleep in the mosque."

"Who told you that Americans have invaded Afghanistan?"

"That is no secret, Uncle. Even the beggars on the street know this. Ask this Mawlana Sahib, and he will confirm it." Mirwais pointed his finger toward the restaurant owner behind the cash register. Ibrahim looked up to find Mawlana rushing out toward the front of the restaurant with a big stick. The women and children who had been sitting along the front window went scattering with their empty aluminum bowls and used plastic bags. While Mawlana came back muttering to himself, Ibrahim told Mirwais to go gather the beggars and tell them to wait. He would order food for everyone.

"The food from this restaurant will only feed them one time," Mirwais said. "If you really want to help, you should give them money so they can go buy their own bread."

Seeing the worthiness of the boy's heart and wanting to oblige him, Ibrahim went out front with Mirwais, and together they passed out a bit of money to all of the poor.

They were gone quite a while, and when they returned, they found that most of the lights in the restaurant had been turned off. Most of the customers had left. Only one ceiling light remained on directly over their own seats.

"Where is our dinner?" Ibrahim asked Mawlana. "You told me fifteen minutes. We've been waiting more than forty-five."

"My helpers went home," Mawlana said while counting his money. "I can't keep them overtime when I don't have any customers. Or if I have cheap customers who don't want to spend any money."

Mawlana Sahib finished counting his money and started turning off the lights around his counter.

"Look at all of these lights. And the waiter is already here beyond his normal hours. All this costs me money."

Ibrahim nodded, not liking the man. A short while later, the waiter came with the two chickens wrapped in separate newspapers.

"Mawlana Sahib said he was late for his prayers and couldn't wait longer. Please take your food out with you. And there is an extra charge for the tea. I had to bring it from the tea house. We don't sell tea here. Our customers drink fresh juice and soda."

Ibrahim paid for the tea and took Mirwais with him to sit at the tables outside McDonalds.

"Do you live in Karachi, Uncle?" Mirwais asked while they ate.

"No, I live in America, Mirwais jaan."

Ibrahim saw that Mirwais was astonished.

"Then what are you doing in Pakistan?" Mirwais asked him.

"I came here to see my Afghans, to see how they are doing, and to talk to them, and to listen to them."

Mirwais was silent and thinking while he ate. Ibrahim watched him.

"What is it you want to tell them?" Mirwais asked after a moment.

"It depends on what I hear from them," Ibrahim said. "But hopefully to share our stories. To share our opinions. To find a way out of this civil war and a way to stop killing our brothers and sisters."

"Uncle," Mirwais said, "may I ask you a question? And please don't get angry with me. If I don't ask, I will be one of the *munafiqeen*. As almighty God says in Holy Quran, if you say something, but have a different feeling in your heart, you are one of the munafiqeen, and there is a harsh punishment for munafiqeen."

"Go ahead," Ibrahim told him with a smile. "You can ask me anything you want, and I will never raise an eyebrow, let alone get mad."

"You are such a nice person," Mirwais said. "Why did you choose to live in America?"

Ibrahim thought for a moment before speaking. "I will answer your question, Mirwais, but only if you too promise not to get upset with me."

"I promise," Mirwais said.

"And also promise not to raise your eyebrows either!"

Both of them laughed.

"Okay," Ibrahim said. "Not only did I choose to live in America. I also chose to become an American. I became an American citizen after I had traveled all over the world, and—"

"But did you go to Saudi Arabia and Sharjah as well?" Mirwais said, cutting him off.

"Yes, I was in Sharjah last week, and I lived in Saudi, before they kicked me out with my wife and our little son, who was born in Saudi Arabia. They wanted to deport us back to Afghanistan and relinquish us to the Communists, who had killed my father and two brothers before I escaped with my wife. But we were fortunate to end up in America."

"Are you a Communist?" Mirwais asked him.

"No, I was never a Communist, but I chose to be an American and raised my hand in front of a judge, saying that I would defend the national interest of America and obey the Constitution of America."

"But you raised your hand in an un-Islamic court," Mirwais said, "and in front of a judge who was not a Muslim."

"It doesn't matter what faith the judge has and what book you swear to," Ibrahim said. "God is the judge, and your conscience is the witness. As you just said, you would be one of the munafiqeen if you said something that you didn't believe in. And remember, according to the holy Koran, there is a harsh punishment for munafiqeen."

Mirwais was perplexed by the man's logic, which was in complete opposition to everything he had heard from his Mawlana Sahib in the mosque about Muslims living in America.

"Do you know of any other Muslim who has converted to become an American?" Mirwais asked him.

"America is the land of many faiths, and also the land of people who don't believe in any faith."

"So if there are Muslims in America, why don't they bomb India? If they have courts and judges, why don't they get married? Mawlana Sahib told me that all Americans are born haraami. They don't get married."

Ibrahim thought long again before speaking. "Let me give you my patu," he told Mirwais. "It is getting colder, and the shops are closed right now, but I want to see you tomorrow and buy you some warm clothes."

Ibrahim unwrapped his woolen shawl and offered it to Mirwais.

"Mawlana Sahib won't let me wear new clothes and shoes," Mirwais said. "And besides, I am a soldier of God. I have to get used to overcoming any difficulty. The real life is the permanent life after death, and it will be a good one for those who are martyred."

"Soldier of God," Ibrahim said. "What do you mean by that?"

"When I am fourteen years old, I will be qualified to get training and go fight for justice in Afghanistan, which will be, insha'Allah, next year."

Ibrahim was silent. A wave of passion overwhelmed his being, digging deep into his heart and rising to the level of an explosion. The innocent cry of this helpless young boy suffering from the confusion of life echoed the sorrows and sufferings of all his people. Ibrahim's mind went searching, trying to find the appropriate phrases to persuade Mirwais out of the magic of his Wahhabi masters.

"It is getting late," Ibrahim said. "Let me take you to the mosque, and I will have a surprise for you tomorrow."

Before noon the next day, Ibrahim showed up at the mosque with a bag of winter clothes and a pair of warm shoes as promised. A boy as young as Mirwais was sitting on the concrete stairs in front of the main entrance and greeted him politely. Ibrahim asked him in Pashto if he knew Mirwais. The young boy responded in Urdu.

"Do you know Mirwais," Ibrahim asked him again in Pashto.

"Do you speak English?" the young boy asked in perfect English with a British accent.

Ibrahim repeated his previous question in English.

"After dawn prayers, Mirwais was lucky enough to be sent to military training," the young boy said.

Ibrahim thought again before speaking. "Masha'Allah, you speak very good English. I brought some clothes for Mirwais. Since he is gone to join the army of mujahideen and serve the will of God, I will give this gift to you, while I pray for his success in his holy mission."

The young boy thanked Ibrahim for his donation to the mosque and told him that he would pass this to the *zakat* committee of the mosque. Ibrahim sat on the concrete floor next to him.

"When is the noon prayer?" he asked the boy.

"Quarter past twelve."

"Where did you learn such good English?" Ibrahim asked him.

"I was born in a town outside London."

"Did your whole family move back to Pakistan?"

"You are asking personal questions," the boy said. "I don't even know you. You are a stranger."

"I am a journalist and want to write a book about our holy jihad. The ambition and sacrifice of young believers like you and Mirwais should be admired. The world should know about it."

"Journalist?" the young boy said. "You are the right person to talk to. I need the world to hear my story."

"What is your name?" Ibrahim asked him.

"I will tell you my story, but not my name."

"It's okay," Ibrahim said gently. "You can tell just your story if that is what you want."

"My parents were born in Kashmir but got married in London. Then, after sixteen years of marriage, they separated when I was four, and I lived with my father. My mother had custody of my two older sisters, who were twelve and fourteen. My mother married a white man, and later on both of my sisters married Britons as well. My father killed my mother out of jealousy and is now serving life in prison. A friend of my father, an imam of the mosque in the UK, gained custody of me after fighting in the court for over two years. I've lived with him and his family for the past two years."

"Where is your godfather now?" Ibrahim asked him.

"We moved here three months ago. He had written consent from my mother that I could go with him and his wife on vacation to Pakistan, but only for two weeks, and here we are three months later."

"You didn't tell me where your godfather is," Ibrahim said.

"Mawlana Sahib is in charge of fundraising for the Taliban. He is here in the mosque most of the time, going home only on Friday nights to visit his wife."

"Do you visit your godmother as well?"

"No, I am not allowed. Mawlana Sahib told me that it is against sharia to see his wife anymore, because I have reached the age of puberty."

"Why did you say earlier that Mirwais was lucky to be sent for military training, when it looks like you have been brought here against your will?"

"That is not true," the boy said with tears in his eyes. "You have misunderstood me. It was not against my will to come here, but it is against my will for him to keep me here. I can't wait to go to jihad and become martyred."

Their discussion was interrupted when the owner of the Sharja Restaurant, came for noon prayers.

"You'd better stop harassing these young kids," he said while coming up the concrete stairs to enter the mosque.

Mawlana said something in Urdu to the young boy as well, who suddenly stood up and shouted at Ibrahim. "I didn't know that you were a sick gay man. I believe what my goduncle said!"

Ibrahim tried to speak to the boy again, but Mawlana hurried him into the mosque.

CHAPTER 20

THERE WERE TIMES AFTER the fighting had stopped in Musa Qala when Laalla and Qamar and Zarghoona heard music from cars passing along the street, and the three of them often sat together discussing what this might mean. Surely the Taliban had fallen, Laalla reasoned, for how else could there be music playing in the streets? But Qamar argued that because the mullah's business in white powder continued to thrive and he continued to bring large sacks full of money home to hide in the back room, the Taliban must still be in power, for how else could the mullah remain in business?

Then one day they heard slogans and speeches from the loudspeakers of passing cars instead of music, and some days later a plane flew over the house. Leaflets in Pashto fluttered down from the sky, and in reading them, Laalla learned for the first time that the Taliban had been defeated and there had been a new Afghan government backed by the Americans for the past four years. What this meant for the mullah and his Taliban friends, she did not know, but the leaflets urged all civilians to leave their homes. A military operation against the terrorists would begin any day now.

The same day that the leaflets fell out of the sky, Mullah Satar came home with a car full of fresh produce and groceries, enough to last them for a long time. A few days later, the fighting commenced, and it continued on sporadically for most of four months.

During this time, there were constantly rumors swirling around, and Laalla often overheard the mullah's conversations. She learned that Tommy had left Kandahar. He had simply disappeared one day and never had come back.

One afternoon, Mullah Satar came rushing home and told his three wives to pack up their belongings. They would be leaving the next morning. He took the bags of white powder and sacks of money out to his car and then returned to lock the women up for the night.

The next morning he returned in a black Toyota SUV. All three of his wives were told to sit in the backseat. Mullah Satar got behind the wheel. There was no driver this time.

All that day and night, they traveled through deserts and dirt roads and sometimes through heavily wooded valleys with green hills high around them. The mullah now had two small phones, not the big satellite phones he had used in the past, and he was on the phone nearly every minute of their journey, sometimes speaking in Urdu, sometimes in Pashto, but from the words he spoke and the tone of his voice, Laalla knew that he was running for his life.

Early the next morning, they came to an asphalt road. A road sign read "State of Baluchistan, Pakistan." After another three hours, they passed through a crowded roadside bazaar, and an hour later they came to a village that looked very much like the village where they had lived in Musa Qala. All the homes had the same high mud walls. There were SUVs and pickups packed with men, all of them turbaned, all of them bearded, all of them carrying rifles as they sped here and there along the bumpy dirt roads.

Some miles beyond the village, the mullah called someone to explain his location and received instructions to detour down a narrow dirt road. The road cut through farmland and led to a metal gate. A young man with a beard and a turban opened the gate. Mullah Satar drove through, and the gate was closed behind him. The young man came up to the SUV, and the mullah rolled down his window to greet him. The young man gave the mullah a large key chain with lots of keys, told him to go with God, and went back into a blue wooden guardhouse that sat next to the gate. Mullah Satar drove ahead to a large house that was surrounded by the usual high mud walls.

Inside, Laalla found the house had twelve rooms with a modern kitchen and many baths. There was electricity, and fans hung from every ceiling. Given these amenities, Laalla somehow expected things would be better here, but unlike in Musa Qala, the three wives soon learned that they were now not even allowed to go into the front yard. Mullah Satar had all the windows of the house painted black and spent most of his time in a back room talking on the phone, mostly in Urdu. From the sound of the conversations, the three wives could tell that his plans were not going well. In the course of things, they did learn one fact for certain. This was the village where Mullah Omar, the leader of the Taliban, and most of his supporters now lived.

Three summers passed, , and then one night Mullah Satar woke his wives and told them to hurry and pack up. They were headed back to Afghanistan once again. There was a scramble to get all their belongings into the car. Qamar and Zarghoona had quickly taken their places in the backseat. Mullah Satar was behind the wheel, growing furious as Laalla stood on the porch facing Mecca and said her prayers.

"We are waiting for you, you daughter of a whore," he called out, and Laalla at last rushed from the porch for fear her husband would soon come to beat her and spit in her face over the delay, but after only a few paces, Laalla saw the flash of white light and heard the explosion.

It was four whole days before she woke again and found that she was lying in a hospital room with machines monitoring her vital statistics. There was an IV stuck into her arm.

A nurse came in and looked encouraged to see Laalla had finally awakened.

"Where am I?" Laalla asked in a feeble voice.

"Wait," the nurse said and ran off. She returned a moment later with a doctor.

The doctor read Laalla's chart and checked her vital statistics.

"What had happened?" Laalla wanted to know.

"You don't remember," the doctor said matter-of-factly.

Laalla shook her head.

"You were in a bomb explosion and are very lucky to be alive." He paused. "Unfortunately, we had to amputate your right leg."

With those words, the moment of the explosion flashed through Laalla's mind. She remembered hurrying to open the car door, the flash of light, and the deafening sound.

"I am very, very sorry," the doctor told her. "But we will fit you with an artificial leg and get you walking again very soon."

The doctor patted Laalla gently on the shoulder and stood up to leave. "You are lucky to be alive."

Laalla nodded, weary, sad, and unable to process what had happened to her. The doctor left the room. The nurse encouraged Laalla to sleep, and she did for another two days.

When Laalla woke again, it was afternoon and she felt very hungry. The nurse went off and brought back food and helped her to eat. When Laalla went to use the bathroom on crutches, she was unable to see what remained of her leg. She only saw the heavily bandaged stub sticking out and then a deep, short scar on her chin when she went to wash her hands.

Later that afternoon, two elite members of the Pakistani military woke Laalla and questioned her about her life with

Mullah Satar and what had happened. In the process, Laalla learned that not only Mullah Satar had died in the explosion but also Qamar and Zarghoona. A bomb had been placed under the mullah's seat and set off by remote control.

After a number of weeks in the hospital, when Laalla's wound had healed sufficiently, the doctors fitted her with a prosthesis for her right leg, and she began the slow process of learning to walk again. The ward was populated with women who had lost one of their limbs—mostly legs and mostly from land mines—so Laalla had much support from those who had gone before her. Then, these women moved on one by one, and it became Laalla's turn to assist the latest arrivals with their rehabilitation in the amputee ward.

For the sake of convenience as much as for medical reasons, the women usually wore their light blue hospital gowns around the ward so their artificial limbs often poked out through their gowns. And as the women sat around talking about their lives, one or another of them sometimes removed an artificial limb to scratch at the stub beneath it.

Laalla was determined in her therapy and perhaps even happy at times, but time and tragedy had taken their toll on her life. Her once-black hair was streaked with gray now. Her eyes had started to acquire dark rings like her mother's. But as she often told herself, at least she now lived as a free person. With a computer at her disposal, she got acquainted with the Internet and was able to learn from afar what was going on in a changing Afghan society and the greater world around it.

As the months passed, Laalla felt old feelings reawakening. She thought of all she had lost. She found hope stirring in her heart for what lay ahead. She thought of her family and very much wanted to find them.

Rather than succumbing to the frustration and boredom of her long rehabilitation, Laalla started teaching the other women in the ward how to read and write. Laalla printed each letter of the alphabet as large as she could on a piece of notebook paper and stood in front of them, having the women repeat the sounds after her. Once they had mastered the letters, Laalla started them in on pronouncing various words.

It was getting on toward the end of summer that year, and there were only four other women left in the ward with Laalla. The youngest was in her early twenties. The oldest was in her late forties. The four women were sitting on their chairs in front of Laalla in their light blue hospital gowns with their artificial limbs sticking out.

Suddenly, Laalla sensed that the women were distracted from the lesson by something behind her, and she turned to see what her own eyes were unable to believe. It was Parwin, standing in the doorway with a smile.

Laalla instantly dropped her papers and hobbled over to Parwin on her cane. They hugged for a long time and then stood at arm's length to look at each other, their eyes filled with tears. Parwin looked down sadly at Laalla's leg and back into her eyes again.

"We both know why I'm here," Laalla said. "But what are you doing in this place?"

"I work here as a nurse," Parwin said. "Runa works here too. Because of her English, the hospital hired her to interface with the European and American donor organizations. She writes grant proposals and takes care of all the fundraising."

Parwin looked to the other women.

"I'm sorry to interrupt, but Khadija here is an old friend from the wars."

The women seemed confused. Parwin looked back at Laalla.

"Khadija was the name given to me by Mullah Satar," Laalla said. "Laalla is my real name."

"Forgive me," Parwin said.

"No, it's okay."

"Then you are Laalla. It is a beautiful name."

The two women stood smiling at each other.

"Perhaps we can talk another time," Laalla said.

"No, no," her fellow patients said. "We're fine. Go get reacquainted with your old friend."

"Yes," Parwin said. "It's time for tea. Let's find Runa and we'll have a nice long chat." Laalla followed Parwin out the door, her cane striking against the vinyl floor as they went.

Laalla actually enjoyed the sound of her cane as she walked down the long corridor. It was the sound of dignity to her, and she carried herself with pride, her back straight, her head up, her graying hair tossed from one shoulder to the other as she went. It made her feel like a free person to move forward on her own. It made her feel proud. It made her feel strong.

She remembered how her father had told her, "There are ups and downs in this life, so if I die one day or we lose each other, don't think that this is the end of the world. Keep hope, and don't ever let misery overcome you."

On the way down the long corridor, Laalla explained much of what had happened to her since the last time the two women had met. She also mentioned the rumors she had heard about Tommy's mansion and that it was assumed Parwin and Runa had escaped into Pakistan, but of course Laalla had never expected to see them again. Once they had located Runa and the two of them had hugged, the three women went together to a break room, and Parwin made tea while Laalla explained to Runa much of what she had already explained to Parwin.

"But I don't understand," Laalla said. "How did you know I was here today? And how come I did not see you sooner?"

"Parwin doesn't work in your part of the hospital," Runa said. "I was browsing through the patient ledger as usual to prepare my quarterly grant proposal when my attention was drawn to a patient's name—Khadija, the widow of Abdul Satar, who was ready to be discharged from the orthopedic rehab ward pending her acceptance by a women's shelter, and I called Parwin right away.

"We have a nice, big apartment," Parwin said, "and you are coming to stay with us."

Laalla at first tried to resist this generous offer, but Parwin would hear nothing of it.

"You are coming to live with us. That is settled. Now tell us more about what happened. I can't believe this monster. Three wives ..."

"We were actually much happier in Pakistan. Aside from the beatings and verbal abuse, we saw little of the mullah. We read from the Koran together. We were exercising together when the mullah was not around. I had even started teaching Qamar and Zarghoona to speak English. Then the end came." Laalla looked down at her feet. She had a blue plastic flip-flop on her left foot and a round, black rubber base supporting her artificial limb.

"Sometimes I cannot believe it is 2009," she said. "One minute it seems like twenty years ago that I last saw you in Kandahar. The next minute it seems like only yesterday when I last saw my parents in Kabul."

"And what of your parents?" Runa said. "Have you never thought to look for them again?"

"Of course, of course. Endlessly, but until I saw that leaflet in Musa Qala, I was unaware of there being a new Afghan government. So it was hard to have any hope. Then we were in Pakistan and locked up behind closed doors again. And then this." Laalla looked again at her feet. "All my energy has been used up simply trying to walk again, but suddenly in these past few weeks, I have felt many old longings bubbling up in my heart. And of course finding my parents is one of them."

"Come," Runa said. "Let's go to my office, and I will make a few calls. If your parents have fled here to Pakistan, then maybe they filed for refugee status, and it should be easy to find them."

Laalla looked both hopeful and sad.

Runa's office was lined with bookshelves, and along with books, the shelves were filled with framed photos of Runa's family. Men and women, young and old, children and grandparents, but all the photos were from another era, from a time when people had families and life was normal in Afghanistan. Laalla and Parwin sat reminiscing amid the dark wood shelves and photographs while Runa made her call.

"There you go," she said, setting down the phone. "It may take months. Who knows, but we have started the process."

The women sat looking at each other.

"So much has happened in our country since we last saw each other," Runa said.

"Yes," Laalla said. "After I woke up from the explosion, I found myself watching television for the first time in sixteen years. And I can hardly believe what I read in the newspapers. Afghans elected a new president. There was even a woman presidential candidate."

"We are wary though," Parwin said. "The government has talked of making peace with the Taliban, so who knows where that will lead."

"Yes," Runa said. "We have all had our disappointments. With the Russians, with the mujahideen government, with the Taliban, and it continues with the Western-backed government now."

Runa stood up and opened a door at the back of her office. "But at least we have some measure of peace today. Come, let me show you our apartment."

"Oh!" Laalla said, seeing that the door led into Runa's apartment. A hallway went down past three bedrooms and two baths. The kitchen was to the right. The living room led out to a nice porch.

"Our meals come right from the hospital kitchen," Runa said.

"Yes," Parwin said with a smile. "We spent too much of our lives in the kitchen already. We have no more interest in cooking."

As the afternoon grew late, Laalla said good-bye to her now old friends and went back to her ward, escorted by Parwin. Two weeks later she completed her rehab and went to live with Runa and Parwin at the other end of the hospital. Very quickly, Runa was able to find Laalla work as an adult literacy teacher with a women's shelter run by an international NGO. This led to the three women establishing their own NGO called Peace Through Education. Runa raised funds in the donor community. Laalla and Parwin did the teaching, and in connection with their shelter, they began to publish a monthly magazine called *Hope*.

With the success of their shelter, Laalla and Parwin rented a large house of their own, spacious enough to live in and provide work space for over twenty employees. Laalla threw herself into promoting adult literacy and human rights with a passion, but all the while, she wondered and waited for news about her family.

CHAPTER 21

LAALLA AND PARWIN TRAVELED by air to Kabul to attend a women's rights conference. Three days of speeches, seminars, and round tables awaited them, but Laalla had hopes of finding some time to look for her family while she was there. It seemed she had already exhausted every possibility in her search for them. The refugee camps in Pakistan had been scoured. Friends and business associates had kept their eyes open in Kabul and throughout Afghanistan.

On arriving at the airport, Laalla was shocked to see the changes that had taken place in Kabul over the past fourteen years. It was just after the presidential election, and the terminal was overrun by everyone from government officials and sharp-looking businessmen carrying black diplomat brief cases in black suits to airport security people shuttling the wealthy in and out of VIP lounges. There were enough military uniforms to make the place look like a bit of a war zone.

Parwin, expecting Laalla to be very emotional about her return to the city of her birth, held onto Laalla's arm very tightly as they came down the stairs into the terminal, but to Parwin's surprise, Laalla was utterly calm in the face of this flurry of officials and businessmen going this way and that.

"What do you think?" Parwin asked her.

"Somehow I never expected so many professional looking people."

"It's how they smuggle all the reconstruction money out of the country," Parwin said with a smile.

Laalla looked at Parwin. "I would laugh at your joke, but I'm afraid there's too much truth in it."

"Sadly, there is."

The two women walked out to the baggage carousel and waited for their luggage

"I have to go see what they've done to my old Macroyan neighborhood," Laalla said on their way out of the terminal.

"But let's check into our hotel first," Parwin said.

"Of course, of course," Laalla said, and they went out to the curb to catch a taxi.

On their way to the hotel in Shar-e-Naw, Laalla saw many children begging in the streets. The sidewalks were packed with street vendors, and women wore burqas even though they were no longer required to do so. In particular, women who were begging wore them so their faces would not be seen.

As the driver went to make a turn, a new SUV went speeding past the taxi, causing him to swerve.

"Dog washers!" he called out as if it were a curse.

"What is that?" Parwin said, leaning over the seat.

The driver dodged another car and cursed again. "That's what we call all these unskilled foreigners and Afghans pouring in from the West. They'd been dog catchers back home. But here, since they can speak English, they all get offered high salaries."

The driver glanced at the two women in his rearview mirror.

"We also have what we call vultures."

A vehicle escorted by armed security guards went racing by, causing the driver to swerve and curse again.

"See, there goes one right now," he said. "A warlord, by his beard, but they can be anything from members of parliament to high-ranking government officials. As long as they condemn the presence of Americans in public, no one thinks to trouble them. But they are the ones sucking most of the reconstruction money out of the country by partnering with the dog washers."

"We belong to neither of these two categories," Parwin said with a grin. "I've never washed a dog before, but I know how to do dishes." She looked at Laalla. "How about you?"

Lost in her thoughts, Laalla came back, not knowing what the context of the question had been and not knowing how to answer.

"Here we are at the hotel," the driver said.

He got out and helped the women inside with their luggage. Parwin paid him, and both of them went to check on their room.

After a brief rest and freshening up, they took another taxi over to the Macroyan district, where the once-empty streets were now bustling with shops and people. Aunt Sakina's bakery had been turned into a combination Internet café and DVD store. The corridor leading up to Laalla's old apartment had a metal gate and two armed guards standing in front of it. The spot where Shabnam had fallen to her death was fenced off. A vase with plastic flowers sat next to a small tree. A red lightbulb hung from one of the tree branches. A pole with newer red flags had replaced the one the neighbors had left there long ago.

"Stop," Laalla told the driver. Parwin got out with her, and the two went over to pay their respects.

After praying, Laalla showed Parwin where her father used to sit and mourn over his daughter.

"A child was killed here by the Russians some thirty years ago," one of the uniformed security guards told her. Laalla nodded. There was no point in explaining. History had been transformed through time into a myth.

She walked with Parwin over to a smart new shopping center across the street. They went into a market and asked if anyone remembered the old bakery, or her family, or Dr. Nazir, but none of them did. There were photos of warlords hanging from the walls of the market, men who had run four years ago in the parliamentary elections, but nobody remembered General Qassim or Shabnam or Aunt Sakina and her bakery.

"Kabul has been given a facelift," Laalla wrote in her diary later that evening, "but it is like wearing a pair of designer sunglasses over a burqa." You turned on the TV channels owned by unscrupulous businessmen and heard warlords casting spurious accusations at their rivals. In the absence of any meaningful media policy, the fledgling democracy was being poisoned by free speech itself. The specter of sectarian violence seemed more imminent, not less. If the Taliban used to beat up women in front of food distribution centers, now they blew themselves up in front of the same places, killing women and children who were still starving. Laalla thought of the turmoil as new flames growing out of the old ashes.

"But at least children are happy," she wrote. Many of them were still begging on the streets and collecting garbage, but they seemed happy. As Laalla had traveled around in the taxi that day, some of the children had come running alongside the car, and she had seen them singing and dancing as they washed cars along the sidewalks. There was a joyful innocence in the air that she had not seen for thirty years.

After completing the conference and visiting several human rights NGOs on the final day, Laalla and Parwin decided to cancel their planned visit to the Afghan Parliament. A just-published human rights report had revealed that many members of the parliament were simply puppets for whatever lawless warlords had financed their campaigns back at home.

Rather than dignify the enterprise with their presence, Laalla decided to get on with the long, frustrating search for her family, and Peshawar was the next place on her list to look. So she and Parwin hired a driver and started for the border, with the lovely high, green mountains looming over the journey.

In the days that followed, Laalla visited all the refugee camps around Peshawar, hoping to find someone who had any knowledge of her family's whereabouts, but she had no luck. What she found instead were countless other families who had been traumatized by tragic circumstances of their own, mothers left in grief, fathers speechless, their daughters frequently the victims of rape or landmines and sometimes both.

Sadly, Laalla learned that in post-Taliban Afghanistan, many of these families had been forced to leave their land and villages—not by rootless gangs or the Taliban this time, but by the very representatives they had elected to parliament. Warlords, who would imprison innocent people solely for the purpose of exacting a ransom from their families, were now being allowed by the coalition government to entrench themselves in the highest positions of power in Afghan society. After a week of searching through the refugee camps and hearing these same stories, a discouraged Laalla finally headed back to Quetta with Parwin.

For years now Mirwais had been appearing to Laalla in her dreams, always with the same innocent appearance and always with the same exact words: "I have joined the Taliban to search for you, Laalla. I left Mom and Sahar and Mina after Dad passed away, and I am looking for you always. I miss you so much." However, in the weeks and months that followed Laalla's return to Quetta, her dreams of Mirwais assumed a new form. He now appeared to her saying, "Visit me in the garrison next to our old apartment in Macroyan." He was sorry that he had gone there. He had been deceived by the Taliban and asked Laalla for her forgiveness. He came to Laalla's dreams and said that he was there and couldn't leave the place anymore, always with those exact same words, always with the same innocent look on his face as before.

"I believe in my dreams," Laalla told Parwin at one point, "but I can't interpret this one, and it leaves me worried."

Parwin too thought that it sounded very strange. "The same dream for so many years, and now this change, where he keeps apologizing for what he did and tells you that he is in Kabul. I am sure there is an interpretation to this, but I don't know what it is."

Both of them were silent for a moment. Then Parwin said, "Why didn't you say something when we were in Kabul? We could have gone to the garrison and checked it out while we were there."

"I didn't want to go anywhere near the place," Laalla said. "I thought it would only open old wounds. The garrison was the old military club, the place where Farid gave me his first love letter and we fell in love, remember? Now that it has been destroyed by mujahideen and used by the Taliban religious police as a barracks, I couldn't stand to see it."

"Well, now it makes perfect sense," Parwin told Laalla. "I can see the dream is somehow reflecting a reality. Your dreams have always reflected reality. Maybe there is a Taliban cell and he wants us to go and discover it."

"I'm trying to find my parents," Laalla said with a sarcastic smile, "not play a female James Bond. Besides, there can't be any Taliban in the garrison. It would be impossible with the place right across the street from the American Embassy."

CHAPTER 22

A YEAR AFTER THE 2009 presidential election and shortly before the parliamentary election, discussions between the government and the Afghan Taliban were initiated. The political tensions in Afghanistan had started once again to tear the country apart. There were those who simply wanted power-sharing at any cost. Others could not imagine giving those medieval barbarians another chance to be in power.

Heated debates took place on the TV and on radio talkshows everyday. Afghan intellectuals wrote articles in the newspapers predicting that any peace talks with the Taliban would usher in a new era of conflict, bringing the nation to the brink of civil war, and could possibly lead to a fragmentation of an already fragile country. Rumors circulated that secret meetings between the Taliban delegation and the Karzai government had been orchestrated by the ISI in Pakistan. There were reports of acid attacks on women by the Taliban and the poisoning of water in girls' schools reminiscent of the last days of Dr. Najibullah's regime before the Soviet withdrawal and the mujahideen domination of Kabul.

The media in Pakistan reported that their government was very supportive of a peace jirga. They were said to welcome this new era of reconciliation. They welcomed any way to end the civil war.

In an interview with the BBC, Hamid Gull, the former ISI general, said, "America is history. Karzai is history. The Taliban are the future. It would be unwise to cut all contacts and goodwill with the future leaders of Afghanistan."

Laalla and Parwin received an invitation to attend another women's conference in Kabul, this time condemning any plans for sharing power with the Taliban, and Laalla spent many sleepless nights with Parwin before departing watching the news, poring back through pre-9/11 reports and analysis, combing through articles and speeches and UN resolutions and the very blueprint for the post-Taliban Afghanistan government, hoping to discredit Pakistan's support for the upcoming peace jirga with the Taliban.

Parwin and Laalla decided to travel to Kabul by bus this time, under burqa and escorted by Akhtar, one of their Pakistani male coworkers. They arrived the day before the conference was to take place and a week before the parliamentarian election. There were many large billboards crowded with photos of parliamentary candidates—warlords, many of them—and many of the faces had long been familiar to Parwin and Laalla.

"I want to see those photos down one day, and instead their bodies should hang on these poles," Laalla griped to Parwin.

"I thought you couldn't play female James Bond." Parwin smiled.

"It's not so funny." Laalla pinched her in the arm. "Look what they did to our lives."

Laalla feared her country was turning back toward its catastrophic past, and the next morning, she felt those fears echoed all around her in the conference hall of the Intercontinental Hotel.

"The world needs to end their delusion that Pakistan is seeking an independent and democratic Afghanistan," Laalla said on stage as part of a panel. She also argued that the peace talk with the Taliban would ultimately turn into a *loya jirga* where the constitution would be amended for the purpose of electing a president for life.

The conference went on delineating and condemning any future power-sharing deal with the Taliban, and after two days of listening to it, Parwin decided to take a break and visit an old acquaintance of hers from Quetta named Farida. Farida ran a local women's shelter and was a women's rights activist in her own right, and Parwin had planned to visit her on the last trip to Kabul with Laalla, but those plans had not worked out.

It was a few hours after lunch when Parwin called Laalla from Farida's shelter. "I am sending Akhtar over to pick you up right now. I want you to leave the conference and come here immediately. I have found one of your sisters."

"What?" Laalla said. "Parwin, I can't hear you. The reception is terrible inside this conference hall."

The phone went dead, so Laalla tried calling Parwin back again and again until she had dropped the call three different times. Knowing by the tone in Parwin's voice that it was something urgent, Laalla walked out of the conference hall only to have the same problem finding a signal outside. She stood there with a cane in one hand and her cell phone in the other, nervously punching on the keys.

A security guard standing next to the entry door saw Laalla's frustration and went over to her. "Do you see those American military vehicles over there?"

Laalla nodded.

"Wait until they leave. When they are in the vicinity, no phones work."

The man nodded hopefully at Laalla's frustrated look. "They should be leaving very soon. They come here every day around the same time for their situation-awareness patrol."

Laalla waited impatiently until the Americans had left and finally got a call through to Parwin.

"What, Parwin? I could not hear inside."

"I said it's one of your sisters. I can't say anything more right now. The whole world is listening to our conversation. Just wait there, and Akhtar is coming with Farida jaan's driver to pick you up."

Parwin hung up, but Laalla called her right back again.

"Which sister of mine?" Laalla demanded, her patience growing thin. "What's her name?"

"Calm down," Parwin told her. "It's your younger sister, Mina. You have waited for fourteen years now. It is only a matter of another fourteen minutes."

A white van showed up a few minutes later, and Akhtar got out to slide open the side door for Laalla. She took her burqa out from a canvas bag and put it on. Akhtar took Laalla's purse and white binder and helped her hop into the van. Once Laalla was safely inside, Akhtar slid the door closed and got back into the front seat.

The white van maneuvered left from the main road, passed the attorney general's office, and stopped in front of a two-story house with a blue guardhouse next to the garage door. Unable to wait for the car to enter the garage, Laalla got out and hurried toward the house as fast as her plastic leg would let her. Parwin and Farida were standing on the brick porch. A sign above the porch read, "Angels House."

"Where is my little Mina? Laalla called out in a shaky voice. "Show me my sister."

Parwin rushed to her and held up her hand. "Ssshh. I want you to keep your emotions under control. It is very important that we do this in the right way. Otherwise her life is in danger, and ours too. It is not the right time to take revenge or seek justice. Just calm down, and let's plan this the right way."

"Farida, this is Laalla," Parwin said. "Laalla, Farida jaan."

"Let's go to my office," Farida said, "and I will have Mina come there to see you."

"She doesn't know about you," Parwin said on the way to the office. "I didn't tell her that you are alive or that you are here. Other women in the shelter cannot know about this either."

In the office, Laalla kept begging for Parwin and Farida to bring her little sister to her immediately.

"I brought her here from the Puli Charkhy women's jail two months ago," Farida explained. "That is where I found her. During my first visit with her at the jail, she told us she had no one and did not want to see her mother or older sister ever again."

"But what happened to my father?" Laalla asked. "Where is Mirwais? Can you please tell me what is going on?"

"I am sorry to tell you this," Farida said, "but Mina was forced into prostitution for years by her mother and older sister. Unfortunately, I have no idea what happened to your father. Mina never told us a thing, but she has told other girls that her brother ran away from home some ten years ago."

Laalla was crying now, and Farida handed her a box of tissues.

"I think some powerful people wanted her to go back and work for her mother as a prostitute," Farida continued. "Probably bribery was involved, but luckily I happened to have two women from an international human rights organization with me on the day I discovered your sister in the jail. The fact that it was election time didn't hurt either."

"No, no, this is not the mother of Laalla and Shabnam," Laalla said, still crying. "I won't believe that my mother and Sahar forced Mina into prostitution. I need to talk to Mina myself.

"Maybe it is a different Mina" Laalla said, looking at Parwin.

"I will bring her," Farida said, leaving the room.

"Farida jaan will help us," Parwin said, "but you must understand this situation puts her in danger as well. The only way to rescue Mina is to forget about your mother and your sister Sahar. From what I understand, it's too late for them, but we can rescue Mina and take her out of this country before your mother and Sahar find out."

Farida entered the room with a young woman, and Laalla knew from the first glance that it was her little Mina. There were the same blue eyes, the same thick, black eyebrows nearly merging above her nose.

"I can't believe it," Laalla said with a kiss and a hug and a long look at her sister. "You are a grown up lady now."

Looking surprised and uncomfortable, Mina pulled her hands free from Laalla's. She had not been told by Farida that the woman waiting to see her claimed to be a sister.

"I'm sorry," Mina said, "but do you mind telling me who you are?"

"I'm Laalla, Mina. Your oldest sister."

"I don't have any sisters," Mina said, in tears now. "And I have no mother or any family anymore."

"Yes you do," Laalla said. "Don't you remember me at all?"

Mina collapsed into the chair behind her and hid her face in her hands. Trembling and in tears, Laalla sat down with her artificial leg splayed out awkwardly to the side, trying to get Mina to look into her face.

"Don't you remember that night when you said you wanted to build schools all over Afghanistan? It was the night before I left, remember?"

Mina looked up.

"Well, I remember your words, and we can do that now. We can teach the mujahideen not to make war. We can teach the Taliban to let women be free and go to school." Laalla took hold of Mina's hands again. "One day we can stand on top of a mountain together and see schools everywhere we look."

When Mina looked down forlornly again, Laalla gently lifted her face back up.

"Look at Aunt Farida and this place. Who could think that Afghan women would have someone to stand up for them in this way? We must keep hope, Mina. I don't know what happened with Mom and Sahar, but I promise you everything will be okay."

"Don't mention Mom and Sahar to me," Mina said. "Please don't remind me of them ever again. After Dad passed away and Mirwais left home, they never even mentioned your name."

It was Laalla's turn to hang her own head now. "Father passed away."

Seeing her sister's sorrow, Mina touched Laalla's hair. "Yes, many years ago now."

"And Mirwais?"

"I don't know where he is," Mina said, "but I have always dreamed of finding him. And I am sure he is still looking for you."

"Oh, Mina," Laalla said. "We are together. There is so much sorrow in this news today, but isn't it wonderful? We have each other again."

She shook Mina's hands. Mina smiled sadly and fought back tears.

"It is such a joy that we have found each other, Mina, and we have all the rest of our lives to make things better now."

"It is true," Parwin said, "but now we must get Farida jaan's advice on how best to proceed."

"To have saved one life," Farida said, "we have accomplished a lot, but I must tell you again: if I let Mina go with you, the commanders who want her are sure to make noise. I am well connected with the journalists and human rights organizations, and this shelter is funded by the Americans, so they look out for me, but someone is sure to make trouble. Even if the government can't put me in jail, I am being threatened all the time. The Taliban accuse me of selling Afghan girls to the foreigners. They say I'm operating a whore house for the Americans. These vultures are only infuriated because they can't rape and kill a woman when she is in my shelter, but they make allegations, and someone always believes them."

"I know," Parwin said, "that by getting Mina jaan out of here, she will rescue tens and maybe hundreds of other women, and she will open her own shelters one day. Won't you, Mina?"

"Yes, I'm sure she will do good deeds," Farida said, "but I think it is best that we get her a passport. I hate to bribe, but I am afraid we will have to do it in this case just to get her out of the country."

Farida looked at Laalla. "If you don't have money with you, I can lend it to you."

"No, we have money," Laalla assured her.

"What if someone comes and asks about her sudden disappearance?" Parwin said. "Perhaps the commander who is after her, or even her mother and sister?"

"I can handle that," Farida said. "By law, she is considered an adult and doesn't need a guardian. We really have the best laws. The problem is they are not being enforced. But please, let's keep this among ourselves. I can't let any of the other women in this shelter know about it. I will have Mina's photos taken today, and you will have her passport by this evening or tomorrow morning at the latest. Money talks fast around here."

"In the mean time, can I take Mina with me to our hotel?" Laalla asked.

"No," Farida said. "I can't let her go to the hotel with you. You must take Mina directly from here to Pakistan. However, you are welcome to stay here with your sister if you like. I will make a bed available in the same room. You can stay here until you are ready to leave for Pakistan."

Unable to feel any happier than she did in that moment, Laalla thanked Farida and said that she hoped one day to make up for her great hospitality and kindness.

"Think of it," Farida said. "You are not only rescuing your sister, you are rescuing a human being. As a practicing Muslim, I know this to be the real jihad. According to the Koran, if you save one life, you have saved the whole of humanity. If you kill one life, it is as if you have killed the whole of humanity. At least, that is what it says in my Koran."

That night at the Angels Shelter, Parwin and Laalla learned how Zia Gull had not allowed Mina to go beyond the third grade in school. This was after Mirwais had disappeared and Sahar had become one of Zia Gull's top girls. By that point, Shah Jaan was addicted to drugs and nothing more than a pimp.

Then Zia Gull was put in jail by Pakistani police, and a man who pretended to be in love with Sahar had persuaded Shah Jaan to go with him and her two daughters to Kabul. That had been five years back, and with drugs so widely available in Kabul, even cheaper than they had been in Peshawar, Shah Jaan's dependency had only become worse and worse.

The pimp who had dragged them to Kabul kept about fifteen girls in a large house and would send them out to work, keeping Mina and Sahar and another two girls at home for his VIP guests. Then the pimp had been killed by a commander, and Sahar had taken charge of the girls. Moving to a smaller house, she managed more than fifteen girls at one time, though only four of them actually lived in the house. The rest lived elsewhere and worked on call. Although Sahar had already started drinking in Pakistan, like Shah Jaan, once they moved to Kabul, her drinking got worse and worse.

In time, Sahar and Shah Jaan had stopped entertaining customers at home and begun sending the women out to service the customers at locations of their choice. Mina cried again while explaining how she had been beaten by customers every time she went on call.

There was a particular commander who always ordered four or five girls on the same night, and once drunk, he would start biting their arms. This was all he ever wanted to do for his personal satisfaction, after which he would toss the women to his gunmen and guards.

One night, this commander sent his men over to pick up Mina alone but she refused to go. In response, Shah Jaan and Sahar slapped Mina across the face and eventually pushed her out the door into the hands of the gunman. On the way to the commander's house, the driver stopped at a supermarket to buy cigarettes. Mina saw a police car through the tinted windows of the car, along with many men and women shoppers coming from the supermarket, and thought this was her chance to escape.

Jumping out the door, she ran screaming to the police car. A crowd of men and women gathered around her and, hearing her story, began shouting at the driver and the gunmen and threatening with retaliation.

Not wanting a confrontation with the police or the crowd, the men fled, and the policemen took Mina with them to the station. However, rather than being saved, she found the officers at the station more brutal then the commander himself. Mina was raped by seven policemen at the station. Then she was thrown into a cell and charged with running away from her husband.

Coming to this part of her story, Mina stopped, her lips trembling, tears trickling down her cheeks, and she threw herself into the arms of Laalla.

"Are you married?" Laalla asked her.

"No," Mina said, "but what does it matter at that point? Once you are in jail, it takes months or years until someone asks why you are there. By that time, the policeman who put you in jail is probably a parliament member or a governor or the chief of police, if not a millionaire.

"Please take me with you," Mina begged Laalla and Parwin in her sorrow. "Mom and Sahar will never change. They are drowning in their sick world of money and drugs and whisky."

"Don't worry, my little Mina," Laalla said. "I will never let you to go back to that life again."

It was a long night for the three women. Laalla shared her story, and then Parwin, until in their shared grief, Mina found a little ray of hope.

The next day, Farida told them she had sent the photos to a broker. He would bring back a passport with a Pakistani visa on it by the end of the day.

"How much do we owe you?" Parwin asked her.

"The whole thing is around $1,600. I paid him already. Here is the receipt."

"Do they truly issue receipts for the bribes they are taking?" Laalla asked her.

"This is called the legalization of corruption," Farida said. "There are hundreds of so-called brokers standing in front of the customs house every day and in front of the passport office and almost every ministry office offering to finish your paperwork and expedite almost any kind of application process.

"Now," Farida told Laalla and Parwin, "you should pack up and get ready to depart tomorrow morning. I will miss Mina, but stay in touch with me. My driver will take you to the bus stop at six o'clock tomorrow morning."

That night, while Laalla and Parwin lay on the floor in their makeshift bed next to Mina, Farida came in, and Laalla explained her dream about Mirwais and the old Taliban garrison.

"Somehow, I feel it is very important for me to go there," Laalla said.

"I don't think it's a good idea to visit that heavily guarded area," Farida told her. "It is now the ISAF HQ. Over fifteen hundred troops are stationed there. Helicopters fly in and out every hour. Security is especially tight after the last suicide bombing attempt on the main gate last year. Besides, you can only—"

"Perhaps you should just pray for him. Your dream makes perfect sense, Laalla," Parwin said, cutting off Farida. "He was deceived by the devil. He was helpless."

Laalla and Mina both had tears in their eyes.

"I will not give up hope," Laalla said.

"No, we shouldn't give up hope," Farida said. "After all, look. You finally found Mina after all these years."

Farida said good night, and Laalla, Parwin, and Mina talked for another hour before they finally fell asleep.

The next morning, the three women thanked Farida and left the Angels Shelter to pick up Akhtar from his hotel and drive to the bus station. The shelter van was parked on the driveway outside the shelter's front yard. Mina got in the backseat first, and then Parwin helped Laalla get in, and she climbed in last.

As Farida's driver put the key in the ignition, the bomb went off. Laalla remembered the white light from before, the feeling of a vacuum just before the deafening sound, and then the peace that followed.

Akhtar was standing a block away as the van was consumed by orange-red flames. He paused long enough to see a column of black smoke rising above it. Then he hopped into the white Corolla, and the bearded man behind the wheel raced off toward the road to Jalalabad. Otherwise, it was a sunny spring day in Kabul. There were little schools sitting on top of the little hills. Kites were flying everywhere in the bright blue windy sky, and all the children were happy. Yet there was fear of a Taliban comeback and the Americans' withdrawal everywhere in the city.